PRASE FOR
SOOTHSAYER AND MIKE RESNICK

This is one of those rare novels that pulls you in so quickly and effectively that you'll end up reading it in a single sitting.

SCIENCE FICTION CHRONICLE

Resnick is one of the top storytellers in the field, and Soothsayer is a wonderfully written, lyrical tale, and I honestly can't think of anything negative to say about it.

AMAZING

This tale bears Resnick's writerly stamp. If you don't feel you've had your money's worth out of it, it will only be because you finished it that quickly. It's that smoothly, eminently readable.

ANALOG

ALSO BY MIKE RESNICK

The Return of Santiago
The Amulet of Power (Lara Croft: Tomb Raider)
The Outpost
Kirinyaga: A Fable of Utopia
Tales of the Galactic Midway
Stalking the Unicorn

The Lucifer Jones Series
Adventures
Lucifer Jones
Exploits
Encounters

The Far Future History Series
Birthright: The Book of Man
Santiago: A Myth of the Far Future
Dark Lady: A Romance of the Far Future

The Widowmaker Series
Widowmaker
Widowmaker Reborn
Widowmaker Unleashed

SOOTHSAYER

Mike Resnick

BENBELLA BOOKS, INC.

DALLAS, TEXAS

First BenBella Books Edition July 2005

BenBella Books
6440 N. Central Expressway
Suite 617
Dallas, TX 75206
Send feedback to feedback@benbellabooks.com
www.benbellabooks.com

Publisher: Glenn Yeffeth
Editor: Shanna Caughey
Associate Editor: Leah Wilson
Director of Marketing/PR: Laura Watkins

Printed in the United States of America

10 9 8 7 6 5 4 3 2 1

Library of Congress Cataloging-in-Publication Data

Resnick, Michael D.
    Soothsayer / Mike Resnick. — 1st BenBella Books ed.
        p. cm.
1. Girls—Fiction. 2. Women prophets—Fiction. 3. Life on other planets—Fiction. I. Title
    PS3568.E698S66 2005
    813'.54--dc22

2004017172

Cover art copyright © Jim Burns
Cover design by Laura Watkins

Distributed by Independent Publishers Group
To order call (800) 888-4741
www.ipgbook.com

For special sales, contact Laura Watkins at laura@benbellabooks.com.

To Carol, as always

And to Susan Allison and Ginjer Buchanan,
fine editors and fine ladies

Contents

Prologue

It was a time of giants.

There was no room for them to breathe and flex their muscles in mankind's sprawling Democracy, so they gravitated to the distant, barren worlds of the Inner Frontier, drawn ever closer to the bright Galactic Core like moths to a flame.

Oh, they fit into human frames, most of them, but they were giants nonetheless. No one knew what had brought them forth in such quantity at this particular moment in human history. Perhaps there was a need for them in a galaxy filled to overflowing with little people possessed of even smaller dreams. Possibly it was the savage splendor of Inner Frontier itself, for it was certainly not a place for ordinary men and women. Or maybe it was simply time for a race that had been notably short of giants in recent eons to begin producing them once again.

But whatever the reason, they swarmed out beyond the farthest reaches of the explored galaxy, spreading the seed of Man to hundreds of new worlds, and in the process creating a cycle of legends that would never die as long as men could tell tales of heroic deeds.

There was Faraway Jones, who set foot on more than five hundred new worlds, never quite certain what he was looking for, always sure that he hadn't yet found it.

There was the Whistler, who bore no other name than that, and who had killed more than one hundred men and aliens.

There was Friday Nellie, who turned her whorehouse into a hospital during the war against the Setts, and finally saw it declared a shrine by the very men who once tried to close it down.

There was Jamal, who left no fingerprints or footprints, but had plundered palaces that to this day do not know they were plundered.

There was Bet-a-World Murphy, who at various times owned nine different gold-mining worlds, and lost every one of them at the gaming tables.

There was Backbreaker Ben Ami, who wrestled aliens for money and killed men for pleasure. There was the Marquis of Queensbury, who fought by no rules at all, and the White Knight, albino killer of fifty men, and Sally the Blade, and the Forever Kid, who reached the age of nineteen and just stopped growing for the next two centuries, and Catastrophe Baker, who made whole planets shake beneath his feet, and the exotic Pearl of Maracaibo, and the Scarlet Queen, whose sins were condemned by every race in the galaxy, and Father Christmas, and the One-Armed Bandit with his deadly prosthetic arm, and the Earth Mother, and Lizard Malloy, and the deceptively mild-mannered Cemetery Smith.

Giants all.

Yet there was one giant who was destined to tower over all of the others, to juggle the lives of men and worlds as if they were so many toys, to rewrite the history of the Inner Frontier, and the Outer Frontier, and the Spiral Arm, and even the all-powerful Democracy itself. At various times in her short, turbulent life she was known as the Soothsayer, and the Oracle, and the Prophet. By the time she had passed from the galactic scene, only a handful of survivors knew her true name, or her planet of origin, or even her early history, for such is the way with giants and legends.

But she had an origin, and a history, and a name, and even a childhood of sorts.

This is her story.

PART 1

The
Mouse's
Book

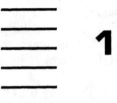

1

Blantyre III was a world of tall towers and stately minarets, of twisting streets and pitch-dark alleyways, of large chimneys and narrow stairways.

In other words, it was a world made to order for the Mouse.

She stood on the makeshift stage at the back of Merlin's wagon now, not quite five feet tall, barely eighty pounds, wearing a sequined tie and tails over her tights, smiling confidently at the assembled crowd as Merlin produced bouquets and rabbits out of thin air. Each of these he handed to her, and each she placed in a special container, since flowers and rabbits were difficult to come by out on the Inner Frontier, and they planned to make use of them a number of times before moving on to the next world.

Then came the cigarette trick. Merlin lit a cigarette, snuffed it out, magically produced four more lit cigarettes, threw them away, pulled yet another out of his ear, and so on, simple sleight of hand, but immensely pleasing to the spectators who had never seen any kind of magic show before.

Then there was the patter, which Merlin kept up incessantly. He told jokes, insulted braggarts, called forth the dark gods to aid him, even read an occasional mind.

And finally, forty minutes into the act, came the *pièce de résistance*.

Merlin had the Mouse climb into a large box, which he then bound with chains and secured with oversized padlocks.

The box, he explained carefully, had a twenty-minute supply of oxygen in it, not a second more.

The Mouse was already out of the box and hiding in the back of Merlin's wagon when he had two bystanders help him attach the box to a pulley, raise it over a large tank of water, and submerge it, promising his audience that the Mouse had only nineteen minutes left in which to escape or die.

He then pulled out some of his more dazzling tricks, those with fires and explosions, which held the crowd captivated while the Mouse slipped into a black bodysuit, wriggled out the hole in the bottom of the wagon, and slunk off into the shadows.

A moment later she was clambering lithely up the side of an ancient building, hiding in the shadow of a turret until Merlin performed his next trick, and then she was inside a window and scampering lightly down a corridor. There was artwork to be had in this house, lots of it, but she decided it would be too hard to smuggle off the planet. Instead she kept racing from room to room until she finally found a woman's dressing room, quickly scavenged through the drawers until she came to a jewelry chest, and plundered it, placing the contents in a leather pouch tied around her waist.

She checked her watch again. Eleven minutes. Time for at least one more house, possibly two.

She raced back to the window through which she had entered, clambered out and up to the top of a minaret, dove through space to the adjacent building, landed catlike on a ledge, and forced open the window of a darkened room.

She realized immediately that she was not alone, that someone or something was sleeping in a corner. She froze, half expecting an attack, but then she heard a snore and she was across the room and into a corridor within five seconds.

She could tell by the numerals on the doors that she was in a rooming house rather than a private residence. It could be better; it could be worse. She could plunder four or five different rooms without having to leave the building, but residents of boardinghouses rarely had anything worth stealing.

She checked the nearest room. It was empty, not only of people but of anything remotely valuable.

The second room was a little better. A man and a woman were asleep in a large bed, and the air smelled of alcohol and drugs. The Mouse found their clothing in a crumpled pile on the floor and extracted three one-hundred-credit notes from the man's wallet. A further search failed to turn up the woman's purse or money, and the Mouse decided that she didn't have enough time to keep looking for them.

She re-entered the corridor with eight minutes remaining on her watch, but just as she did so an elderly woman turned on the light and wandered out to use the only bathroom on the floor. She shot into the stairwell, heard voices coming up from the floor below and realized that at least one of the rooms had a door open, and crouched in the shadows, waiting for the stiff-limbed old woman to make her way down the corridor to the bathroom. It took the old woman almost two minutes, and the Mouse decided that it was time to start heading back. She found an unlit fire exit in the rear of the building, climbed down to the ground, kept to the shadows until she was opposite Merlin's wagon, waited for him to captivate the crowd with one final trick that shot fireworks in every direction, then slithered under the wagon and entered it from beneath.

She placed her pouch carefully inside a production box, so that even if a policeman opened the top of the box he'd have a difficult time finding anything that was hidden in it. Then, with two minutes to go, she donned a black hood and insinuated herself onto the stage.

Merlin was toying with the spectators, half convincing them that the Mouse was mere seconds from drowning or suffocating if she couldn't escape, and finally he led them in a countdown. When they reached the instant when her oxygen was theoretically used up, Merlin and his black-hooded assistant pulled the box out of the water and hacked away its chains—and revealed not a dead Mouse, but an Antarean bird of many colors, which spread its wings, hopped out of the box, walked over to the Mouse, and pulled her hood off—its one and only trick.

The crowd applauded wildly, Merlin passed his hat for donations, and finally the audience dispersed, leaving them there in the middle of the now-empty street.

"Well?" asked the magician. "How did you do?"

"Some credits, some jewelry," replied the Mouse. "Nothing special."

"That's the problem with this world," said Merlin. "There *is* nothing special to it." He stared contemptuously at the houses. "All these stately façades, and each boudoir with its own façade of costume jewelry. Six nights without a major score. I'm for calling it quits."

The Mouse shrugged. "Suits me. Where to next?"

"Westerly is the next human world."

"Westerly is an alien world," she corrected him.

"It's got about twenty thousand humans living in a kind of free zone right in the heart of their biggest city," said Merlin. "We can refuel there."

"We can refuel right here."

"We're going to," explained Merlin patiently. "But Westerly should make a nice one-day stop along the route. Who knows? Maybe we can pick up some fresh fruit. *That's* something we can't get on this particular dirtball."

She shrugged again. "All right. Westerly it is." Merlin began driving the show wagon back to the spaceport. "What do the natives call it?" continued the Mouse.

"Call what?" he asked distractedly.

"Westerly."

"Well, the human natives call it Westerly."

"Thanks a heap."

"You couldn't pronounce what the aliens call it. It's listed on the star maps as Romanus Omega II." He paused. "It's an oxygen world, of course."

"Any idea what the natives are like?"

"I imagine they breathe oxygen," he said. "What difference does it make? We're only going to perform for a human audience."

"*You* don't crawl down chimneys or through sewers," she replied. "If I'm going to run into an alien in tight quarters, I want to know what my options are."

"Same as always: run like hell."

They rode in silence until they reached the spaceport, then loaded the wagon into Merlin's brightly decorated ship. Once they had taken off and laid in a course to Westerly, the Mouse relaxed with a beer while Merlin began running the gemstones she had stolen through the computer's spectrographic sensors. When he finished he cross-checked them against his current jeweler's reference guides and finally placed tentative values upon them.

"Could have been worse," he said at last. "I do wish you'd get over your compulsive urge to always grab the biggest stones, though. So many of them really aren't worth the trouble."

"What about the diamond bracelet and the sapphire necklace?" she asked without looking up.

"They were very nice pieces. But those beads that look like pearls—absolutely worthless."

"You'll find some pretty little girl to give them to, once we get back to the Frontier," said the Mouse.

"I shall certainly try my utmost," agreed Merlin. "But that in no way alters the fact that they won't bring a credit on the black market."

She sipped her beer thoughtfully. "We don't want credits, anyway, not the way the Democracy's going these days. If I were you, I'd sell this stuff for New Stalin rubles and Maria Theresa dollars."

"Then we're going to have to wait a few weeks. As long as we're within the Democracy, people are going to want to pay us with credits."

"Then you'd better charge more, because credits don't spend very well out where we're heading."

"I don't tell you how to steal them; don't you tell me how to unload them."

The Mouse stared at him for a moment as he practiced making the jewels appear and disappear beneath a colorful silken scarf, then went back to concentrating on her beer. It had been a long week, and she was tired, and her left knee was throbbing from where she'd banged it against a turret two nights ago. In fact, her whole body hurt from the chores she kept giving it. It really was time for a vacation, and as she sought out her bed and drifted off to sleep, she found herself hoping that they could make a big enough killing on Westerly so that she could afford to take a few months off.

Westerly, decided the Mouse, was like most alien worlds. At first glance it seemed to make perfect sense; it was only when you looked more closely that it seemed less and less reasonable.

"Well, what do you think?" asked Merlin as he drove the show wagon down the main street of Westerly's human enclave.

"I don't like it," replied the Mouse.

"What's the problem?"

"Look at the way the streets all twist and turn back into themselves," she said. "There are some skyscrapers with no windows or doors at all, and some little one-story buildings that are *all* glass and have fifteen doors. I don't know if I can figure it out in ten minutes."

"Just stick to the human buildings," said Merlin. "We don't want any alien objects, anyway."

"It's not that simple," she said. "Which ones *are* the human buildings? If I pick the wrong one, I could get lost inside of it for an hour or more. I have a horrible feeling that every corridor ends in a blank wall and that every staircase forms a continuous loop."

"You're overreacting," said Merlin.

"I don't think so," she said, "and it's *my* opinion that counts." She paused. "Your information was wrong. This planet never saw twenty thousand men at one time. I'd be surprised if they've got a thousand in residence."

"Let's compromise, then," said Merlin, bringing the wagon to a halt.

"How?"

He jerked his head at a large steel and glass building just across the street. "The Royal Arms Hotel," he said. "Human-owned, human-run. We've got all day to study it. Let's go in, have lunch, and walk around a bit. If you're comfortable with it by nightfall, it's the only place you'll have to hit."

She nodded her agreement. "Fair enough," she said.

"I'll join you as soon as I can find a place to leave the wagon."

While she was waiting for him, she walked entirely around the hotel, and located what would be her means of ingress later that night: a ventilation shaft attached to a basement laundry. There was a grate covering it, and room enough to park the wagon right over it. She had already entered the lobby when Merlin caught up with her.

"Well?" he said. "Learn anything?"

"Two things," she replied. "First, I know how I'm getting in."

"Good."

"And second," she continued, indicating a Robelian and a trio of Lodinites, "they've got more than just men staying here."

"They'll have their own floors," replied Merlin with a shrug. "It just means we have to be selective."

"What about the locks?"

"They should be standard, keyed into the house computer so they can change combinations on a moment's notice." He paused. "If you forget half of what I've already taught you, it might take you thirty seconds to crack one of them."

"You don't mind if we check them out *before* tonight?"

He shrugged. "Whatever you wish."

"Has it occurred to you that *you* could probably loot fifty guest rooms between now and dinnertime?" she suggested.

He shook his head. "We've been through all that before. The only reason we've never been arrested is because we do our looting *only* during the time we have an alibi."

She made no reply, but kept looking surreptitiously into corners, down corridors, behind room dividers. From what she could tell—and she couldn't be certain until she examined some of the rooms—it appeared that most or all of the human guests used the airlifts to the right of the registration desk, which put them on levels four through nine. Levels two and three were reached by gently ascending ramps to the left of the registration desk and seemed to be of interest only to Canphorites, Lodinites, and Robelians.

"Well, at least they're all oxygen-breathers," she muttered. "I hate it when they change environments." She turned to Merlin. "Have you spotted the service lifts yet?"

He frowned. "There don't seem to be any."

"There must be. They'd never let the maids go up in the same airlift as the paying customers." She paused. "Maybe you'd better go tell the management that we're here to put on a show for their customers tonight, before they think that we're casing the premises."

"And what will you be doing while I'm explaining away our presence?" asked Merlin.

"Casing the premises," she replied with a smile.

Merlin approached the front desk, and the Mouse took an elevator to the seventh level, made sure that the locks were a type she could pick, tried to take the lift down to the basement to inspect the laundry, found that it stopped at the lobby, and finally rejoined the magician just as he was emerging from the day manager's office.

"All set?" she asked.

"They won't give us any problems, and it'll justify our hanging around the hotel for the rest of the afternoon."

"Good. Let's start by having some lunch."

He agreed, and a moment later they entered the main-floor restaurant. Only two other tables were occupied, and Merlin nodded toward the farthest one.

"See that alien over there?" he whispered, indicating the lone being at the table.

"The humanoid with the bad complexion?" she asked.

Merlin nodded. "The one who's dressed all in silver. Steer clear of him."

"Why?"

"Wait'll he reaches for something and you'll see."

As if on cue, the alien signaled for a waiter, and she could see that he had once possessed four arms, but that one had been amputated.

"What kind of race does he belong to?" she asked.

"I don't know—but unless I miss my guess, that's Three-Fisted Ollie."

"Never heard of him."

"Just keep out of his way."

"Outlaw?"

"Bounty hunter. They say he's killed more than thirty men and that he never takes contracts on his own race." The magician paused thoughtfully. "I wish I knew why he was on Westerly; he usually operates on the Inner Frontier."

"Unless he's hunting for us."

"Come on," said Merlin. "There's not a warrant out on us anywhere in the Democracy."

"That you know of," she said.

"That anyone knows of," he replied confidently. "Anyway, if you run into him tonight, just apologize and get the hell out of his way quick."

The Mouse nodded and punched her order into the small menu computer. A moment later Merlin prodded her with his toe.

"What now?" she asked.

"Don't turn around or pretend to notice him—but do you see who just joined the alien?"

She turned her head.

"I said don't look directly!" hissed Merlin.

"All right," said the Mouse, staring directly into Merlin's eyes. "It's a big bearded human with a small arsenal hanging down from his belt. I assume you know *him*, too?"

"It's Cemetery Smith."

"Another bounty hunter?"

Merlin shook his head. "A hired killer. One of the best."

"So why are an alien bounty hunter and a professional assassin sitting fifty feet away from us?" asked the Mouse.

"I don't know," said the magician nervously. "They should both be on the Frontier, and they sure as hell shouldn't be talking to each other."

"Are they after us?" asked the Mouse calmly, even as she searched for exits and mentally calculated her chances of reaching them.

"No. These guys don't fool around. If they wanted us, we'd already be dead."

"What do you want to do about tonight?" she asked. "We can give the hotel a pass and just take off."

"Let me think about it," said Merlin. He lowered his head and stared at his interlocked fingers for a long moment, then looked up. "No, there's no reason to cancel out. They're not after us, and we don't represent any competition to them. We're thieves, they're killers."

The Mouse shrugged. "Makes no difference to me."

"I wonder who they're after?" mused Merlin as the human got to his feet, said something to the alien, and walked out into the hotel lobby. "Whoever it is, he must be damned good if it takes the two of them together to hunt him down."

They ate in silence, and then, as twilight approached, the Mouse began passing out holographic fliers announcing the magic show that would shortly be performed on the street outside the hotel.

By sundown, when Merlin began producing bouquets and birds and rabbits with professional élan, they had attracted a crowd of about sixty, all but a handful of them humans. Merlin continued to bedazzle the crowd, the Mouse performed her two or three simple illusions to a smattering of applause, and then Merlin put her into the box and began securing the locks, even as she rolled out the false back. By the time he had maneuvered it into the water tank, she was beneath the surface of the street, crawling through the ventilation shaft into the laundry. There were two women on duty, and it took her a minute longer than she had anticipated to reach the enclosed fire stairs. She raced up the stairs to the fourth level, then emerged and began checking for unlocked doors. She found one, quickly looted the room of its few valuable items, and then broke into another room. This one provided even less booty, and she soon emerged into the corridor. According to her watch, she had time for perhaps two more rooms if she was fast enough, one more if she had to hunt for its treasures.

Then, suddenly, she heard a door open, and she shot into the stairwell. There was no reason to wait for the resident to traverse the corridor and reach the airlift when all she had to do was climb another floor and loot two rooms on the fifth level—but some instinct warned her not to climb any higher. Perhaps it was the press of time, perhaps it was the possibility of running into Cemetery Smith, but whatever the reason, she found herself waiting for the fourth-level corridor to become empty rather than ascending to the fifth.

"Goddamn it!" bellowed a voice, and she peeked into the fourth-level corridor.

Evidently whoever had opened the door had managed to lock himself out of his room, because now he was cursing at the top of his lungs and pounding on his door. Other doors cracked open as curious residents sought the reason for the disturbance, and the Mouse pulled her head back into the stairwell, convinced that the fourth level wouldn't be safe for her until long after she had to return to the magic show.

She took two steps up the stairwell, then heard still more noise on the fifth level as the sounds of cursing and pounding rose through the building, and she immediately reversed her course, racing down to the second level, well below the noise.

She stepped cautiously into the corridor, which was a bit wider than the human section, and began checking the doors.

The first two were locked, the third had a hideous growling sound emanating from behind it. It was as she approached the fourth door that she heard a sound that had no business being in the alien section of the hotel: the sobbing of a human child.

It took her less than twenty seconds to pick the lock and leap into the darkness of the room before the door could slide shut behind her. She pulled out a tiny flashlight and began inspecting the premises. There was an oddly shaped couch and chair that no human could ever sit in, a table on which were placed six bronze artifacts that were absolutely meaningless to her, and another table with the remains of an alien meal on it.

Then her light caught a slight movement in the corner of the room. She immediately turned and focused it, and found herself staring at a small blonde girl manacled to the heavy wooden leg of an immense chair.

"Help me!" pleaded the girl.

"Are you alone?" whispered the Mouse.

The girl nodded.

The Mouse crossed the room and set to work on the girl's manacles.

"What's your name?" asked the Mouse.

"Penelope," sniffed the girl.

"Penelope what?"

"Just Penelope."

The manacles came apart and dropped to the floor, and the Mouse stood up and took her first good look at the girl.

Penelope's blonde hair seemed to have been haphazardly cut with a knife rather than a shears, and it obviously hadn't been washed in weeks, or perhaps months. There was a large bruise on her left cheek, not terribly miscolored, obviously on the mend. She was thin, not wiry and hard like the Mouse, but almost malnourished. She was dressed in what had once been a white play outfit that was now grimy and shredded from being worn for weeks on end. Her feet were bare, and both her heels were raw.

"Don't turn the light on," said Penelope. "He'll be back soon."

"What race does he belong to?"

Penelope shrugged. "I don't know."

The Mouse pulled a dagger out of her left boot. "If he comes back before we leave, I'll have a little surprise for him, that's for sure."

Penelope shook her head adamantly. "You can't kill him. Please, can't we leave?"

The Mouse reached out a hand and pulled Penelope to her feet. "Where are your parents?"

"I don't know. Dead, I think."

"Can you walk?"

"Yes."

"All right," said the Mouse, heading toward the door. "Let's go."

"Wait!" said Penelope suddenly. "I can't leave without Jennifer!"

"Jennifer?" demanded the Mouse. "Who's Jennifer?"

Penelope raced to a corner of the room and picked up a filthy rag doll. "This is Jennifer," she said, holding it up in the beam of light. "Now we can go."

"Give me your hand," said the Mouse, ordering the door to slide into the wall.

She stuck her head out into the hall, saw no movement, and quickly walked to the stairwell, practically dragging the weakened little girl behind her. Once there, they walked down to the basement level and made their way to the laundry room.

"Now listen carefully," whispered the Mouse. "I want you to crawl on your hands and knees, just the way I'm going to do, behind this row of laundry carts, until we reach that vent. Can you see it?"

Penelope peered into the semi-darkness and shook her head.

"I'll let you know when we're there. Once we reach the vent, I'm going to boost you up inside it. It's narrow and it's dark, but you won't get stuck, because that's how I came in and I'm bigger than you are."

"I'm not afraid," said Penelope.

"I know you're not," said the Mouse reassuringly. "But you have to be absolutely silent. If you make any noise, the maids who are running the washing machines on the other side of the room might hear, and if they come over to investigate, I'll have to kill them."

"It's wrong to kill."

"Then don't make any noise and I won't have to," said the Mouse. "Are you ready?"

Penelope nodded her head, and the Mouse began crawling toward the vent. When she reached it she turned to see how far Penelope had gotten and was surprised to find the little girl almost beside her.

The Mouse made sure that the maids were still busily loading and unloading the washers and dryers, put a finger to her lips, then lifted Penelope into the vent. The little girl writhed and wriggled and finally made it to the right angle where the vent left the building and went beneath the street.

The Mouse was about to follow her when she heard a plaintive whisper.

"I can't find Jennifer!"

"Keep going!" hissed the Mouse. "I'll find her."

She waited for a moment until she could hear the child wriggling forward again, then climbed into the vent herself. She came upon the rag doll wedged into a corner as the vent turned out of the building, tucked it into her belt, then continued crawling until she caught up with Penelope, who had reached the grate beneath Merlin's wagon and didn't know what to do next.

The Mouse quickly removed the grate, boosted Penelope into the wagon, and followed her, leaning back down through the false floor to reattach the grate.

"Wait here," she instructed the child. "And don't make a sound."

She donned her black hood and made it to the act's finale with no more than ten seconds to spare. When it was over, and most of the crowd had dispersed, she led Merlin back inside the wagon.

"What kept you?" asked the magician. "You cut it awfully close."

"I hired an assistant," said the Mouse with a smile.

"An assistant?"

The Mouse pointed at Penelope, who had buried herself under a bag of props.

"Good God!" muttered Merlin, lifting the bag. "Where the hell did you find her?"

"Chained to a bed in an alien's room."

The magician squatted down next to the little girl and examined the bruise on her cheek. "You've had a hard time of it, haven't you?"

She stared at him without answering.

"Has she got any family on Westerly?" Merlin asked the Mouse.

"I don't think so."

"What was she doing here?"

"I don't know," said the Mouse.

"Hiding," said Penelope.

"He doesn't mean now, Penelope," said the Mouse. "He meant when I found you."

"Hiding," repeated Penelope.

"You mean the alien who stole you was in hiding?"

She shook her head. "He was hiding me."

The Mouse nodded. "From your parents."

Penelope shook her head again. "My parents are dead."

"From the authorities, then," said the Mouse.

"No."

"Then from who?" asked the Mouse in mild exasperation.

Penelope pointed a thin, wavering finger out the wagon's only window to the doorway of the hotel, where Cemetery Smith and Three-Fisted Ollie were speaking in loud angry voices to the doorman.

"From *them*."

2

Penelope was sound asleep, clutching her rag doll to her chest, as the ship sped through the void to the dry, dusty world of Cherokee. The Mouse had fed and bathed her, and put a healing ointment on her feet, and had finally gone to the ship's cluttered galley, where she found Merlin sitting at the dining table. He had a small mirror set up opposite his hands and was studying it intently as he went through his repertoire of card tricks.

"Well?" he asked.

"Well what?"

Merlin put the deck of cards in his pocket. "Did she say anything?"

"Of course she did," answered the Mouse. "She's not mute, you know."

"Anything *useful*?" he persisted. "Like why anyone would hire two such expensive killers to hunt her down?"

"We've gone over this before," said the Mouse wearily. "She's very young and very confused." She commanded a cabinet to open and withdrew a bottle and a glass. "It's far more likely that they were after her abductor. Look at it logically: the alien kidnapped her, the family decided not to pay any ransom, and they hired a pair of killers to get her back."

"If you're right, we've got to unload her quick," said Merlin. "If there's a reward, we claim it on Cherokee. If there isn't, we get rid of her before they send Smith and Ollie after *us*."

"There *aren't* any authorities on Cherokee," she pointed out while pouring herself a drink. "It's an Inner Frontier world. That's why we chose it."

"It's got a post office covered with Wanted posters, and it's got a powerful subspace radio transmitter," responded Merlin. "We can at least find out if a reward has been offered."

"I don't know if there will be a reward in the usual sense," said the Mouse, "but someone is offering something, or Cemetery Smith and Three-Fisted Ollie wouldn't have been after the kidnapper." She paused. "If she's valuable enough to interest professional assassins and bounty hunters, the family must be awfully rich. My guess is that they're trying to keep it quiet. Maybe she's got brothers and sisters; there's no sense advertising that their security is flawed."

"Then how will we find out who she is and who she belongs to?" said Merlin. "We can't just post an advertisement that we've stolen this little blonde girl from an alien kidnapper. Smith and Ollie would be hunting for *us* five minutes later." He stared thoughtfully at his lean, white fingers. "I don't know. We may have bitten off more than we can chew."

"What did you want me to do?" asked the Mouse irritably. "Leave her where she was?"

"No, I suppose not." Merlin sighed deeply and lit a small cigar. "But I'm starting to get a very bad feeling about this."

"I don't see why," said the Mouse, downing her drink.

"Because we're a couple of small-timers. If Cemetery Smith and Three-Fisted Ollie are involved in this, then we're in over our heads. And I have a feeling that there's more to this than meets the eye."

"For instance?"

"I don't know," he admitted. "But I can't help remembering the look on her face when she pointed to those two killers—like she'd seen them before."

"Perhaps she had," agreed the Mouse. "So what? Maybe they took a shot at her captor and missed, and in her confused state she thought they were shooting at her."

"*That's* the problem," said Merlin.

"What is?"

"Those guys don't miss." He paused and rubbed his chin thoughtfully. "And there's something else, too."

"What?"

"Bounty hunters aren't much for sharing. Do you know how much money someone had to put up to get them to work together?" He stared at her, a troubled expression on his face. "If she's worth *that* much, why haven't we heard about her before?"

"When you're *really* rich, you don't brag about it—you hide it."

"I don't know," said Merlin. "You've got an answer for everything . . . but I still don't like it."

"I'll tell you what," she said. "When we set down on Cherokee, we'll make some very discreet inquiries and see if we can find out who she is and who wants her . . . and we'll keep doing it, carefully and discreetly, on every world we hit until we get an answer. In the meantime, she can shill for the act. Will that satisfy you?"

"I suppose so. The question is: will it satisfy *her*?"

"What do you mean?" asked the Mouse.

"What if she wants to go home right now—wherever home is," said Merlin. "You told me that the alien kept her chained up. What if she tries to get away from us?"

The Mouse shook her head. "She thinks I saved her—which in fact I did. I can keep her contented."

"I just don't think of you as the motherly type."

"Why don't you let *me* worry about that?"

"As long as *some*one's worrying about it," said Merlin.

They sat in silence for half an hour, the Mouse reading a newstape, Merlin practicing his sleight of hand with a trio of coins. Then they heard Penelope moan, and the Mouse went to her cabin to check on her.

"What's the matter?" she asked as she approached the girl's bed.

Penelope looked confused. "I thought I was back where you found me."

"It was just a dream," said the Mouse soothingly.

"I'm frightened," whimpered Penelope.

"There's no need to be. You're safe now."

Penelope shook her head.

"But you are," continued the Mouse. "Tomorrow we'll be landing on a new world, and we've decided to let you start learning the act so you can help us. Won't that be fun?"

"They won't let me."

"*Who* won't let you?"

"Everybody."

"No one on this world even knows you," said the Mouse.

"Someone will. Someone always does."

The Mouse frowned. "How many worlds have you been to?"

Penelope held up both hands, studied them, and then bent two fingers on her right hand.

"Eight worlds?"

Penelope nodded.

"And somebody always knew you on each of these worlds?"

"On most of them."

"Who knew you?"

"Men."

"Just men?"

"*Bad* men," said Penelope.

"Men with weapons?"

"Some of them."

"You've had a tough time of it, haven't you?" said the Mouse. "Try to go to sleep now. Things will look better when you wake up."

She gave the little girl a hug and then left the cabin.

"Well?" asked Merlin when she rejoined him.

"Bad dream."

He shrugged. "I suppose she's entitled to it."

"She is. Do you know that they've been chasing her kidnapper across eight worlds?"

"She told you that?" asked Merlin.

"Yes."

He frowned. "That's another thing that doesn't fit."

"Why not?"

"If this alien was good enough to keep one step ahead of Cemetery Smith for eight worlds, how come you were able to just walk right in and grab her?"

"He didn't know I was there. Nobody did."

"And he didn't take any precautions against an unknown bounty hunter coming in the back door? I find that just a little bit hard to believe."

"He obviously didn't have any confederates," replied the Mouse. "Or else they were killed by bounty hunters. At any rate, he couldn't watch her every minute of every day."

"I gather he'd been doing just that on eight different worlds."

She looked annoyed. "Why is it that whenever you find yourself in a new situation, you suddenly become the most paranoid man I've ever known?"

"*New* I don't mind," responded Merlin, waving his hand in the air and producing a bouquet of flowers. "I don't even mind *strange*. But this situation feels more than new and strange: it feels *dangerous*, and *that* I don't like."

"Well," said the Mouse after a moment's silence, "I don't know what we can do about it. She's here, and until we can return her to whoever's paying Cemetery Smith and Three-Fisted Ollie to find her, she's staying here."

"We'll see."

"I mean it, Merlin," she said firmly. "After what she's been through, I'm not about to abandon her on some Frontier dirtball with no friends or family to look after her."

"All right," he said resignedly. "I know that tone of voice. She stays until we find out who will pay to get her back."

"You needn't look so unhappy about it," she added.

"Why not?" replied Merlin. "I've got the same questions now I had an hour ago; none of them have gone away just because you've always got a smooth answer for everything." He paused. "The only thing that's changed since this conversation began is that now we've got another mouth to feed."

"A very little one."

"A very well traveled, very enigmatic little one," he corrected her.

3

The ship touched down on a barren strip of ground a mile beyond Cherokee's only Tradertown. Ordinarily Merlin and the Mouse would have taken a room at the local hotel, just to get away from the monotony of their cramped quarters, but they didn't want to advertise the fact that a little blonde girl was traveling with them, so they decided to sleep in the ship.

They touched down in the middle of the night, and when the harsh yellow sun rose over Cherokee's bloodred sand dunes and barren, rocky hills, they left Penelope behind and walked into town.

Like most of the Inner Frontier's Tradertowns, this one had sprung up around the planet's first bar and whorehouse. There were a pair of small hotels, a couple of restaurants, a second whorehouse and three more bars, a hangar for private spaceships, a post office that functioned not only for Cherokee but for every habitable world within five light-years, a now-defunct government office for registering mining claims, a safari outfitter, seven import/export companies, a small brewery, two general stores, and perhaps fifty modular domed houses.

Once Cherokee had been a mining world, but after its limited supply of diamonds and fissionable materials had been exhausted, its primary reason for colonization had vanished, and it was now used mainly as a trading post and refueling depot for excursions to Far Hebrides, Oceana III, and other more interesting planets closer to the Galactic Core. A few thousand people had remained on Cherokee, but it was as close to being deserted as a planet could become while still inhabited by some sentient life-forms

The Mouse stopped at the post office and checked the various posters, hoping to find some mention of a missing blonde girl, but saw nothing but the holographs of wanted criminals. Finally she left and walked into the largest of the taverns and waited for Merlin, who was trying to get some news concerning Penelope's family from the subspace transmitting station.

The tavern was quite large. There was a long hardwood bar running down one side of it, a handful of gaming machines in the rear, and a number of large round tables clustered in the middle. A trio of overhead fans spun lazily, recirculating the warm air. A holograph of a buxom nude brunette hung over the bar, punctured by hundreds of darts. The floor was covered with the omnipresent red dust of Cherokee, and traces of it seemed to hang in the still air of the tavern.

The clientele was similar to most of the Tradertowns that the Mouse had visited, a mixture of aliens and humans, some obviously wealthy, others just as obviously poor, all chasing the dream of instant riches that life on the Inner Frontier always promised and rarely delivered.

Two Lodinites, their red fur rippling despite the lack of air circulation, were seated at one table, playing *jabob*, a card game that was becoming increasingly popular on the Inner Frontier. There was a tall, emaciated Canphorite sitting alone in a corner, obviously waiting for someone to join him. The rest of the customers, clustered together in twos and threes, were Men. Some were garbed in silks and satins, with shining leather boots and sparkling new weapons; others, those who had not yet struck it rich, or, more likely, had squandered what they had earned, wore the dusty working outfits of prospectors. A couple of girls from the whorehouse next door were drinking at the bar, but by some sort of mutual understanding, none of the men approached them or even paid any attention to them while they were on their equivalent of a coffee break.

The Mouse sat down at an empty table, spent a few restless minutes waiting for Merlin, and finally ordered a container of the local beer. It tasted bitter, but it quenched the thirst she had built up walking through the hot dusty street, and she quickly finished it and ordered another.

A moment later Merlin entered and came over to join her.

"Any luck?" he asked, sitting down on a straight-backed chair.

"No. How about you?"

He shook his head. "Not a damned thing. What do we do now?"

"We do our act tonight, and then leave. This world's only good for one day. Hell, I doubt that I'll be able to steal enough to pay for our fuel."

"And the girl?" continued Merlin.

"She can't stay here," said the Mouse adamantly. "She'll come along until we can collect a reward or find a safe place to leave her."

"It had better be soon," said Merlin. He got up and walked over to the bar to order a drink. As he returned and sat down, a tall, slender man turned away from the bar and approached their table. His coal-black outfit was carefully tailored and remarkably free of dust, his boots were made from the pelts of some exotic white and blue arctic animal, and he carried a small hand-axe tucked in his belt.

"Mind if I join you?" he said, pulling up a chair, wiping a trace of red dust from it with a linen handkerchief, and sitting down.

"Do we know you?" asked Merlin suspiciously.

"I sure as hell doubt it," said the tall man. "But *I* know *you*."

"Oh?"

The man nodded. "You're that magician who hits the Inner Frontier worlds, aren't you?"

"Who wants to know?"

"My name's MacLemore," said the man. "Hatchet Jack MacLemore. Maybe you've heard of me?"

"I'm afraid not," said Merlin.

"Well, it's a big galaxy," said MacLemore with an easy shrug. "No reason why you should have." He paused. "And you're Merlin the Magician, right?"

"Merlin the Magnificent," the magician corrected him. "And this is my assistant," he added, gesturing toward the Mouse.

"I'm pleased to meet you," said the tall man, smiling at her.

"Where was it that you saw me perform?" asked Merlin.

"Oh, I never saw you perform," said MacLemore. "Magic doesn't interest me much."

"I must have misunderstood you," replied Merlin. "I thought you said you had seen me."

"I said I knew who you were," said MacLemore. "That's not the same thing at all." He paused. "Anyway, I'd like to buy you a beer and maybe do a little business with you."

"What are you selling?" asked the Mouse, surreptitiously withdrawing her knife from her boot, but keeping her hands beneath the table.

MacLemore smiled. "I'm not selling anything, ma'am. Selling's not my business."

"All right," she said coldly. "What are you buying?"

The smile remained in place. "Well, truth to tell, buying's not my business, either."

"Just what *is* your business?"

"Oh, a little of this and a little of that." He turned to Merlin. "You were on Westerly a couple of days ago, weren't you?"

"What concern is that of yours?" demanded Merlin.

"Where you go makes no difference to me," said MacLemore. "Westerly's as good a world as any, and probably better than most." Suddenly he leaned forward, staring intently at the magician. "But while you were there, you took something that didn't belong to you." He paused briefly. "And *that's* my business."

"I don't know what you're talking about," said Merlin.

"Oh, I think you do," replied MacLemore. "I'm talking about something you took from an alien's room."

"I'm a magician, not a thief," said Merlin. He paused and returned MacLemore's stare. "But just out of curiosity, how much is this missing object worth?"

"I think you know, or you wouldn't have taken it."

"I didn't take anything."

"I thought we were talking business," said MacLemore. "And here you go, insulting my intelligence. It's enough to make a man take offense." He smiled again, a smile that started and ended with his lips. His eyes remained cold and hard.

"I assure you that no offense was intended," said Merlin. "As for talking business," he continued carefully, "I haven't heard any offers yet."

"You're still alive," said MacLemore. "That's not necessarily a permanent condition."

Merlin looked more annoyed than frightened. "I've been threatened by experts." He reached into the air, snapped his fingers, and suddenly he was holding a small laser pistol that was aimed between the tall man's eyes.

"That's very good," admitted MacLemore. "Maybe I ought to take more of an interest in magic."

"Maybe you ought to take less of an interest in other people's affairs," said Merlin.

"You might as well deal with me," said MacLemore. "You're going to have to deal with *someone* before you leave the planet."

"Nobody else knows we're here."

MacLemore chuckled in amusement. "How do you think *I* knew it—or do you think I live on this dirtball?" He turned to the Mouse. "You're going to run into a lot of people who aren't as friendly and reasonable as I am, ma'am. Maybe you'd better tell your friend to deal with me while he can."

"I still haven't heard any offers," said Merlin. "Either tell me what you're after and how much you're willing to pay for it, or go bother someone else."

"I've already made you a handsome offer: you get to live."

"You seem to forget who's holding the gun."

MacLemore shrugged. "It's not the kind of thing I'm likely to forget," he replied easily. "Hell, everyone in this tavern knows you're pointing a laser pistol at me." Suddenly he smiled. "But you don't know which two of them are my partners."

"Mouse?" said Merlin, never taking his eyes from MacLemore. "Any suggestions?"

"He doesn't have any partners," said the Mouse coldly. "Men like him always work alone."

"My feelings precisely," agreed Merlin.

"If he doesn't get up and walk away, kill him," said the Mouse.

"There are a lot of witnesses," said MacLemore, suddenly tense.

"They don't give a damn about any of us," replied the Mouse.

"Forgive my saying it, but you're a bloodthirsty little lady, ma'am," said MacLemore, his right hand inching down to the hand-axe he had tucked in his belt.

Suddenly the Mouse stood up and threw her knife at him. It caught him in the right shoulder, and he shrieked in pain.

"Nobody does that to Hatchet Jack!" he bellowed, awkwardly trying to withdraw the axe with his left hand.

There was a brief buzzing sound as Merlin fired his laser pistol, and MacLemore collapsed across the table, his head smoking and sizzling.

"Wonderful," muttered Merlin, staring at the humans at the bar, who had all turned to see what was happening. "What now?"

"Now we get the hell out of here," said the Mouse, retrieving her knife with a hard jerk.

"Start walking to the door."

She nodded and did as he said, while he faced the assembled spectators.

Nobody moved. The silence was almost palpable, broken only by the creaking of the overhead fans as they continued to turn slowly.

"He threatened us," said Merlin at last, starting to back toward the door. "It was self-defense."

The bartender, who had been totally motionless, picked up a glass and began wiping it absently. "No one's prepared to argue that point while you've got a gun trained on us, mister," he said. "And no one's going to weep bitter tears over Hatchet Jack's grave, either."

"I'm delighted you're being so reasonable about it," said Merlin, reaching the door.

"You got the gun."

"Just remember that."

"Got a bit of advice for you, though," said the bartender.

"What is it?"

"I wouldn't try using that gun on the next fellow who comes to talk to you. There won't be enough of you left to bury."

"Who else is looking for me?"

"You'll find out soon enough," said the bartender. "I don't know what you've got, mister, but some pretty dangerous people don't want you to keep it."

"Who?"

"You'll know 'em when you see 'em."

"If you see them first," said Merlin, "tell them that I'm a peace-loving man and that anything I've got is for sale."

"I'll do that," said the bartender. "Now you can do me a favor and get the hell out of here before they find you. I don't want my tavern all shot up."

Merlin waved his laser pistol in the air. "If anyone follows me, he's going to wish he hadn't."

"You made your point," said the bartender. "Just leave."

Merlin backed into the street. "Did you hear all that?" he asked the Mouse.

"Yes," she answered. "We'd better get back to the ship fast—if it's still there."

"Damn!" muttered Merlin. "I hadn't thought of that. If we didn't have the girl with us, of course they'd go to the ship!"

They began walking rapidly out of the Tradertown, keeping to the shadows cast by the buildings wherever they could, wary of any possible ambush.

"How did word of what we did get here so fast?" demanded Merlin, increasing his pace.

"Her family must be even richer than I thought," said the Mouse.

"Right at this moment, anyone who wants her can have her, as far as I'm concerned," said Merlin. "That's the first time I've ever killed a man. I don't care how big the reward is, she's not worth the trouble."

"The first time?" said the Mouse, surprised.

"Yes."

"You handled yourself very well."

"It was like some big game of upmanship until you threw your knife at him," replied Merlin. "Then I just pulled the trigger without thinking."

"That's the best way," said the Mouse. "Start thinking about what you're going to do, and you start thinking about what might happen to you, and then you start hesitating, and before you know it you're dead."

"You talk about it like it was a daily occurrence. I've just killed a man!"

"He was going to kill us," said the Mouse with a shrug.

"But—"

"Stop worrying about him. We may have to kill a few more before we get off this planet."

"Let's just give them the girl."

"First they have to ask for her. Since they've probably figured out that she's in the ship, they may not bother."

"Wonderful," muttered Merlin.

They reached the edge of town. Merlin looked back to make sure no one had emerged from the tavern yet, then peered off in the distance, where the sun was glinting off the ship.

"It's still there," said the Mouse, half surprised.

"God!" he said. "It looks a lot farther away than it looked this morning."

"One of the reasons I teamed up with you is because you're good in a crisis," said the Mouse. "But you approach one about as badly as any man I've ever known."

Merlin made no reply, but merely glared at her for a moment and continued walking. When they were within five hundred yards, he stopped again.

"I don't like it," he said. "We're sitting ducks. There's nowhere to hide, and the sand makes it impossible to move quickly if we have to."

"The sooner we get there, the sooner you won't have to worry about it," said the Mouse.

"I'm not that anxious to get my head blown off."

"Has it occurred to you that if someone at the ship was planning to kill us, they would have already done it? This isn't beyond the range of any long-barreled weapon I know of: projectile, laser, sonic, or molecular imploder."

Merlin frowned. "You're right."

"Feel better?"

"Less like a target, anyway. Whoever's looking for the girl is at least willing to let us get close enough to talk to him."

"And if we can get that close . . ." said the Mouse.

Merlin increased his pace. "Yes, I feel much better."

"Somehow I knew you would."

When they got to within three hundred yards, the magician slowed down again.

"Now what?" asked the Mouse.

"I don't see anyone."

"So?"

"If they're inside the ship, they've already got the girl, and they don't need us anymore."

"Then why haven't they shot us?" she asked.

"Why take a chance of missing at a quarter of a mile when they can wait for us to reach the ship and blow us away from ten yards?" he retorted.

"What do you propose to do, then—stand out here until you die of heatstroke?"

"I don't know."

"Well, you can do what you want," said the Mouse. "I'm going to the ship."

Merlin, muttering to himself, fell into step beside her. Then, when they were one hundred fifty yards away from the ship, the Mouse stopped and, shading her eyes with her hands, stared straight ahead.

"What now?" asked Merlin.

"I'm not sure. It's so bright . . . but I *think* I see two bodies at the foot of the ship."

"Are they moving?"

She shook her head. "They look dead."

"That's crazy," said Merlin. "We haven't got any guardian angels on this planet. On *any* planet, for that matter."

"Maybe they had a falling-out," said the Mouse.

"Well, let's find out."

They approached the ship cautiously, but the Mouse had been right: two men, both heavily armed, lay dead at the base of the ladder leading to the entry hatch.

"That's very strange," said the Mouse. "Neither one of them tried to use his weapon."

"What killed them?" asked Merlin.

"The one on the right looks like he broke his neck. There's not a mark on the other one that I can see."

"The hatch is unlocked," said Merlin. "Do you suppose there's another one in there?"

"There's only one way to find out," said the Mouse, climbing up the stairs and entering the ship.

"Penelope!" she called. "Are you all right?"

Suddenly the little blonde girl, her rag doll clutched in one hand, raced out of her cabin and threw herself into the Mouse's arms.

"Please don't leave me again!" she sobbed. "I was so frightened!"

"It's all right now," said the Mouse, stroking her hair. "Nobody's going to harm you."

"Is there anyone else aboard the ship?" asked Merlin, climbing through the hatch.

Penelope shook her head. "Just me."

The Mouse set her down on the deck and knelt next to her. "Tell me what happened," she said.

"Two very bad men came to the ship after you left," said Penelope.

"I know."

"I think they wanted to take me away."

"I think so, too," said the Mouse.

"I'm glad they died."

"So am I," said the Mouse. "But *how* did they die?"

"After you left, I got lonely, so I took Jennifer outside to play, but there weren't any other little girls around." She looked as if she were about to burst into tears again. "There wasn't *anyone*." She paused. "Do we have to stay on this world?"

"We'll be leaving in just a few minutes," said the Mouse. "Now, what happened to the two men?"

"I saw them coming out to the ship and I got scared and ran inside, but I left Jennifer on the stairs to the door."

"You mean the entry hatch?"

"The door," repeated Penelope, pointing to the open hatch. "One of them started climbing the stairs, but he tripped on Jennifer and fell down and didn't move."

"And the other man?"

"He knelt down next to the first man to see if he was alive, and something bit him."

"Something? What kind of thing?"

"I don't know. It lives under the sand. He screamed and grabbed his hand, and then he died, too." She stared out the hatch. "They were very bad men."

"Merlin," said the Mouse, "check him out."

The magician went back outside while the Mouse soothed the little girl, then re-entered the ship a moment later.

"He's got some kind of bite on his hand, all right. It's swollen up and miscolored. He was lying on it or we'd have spotted it right away." He uttered a low whistle and shook his head in wonderment. "Boy! Talk about dumb luck!"

"I'm not dumb!" said Penelope heatedly.

"No," said Merlin. "But you sure as hell are lucky." He turned to the Mouse. "I recognize the one with the broken neck."

"Bounty hunter?"

"From time to time. A killer, anyway."

"We've got some serious planning to do," said the Mouse.

"I agree," said Merlin. "The next guy to come along isn't going to trip on a doll or get bitten by some alien snake." He locked the hatch, entered the control room, and activated the ship's engines. "But before we talk, the first order of business is to get the hell off the planet before somebody else comes looking for us."

"Right," said the Mouse, strapping Penelope and herself down as the ship began climbing through the atmosphere. Once they were safely in space, Merlin set the controls on automatic and joined the Mouse in the galley.

"If they know we landed on Cherokee, they must know the ship's registry number," he said. "And if they know that, they'll be able to find us wherever we go."

"We can't afford a new ship, and I don't think trying to steal one would be the brightest thing we ever did."

"I agree."

"Then what did you have in mind?" asked the Mouse.

"Let's go deeper into the Inner Frontier. I'll touch down on five or six worlds and drop the two of you off on one of them."

"And what about you?"

"I'll lead them a merry chase while you try to find out who she belongs to." The Mouse opened her mouth to protest, but Merlin held up his hand. "Look," he said, "I'm happier running away from trouble and you're happier confronting it. This makes sense all the way around."

"How will we keep in touch?"

"We won't," said Merlin. "If they've got our registry number, they can monitor every message the ship sends and receives. We'll choose a place to meet, say, thirty Galactic Standard days from now."

"What if they catch you first?"

"Well, it's not my favorite scenario," he admitted, "but if they don't blow the ship to hell and gone, they're going to find out that I haven't got the girl."

"They'll make you tell them where we are," said the Mouse. "You're not very good about pain, and even if you were, there are drugs that'll make you tell them everything you know."

"I know," he said. "That's why you're going to catch the first ship off the planet I leave you on. What I don't know, I can't tell them."

"You can tell them where we plan to meet thirty days from now," the Mouse pointed out.

Merlin frowned. "I hadn't thought of that." He shrugged. "Well, I suppose I just can't let them catch me."

"Not good enough," said the Mouse. She was silent for a moment. "I have it."

"Yes?"

"I won't meet you in thirty days—but if you'll tell me where you're going to be, I'll see to it that someone you've never seen before, someone you don't know, will find you and tell you where to meet us. But he'll only approach you once he's made sure you're alone, and not being observed. If he's not satisfied, he won't make contact, and we'll wait another thirty days before trying again."

"I like to think of myself as ruggedly masculine and quite distinctive," said Merlin wryly, "but the fact of the matter is that I look just like anyone else. How will you be sure he'll be able to spot me?"

"You're a magician. Put on a show."

He grinned. "You know, it's been so long since I did a legitimate performance, I never thought of that."

"Well, it's time we *started* thinking," said the Mouse grimly. "Someone is sure as hell putting a lot of thought into hunting us down."

4

Merlin touched down on Binder X, one of the more populous worlds of the Inner Frontier, just long enough to drop off the Mouse and Penelope, then headed toward the Galactic Core.

Within three hours, the Mouse and Penelope were on their way to Evergreen, a lush jungle world which had been opened up only two decades earlier. They spent one night there, then boarded the next ship to Solomon, a mining planet that had yielded the three largest diamonds ever discovered. The spaceport was in the small but bustling city of Haggard, and by nightfall the Mouse had obtained a room in a nondescript hotel.

"How much longer do we have to keep running?" asked Penelope wearily as the Mouse began unpacking their single piece of luggage.

"Until I'm sure no one is following us."

"I'm hungry."

"Wash your hands and face, and I'll take you downstairs for dinner."

The girl walked into the bathroom, did as she had been instructed, and then emerged, holding up her hands for the Mouse's inspection.

"Very good," said the Mouse.

"Good," said Penelope. "I want you to like me."

"I'd like you just as much if your hands were dirty," said the Mouse. "After all, you're a very likable little girl. I just wouldn't shake hands with you."

"Do you really like me?"

"Yes, I really do."

"I like you, too." The little girl paused. "Will you always be my friend?"

"Of course," said the Mouse. "Why shouldn't I be?"

"I don't know," said Penelope. "But lots of people pretend to be my friend, and then they aren't."

"Oh?" said the Mouse. "Who?"

"Lots of people."

"Do you want to talk about it?"

Penelope shook her head. "I'm hungry. So is Jennifer."

"Me, too," said the Mouse. "Bring Jennifer along, and let's go get some dinner."

They left the room, took the airlift down to the lobby, and entered the restaurant. The Mouse scanned the faces of the diners, not quite knowing what she was looking for, but hoping she would be able to spot someone who was after Penelope, either by the telltale bulge of a weapon or by some surreptitious look. But everyone carried weapons on the Inner Frontier, and nobody paid her or the girl any attention.

They punched out their orders on a computer—the Mouse had to help Penelope read some of the dishes—and then settled back to await their meal.

"If we're going to be friends forever," said the Mouse, "I should know a lot more about you. We've been so busy running for the past few days that we've hardly had a chance to get to know each other."

"And *I* should get to know more about you, too," agreed Penelope.

"That seems fair enough."

"Why are you called the Mouse?"

"Because I'm so small," answered the Mouse. "And because I can go places where most people don't fit."

"Like the laundry vent?"

The Mouse nodded. "Exactly."

"Why were you there?" asked Penelope.

"Because that's where Merlin put on his magic show."

"I like his tricks," said Penelope. "They're fun." She paused. "Is he your husband?"

The Mouse chuckled. "No, thank God. He's just my business partner."

"Do you love him?"

"No."

"Do you like him?"

"Yes."

"More than you like me?"

"I hardly know you yet, Penelope," said the Mouse. "But I'm sure that after we get acquainted, I won't like anyone better than I like you."

"I hope so," said Penelope.

"Now it's my turn to ask you some questions."

"All right."

"What's your home world?"

"I don't know."

"I don't mean the world you were born on. I mean the one you live on."

"Oh. Solomon."

"That's the world we're on now," the Mouse pointed out.

"Then it's my home world now."

"Let me try it a different way. Where did you grow up?"

"All over."

The Mouse frowned. "Where did your parents live?"

"With me."

A waiter arrived with their dinners, and the Mouse put off further questions until they finished eating. Then, while they were waiting for dessert, she tried again.

"Do you know why the alien kidnapped you?"

"What is *kidnapped*?" asked Penelope.

"Why he stole you from your family?"

"He didn't. He stole me from Jimmy Sunday." She paused, considering her answer. "He *saved* me from Jimmy Sunday," she amended, "but he was very mean to me."

"Jimmy Sunday?" repeated the Mouse. "He was a bounty hunter. I remember hearing that they found his body on Glennaris V."

"Glennaris IV," Penelope corrected her. "No one lives on Glennaris V."

"And you say the alien stole you from him and killed him?"

"He *saved* me from him," repeated Penelope. "Jimmy Sunday was going to hurt me." She paused thoughtfully. "I don't know who killed him."

The Mouse looked puzzled. "Why would he want to hurt you?"

Penelope shrugged. "I don't know."

"Maybe you just thought he was going to hurt you. He was probably a gruff man."

"He was going to kill me," said Penelope adamantly.

"That doesn't make any sense."

"Those two men on Cherokee were going to kill me, too."

"No, they weren't," said the Mouse. "They were going to take you away from us and return you to your family."

"I don't have any family."

"You must have someone—a cousin, an uncle, something."

Penelope shrugged. "Maybe."

"Anyway, they weren't going to kill you. Someone has offered a lot of money for anyone who finds you and returns you to them. Nobody can collect it if you're dead."

"You're not going to return me, are you?" asked Penelope fearfully.

"Of course not," lied the Mouse. "But I have to find out who wants you back, so I can tell them that you're safe and that you'd rather stay with me." She paused. "Who do you think wants you back?"

"Everybody," said Penelope. "Especially the Number Man."

"The Number Man?" repeated the Mouse. "Who's that?"

"I don't know."

"Why do you call him the Number Man?"

"Because his name is a number."

"It is?"

Penelope nodded. "32," she said.

"Maybe it's a code."

"Everyone called him that."

"Who is everyone?"

"Everyone in the building."

"What building?"

"I don't know."

"Where was this building?" asked the Mouse.

"Far away," said Penelope. "On a big planet with lots of buildings."

"If I named the planet, would you know it?"

"Yes."

"Earth?"

"No."

"Sirius V?"

"No."

"Deluros VIII?"

"That's it," said Penelope.

"You've been to Deluros?"

Penelope nodded. "It's a big world."

"The biggest," agreed the Mouse. "Did you live there?"

Penelope shook her head. "The Number Man took me there."

"Why would someone take you to the capital world of the Democracy?"

"I don't know."

"How long were you there?"

"A long time."

"A week? A month? A year?"

Penelope shrugged. "A long time."

"Did you like it there?" asked the Mouse.

"No. Everybody wore uniforms and they weren't nice to me. They wouldn't play with me."

"How did you leave?"

"Somebody stole me."

"Jimmy Sunday?"

Penelope shook his head. "No. Before him."

The Mouse was silent for a moment, trying to understand what she had been told, and to determine how much of it was true.

"It's my turn," said Penelope.

"Your turn?"

"To ask you more questions."

"All right," said the Mouse.

"Were you always called the Mouse?"

"No. I had a real name once."

"What was it?"

The Mouse smiled a bittersweet smile. "That was a long time ago, and I never think about it anymore."

"How long ago?"

"Very."

"How old are you?" asked Penelope.

"Thirty-seven Standard years."

"You're much older than Merlin," observed Penelope.

"Not *that* much," said the Mouse defensively. "Six or seven years, that's all."

"What did you do before you met him?"

"All kinds of things," said the Mouse.

"Were you ever married?"

"No."

"Did you ever want to be?"

The Mouse shrugged. "I thought I did once. I was wrong."

"Is that when you became the Mouse?"

The Mouse smiled. "Not quite."

"How does Merlin do his tricks? Are they really magic?"

"No, not really; they're just illusions. And he never tells me how they work."

"But he's your friend, isn't he?"

"Yes."

"Then he should tell you."

"But because I'm his friend, I never ask."

"I don't understand," said Penelope.

"When you get a little bigger, you will." Suddenly the Mouse became aware of a large man staring at them through the doorway that faced the lobby. When she met his gaze he looked away.

"Penelope," said the Mouse softly, "I want you to turn your head very slowly and tell me if you recognize the man standing by the pillar just beyond the door. Not quickly, now; just casually, as if you're bored and are looking around."

Penelope did as she was instructed, then turned back to the Mouse.

"Have you ever seen him before?" asked the Mouse.

Penelope shook her head. "No."

"You're sure?"

"Yes."

"I may be wrong, but I've got a feeling that he's staring right at us." She reached out and took Penelope's hand in her own. "There's no reason to be afraid. He won't make a move while there are so many witnesses. We're safe for the moment."

"I *knew* it wouldn't stop," said Penelope unhappily.

The Mouse let go of Penelope's hand and began checking her weaponry beneath the table: the knife in her boot, the acid spray in her pocket pouch, the tiny sonic pistol tucked beneath her belt. When she was sure everything was in order, she instructed the computer to bill her room, then got to her feet.

"Well, we might as well find out if I'm right or wrong," she announced. "Stay near me, but always keep me between you and that man, do you understand?"

"Yes."

"And don't be afraid. No one's going to hurt you."

"I won't be afraid," promised Penelope.

The Mouse took Penelope by the hand and walked out of the restaurant toward the airlift. The large man fell into step about forty feet behind them.

"Damn!" muttered the Mouse under her breath.

She pulled Penelope onto the invisible cushion of air and let it propel them to the eighth floor. The large man took the airlift just to the left, about ten seconds behind them.

They stepped off at the eighth floor and began walking toward their room. The large man remained some forty feet behind them.

The Mouse reached her door and began entering the computer lock combination, then felt a small hand on her wrist.

"Don't," whispered Penelope.

The Mouse turned to her.

"There's someone inside."

"How do you know?" asked the Mouse.

"I just know," said Penelope with total conviction.

The Mouse took her at her word, grabbed her hand again, and began walking down the corridor, away from the large man.

"There'd better be a stairway!" she muttered.

They turned a corner and saw an exit sign above one of the doors.

"Faster!" said Penelope, breaking into a run, and the Mouse followed suit.

They entered the stairwell and the door slammed shut behind them, just as the large man reached the corner. The Mouse pulled her knife out and crouched in the shadows, waiting.

"That won't work!" whispered Penelope.

"It'd damn well better work!" said the Mouse.

"It won't," she repeated. "Follow me."

She darted down the stairs, and the Mouse raced after her. When she reached the fifth floor, they could hear the large man coming down the stairs behind them.

On the fifth floor, Penelope stopped and looked into the darkness behind the door for an instant, then reached into the shadows and grabbed a broom.

"You go first," she said.

"Not a chance!" whispered the Mouse, tightening her grip on her knife.

"You can't hurt him with a knife!" hissed Penelope. She held up the broom. "*This* will stop him."

The Mouse stared at her as the little girl placed the broom on the stairs, then ran down to the next landing.

"Hurry!" urged Penelope as the large man came into view.

The Mouse raced down to the landing, then turned and prepared to do battle.

The man had a sonic pistol in his hand, and as he surged down the stairs he was so intent upon his quarry that he didn't see the broom until he tripped over it. He careened off a wall, grunted in surprise, then fell heavily down the stairs, bellowing in pain. As he rolled onto the landing, the Mouse crouched down and expertly slit his throat.

Suddenly Penelope began crying and wrapped her arms around the Mouse.

"Won't they ever *stop*?" she whimpered.

The Mouse, breathing heavily, stroked Penelope's blonde hair for a moment, then stepped back and held the little girl's face between her hands.

"Don't *ever* disobey my orders again," she said. "I told you to keep me between you and him."

"Now *you're* mad at me, too!" wept Penelope. "I thought we were friends."

"We *are* friends," said the Mouse. "That's why I'm mad at you. You might have been killed because you didn't obey me."

"But your knife wouldn't have hurt him," protested the little girl.

"Hurt him? It killed him."

"But you wouldn't have cut his neck. You would have stabbed his chest or his belly."

"It would have killed him just as dead."

Penelope shook her head. "It wouldn't have hurt him," she repeated stubbornly.

"Why do you keep saying that?" demanded the Mouse.

"Look," said Penelope, pointing to the dead man.

The Mouse knelt down and examined him, then looked up, surprised.

"He was wearing body armor!" she exclaimed.

"That's what I was trying to tell you."

"But it was hidden under his tunic," continued the Mouse. "How did you know it was there?"

"I didn't."

"But you said you did."

Penelope shook her head again. "I said I knew your knife wouldn't hurt him."

The Mouse frowned. "But you didn't know why?"

"No."

"And how did you know there was a broom behind that door?"

Penelope shrugged.

"I thought we were friends," said the Mouse. "Friends don't keep secrets from each other."

"I saw it," said Penelope.

"You've never been in this stairwell."

"I know."

"Then how could you have seen it?" persisted the Mouse.

"I saw it"—Penelope pointed to her head—"in here."

5

"Let me get this straight," said the Mouse. "Are you telling me that you can see the future?"

"There are lots of futures," said Penelope. "I don't see all of them."

"What *do* you see?"

"I see what's going to happen next . . . sometimes."

"But you were wrong," said the Mouse. "You saw me stabbing the armored vest, and I didn't."

"I try to make the best future happen," said Penelope. She frowned. "But it doesn't always work. People still try to hurt me."

"You mean you could see what would happen if I tried to stab him, and also what would happen if I didn't?"

"It's not like reading a book," explained the girl. "I could see that if you stabbed him, he'd kill us. So I ran, and when we came to the fifth floor, I saw that if I picked up the broom and placed it a certain way on the staircase, he'd trip over it."

"And what about our room?" continued the Mouse. "Did you see someone inside it?"

Penelope nodded. "There was a man there. If we had gone in, he'd have shot us."

"How did you ever get captured by Jimmy Sunday or the alien or this man you call 32?"

Penelope shrugged. "Sometimes I can't get away in any of the futures I can see."

"How long have you been able to do this?"

"Do what?"

"See into the future."

"Always, I guess."

"How far ahead can you see?"

"It changes."

"A minute? An hour? A week?"

"Not a week," answered Penelope. "Usually just a few seconds. Sometimes maybe a minute." She paused. "And I can't always do it. Usually just when I have to."

"Like when someone's going to do something bad to you?"

"Yes."

"How does it work?" asked the Mouse. "Do you read their minds?"

"No. I just see what's going to happen, and then if I don't like it, I try to change it."

"That's quite a gift," said the Mouse. "Now I know why they want you back so badly."

"I don't want to go back," whined Penelope. "I want to stay with you."

"Nobody's sending you back," said the Mouse. She suddenly became acutely aware of the dead man at their feet. "We've got to get out of here." She began walking down the stairs.

"What about our clothes?" asked Penelope.

"Is the man still in our room?"

"I don't know."

"It's not worth the risk. We'll buy some new clothes on the next world. Come on."

They descended to the lobby, walked out the front door, and hailed a landcab.

As it approached the spaceport, Penelope tugged at the Mouse's sleeve.

"We shouldn't get out here," she said. "It's not safe."

"You're sure?"

Penelope nodded.

"But we have to get off the planet. Can you see how they plan to attack us?"

"No. I just know it's not safe."

"Then you don't know if we can elude them?"

"What does *elude* mean?"

"It means to keep away from them."

"I don't know," answered Penelope.

"All right," said the Mouse. "We'll play it safe." She leaned forward and instructed the driver to take them to the vehicle rental section. Once there, she paid off the driver and rented a landcar.

They drove through the streets of Haggard, found an all-night grocery store, bought a dozen sandwiches and a few drink containers, and then headed out of town.

"Where are we going?" asked Penelope, hugging Jennifer protectively.

"Away from anyone who wants to hurt you," answered the Mouse.

"Good," said Penelope. "You're my only friend." She leaned against the Mouse and was sound asleep a moment later.

The Mouse drove through the night. The vegetation became increasingly sparse, and by sunrise she found herself on the outskirts of a vast desert. She pulled off the road, brought the vehicle to a stop, and began sorting through maps on the viewscreen.

"Where are we?" asked Penelope, waking up and rubbing her eyes.

"I'm not sure," said the Mouse, still going through maps. "Ah, here we are."

"Where?"

"The Devil's Anvil."

"What's that?"

"That's the name of the desert." She pointed to a tiny dot in the middle of it. "And this is a village called Ophir." She hit two buttons on the vehicle's computer, and the map was replaced by a readout. "One bar, one store, one hotel."

"Why would anyone build a city in the middle of a desert?" asked Penelope.

"Good question," said the Mouse. "Let's find out." She issued another command to the computer. "Hmm. We may be in luck."

"Why?"

"Because there's a diamond pipe about five miles from Ophir."

"What's a diamond pipe?"

"A mine," replied the Mouse. "They're still pulling diamonds out of it, or Ophir would be a ghost town."

"Why does that make us lucky?" persisted Penelope.

"Because where there's that kind of money, there's usually a ship or two. No mine owner is going to drive three hundred miles into the Devil's Anvil to check on business."

"He'd take a plane, not a spaceship."

"Maybe," said the Mouse. "But if he's from off-planet, he'll have a ship—and between you and me, I don't know why anyone would choose to live on this ugly little dirtball if he could afford to live somewhere else."

"And if he owns a diamond mine, he can afford to live somewhere else," concluded Penelope, inordinately proud of herself for following the Mouse's train of thought to its logical conclusion.

"Right," said the Mouse. She sighed. "Well, there's no sense wasting any more time. Let's go."

She pulled back onto the road and headed off across the Devil's Anvil.

After about sixty-five kilometers the road vanished, and the Mouse immediately slowed down.

"You can keep going fast," said Penelope. "The ground is hard here."

"I know," said the Mouse. "But if I don't slow down, we're going to leave a cloud of dust and sand, and that will make us easier to spot if anyone's following us." She turned to the girl. "Are they?"

Penelope shrugged. "I don't know."

"Well, since we don't know that they aren't, we'll do it the safe way."

"But it's hot."

"The air conditioner can only do so much," answered the Mouse. "The ground temperature must be close to sixty degrees Celsius. Just try not to think about it."

Penelope was silent for a moment. Then she turned to the Mouse. "The more I try not to think about it, the more I do," she complained.

"Then take a nap."

"But I just woke up."

"Then let's talk," said the Mouse. "Maybe that will take your mind off the heat."

"All right," agreed Penelope.

"Tell me about this man called 32."

Penelope shook her head. "I don't want to talk about people who were mean to me," she said adamantly.

"Suits me," said the Mouse. "Who *hasn't* been mean to you?"

"You and Merlin."

"There must have been someone else in your whole life."

The little girl was silent for a moment, lost in thought. "Maybe my mother," she said.

"Only maybe?"

"She let them take me away."

"She may not have had a choice."

"*You* had a choice," Penelope pointed out. "You didn't have to save me, but you did."

"You're not saved yet," said the Mouse. "First we've got to get off this world and connect with Merlin again."

"And then what?"

The Mouse shrugged. "I don't know."

"You won't make me go back?"

"No, I won't make you go back," said the Mouse. "I already told you that."

"Lots of people tell me things." Penelope paused. "Most of them lied."

"You're too young to be that cynical."

"What does that mean?" asked Penelope.

The Mouse sighed. "It means too many people have lied to you."

"We're talking about me again," complained Penelope. "I thought we were going to talk about you."

"I have a better idea," said the Mouse. "Let's talk about us."

"Us?"

"You and me."

"What about us?" asked the girl.

"Well, we're a team now."

"We are?" said Penelope, her face brightening.

The Mouse nodded. "We're together, aren't we?"

"Yes."

"And the same men who want you are after me, right?"

"Right."

"And if we get away, you're going to work with Merlin and me, aren't you?"

"I guess so."

"That makes us a team."

Penelope considered the statement for a moment, then smiled. "I like being a team with you."

"I like it, too," said the Mouse. "And the first rule of being on a team is that you never keep secrets from your teammates."

"I don't know any secrets."

"*Everyone* knows some secrets."

"Not me."

"Even you," said the Mouse. "For example, you never told me where Jennifer came from."

Penelope looked at the battered doll, which was propped up next to her.

"My mother gave her to me."

"Where?"

"In the living room, I think."

"I mean, on what world?"

Penelope shrugged. "I don't remember."

"How did she die?"

"Jennifer's not dead. She's right here with us."

"I meant your mother."

"I don't know if she's dead," answered the girl.

"But you think she is."

Penelope nodded.

"Why?"

"Because she would have saved me if she was alive."

"Not if she didn't know where you were."

"*You* found me."

"I wasn't even looking for you," said the Mouse. "It was just a lucky accident." She paused. "If that's the only reason you have, then your mother might very well be alive. How about your father?"

"They took him away."

"They?" repeated the Mouse. "Who?"

"The men who came with 32. He didn't want them to take me, so they took both of us."

"And you haven't seen him since?"

"No."

"If your mother *is* alive, she must be looking for you."

"I don't think so."

"Why not?"

"She's afraid of me."

"Of you?"

"Yes."

"Why?" asked the Mouse.

"Because I'm different."

"You mean because you can see the future?"

Penelope nodded. "I used to think everyone could do it, so I talked about it. My mother didn't believe me, so I showed her that I was telling the truth. Then she was afraid."

"And your father," said the Mouse. "Was he afraid of you, too?"

"No."

"What did he do for a living?"

"I don't know."

"Was he rich?"

"I don't know." Penelope frowned. "We're talking about me again."

"We're talking about secrets," said the Mouse. "And now I'm going to tell you one."

"What is it?" asked Penelope eagerly.

"Someone very rich is trying to find you."

"You told me that already ... but you didn't tell me why."

"Because you can see the future."

"What good does seeing the future do?" asked Penelope. "Everybody keeps chasing me, and no matter how hard I try to get away, sooner or later they catch me."

"Did you ever make a bet on anything?" asked the Mouse.

"No. My parents didn't like betting."

"But you know how it works?" continued the Mouse. "I say something is going to happen one way, you say it's going to happen another, and whoever turns out to be right wins the bet."

"I know."

"A person who could see the future would know in advance which side to bet on."

"It doesn't work that way," said Penelope.

"Oh?"

"When 32's people were making me do all those things, they tried to make me say how a coin would land or what numbers would be on some dice after they rolled them."

"And you couldn't do it?"

"Sometimes I could."

"Even if you just guessed like everyone else, you'd be right half the time on a coin flip," said the Mouse.

"I mean, sometimes I could see in my mind how the coins or the dice would land."

"But only sometimes?"

"Only sometimes."

"Were you ever wrong?" asked the Mouse. "I mean, on those times when you could see the coins in your mind?"

Penelope shook her head.

"That's why this rich person wants you," said the Mouse. "You don't have to know the right answer every time you tell him how to bet or invest. You just have to be right on those occasions that you *do* see the future."

"I wish I couldn't do it," said Penelope, frowning. "Then maybe everyone would leave me alone."

"But you saved my life by doing it," noted the Mouse.

"They wouldn't have been trying to kill you if I couldn't do it," said Penelope. "I wish I were just a normal little girl."

"But then we'd never have met," said the Mouse, offering her a reassuring smile.

Penelope sighed deeply. "I forgot about that," she admitted. "But I wish everyone would leave us alone."

The Mouse shrugged. "We'll just have to find a place where they will."

"Maybe we'll be a safe at Ophir," suggested the girl.

"Nobody's safe in a mining town," answered the Mouse. "Everyone thinks everyone else is after their goods, and nobody ever trusts anybody. I'll be happy if we just live long enough to borrow or steal a ship." She paused. "God, it's getting hot in here!" She slammed her hand against the vehicle's air conditioner. "I wonder if this thing is still working."

Penelope reached a small white hand toward one of the vents. "It is." She paused. "Kind of," she added.

"They must be pulling some damned big diamonds out of the ground to be worth living out here in this heat," said the Mouse. She paused. "Well, we've each told the other a secret. Now I think we'd better invent one."

"Invent a secret?" repeated Penelope uncomprehendingly.

The Mouse nodded. "We need a secret signal so I'll know if someone wants to harm us."

"Like a secret code!" said Penelope excitedly. "Like the stories I saw on the video!"

"Just like them."

"How about if I do *this*?" suggested Penelope, screwing up her face in such a grotesque expression that the Mouse laughed out loud.

"It wouldn't be secret for very long."

"I could pretend to sneeze."

"No," said the Mouse. "We need something that doesn't draw attention to you. Try scratching your chin."

Penelope made a claw of her left hand and scratched her chin vigorously.

The Mouse shook her head. "Use one finger, and do it very gingerly."

The little girl did as she was instructed.

"That's it. If anyone is going to try to hurt us, that's what I want you to do."

"But what if I'm in another room, or you can't see me?" asked Penelope. "Maybe I should whistle a song."

"It will attract too much attention."

"But if someone wants to kill us, shouldn't we want to attract attention?"

The Mouse grimaced. "I'm not big enough to fight off an attacker; I just want a little warning so we can sneak out before they pounce." She paused. "Besides, someone has offered an awful lot of money for you. Attract enough attention in a town like Ophir, and four out of every five men who figure out who you are will be more likely to kidnap you than save you."

Penelope fell silent and practiced gently scratching her chin, and the Mouse increased their speed and tried to ignore the constantly increasing heat within the vehicle.

Two hours later they arrived at the tiny outpost of Ophir.

6

The Mouse walked into the bar, Penelope at her side, and breathed a sigh of gratitude as a wave of cold air swept over her. There were twelve large, well-worn tables made from a local hardwood, all of them empty at midday, and she collapsed into a chair at the closest one. The walls were covered with holographs of military heroes, sports heroes, and plump nude women, none of which particularly impressed her.

The bartender, a short, burly man with a noticeable limp and a sparse mustache that made his upper lip appear dirty rather than hairy, nodded a greeting to them.

"I don't know how anyone lives out here," said the Mouse. "I've felt cooler ovens."

The bartender grinned. "We don't reach the heat of the day for another couple of hours. You'll get used to it."

"Why would anyone want to?" replied the Mouse. She peered at his stock behind the bar. "What have you got to drink?"

"You name it, we've got it."

"We'll need a room, too."

"It's yours, *gratis*."

"You don't charge for your rooms?" said the Mouse, puzzled.

"The next room I charge for will be the first," said the bartender.

"How do you make a living?"

"Oh, I manage," said the bartender. "By the way, my name's Ryan—Banister Ryan."

"Banister?" repeated the Mouse. "That's an unusual name."

Ryan chuckled. "Oh, it's not my real one. They gave it to me the first year I was here."

"Why?"

He leaned forward, resting his large hands on the polished surface of the bar. "Some drunk was causing a disturbance, so I asked him politely to desist. He didn't"—Ryan smiled at the memory—"so I ripped a banister off the staircase and cracked him over the head with it. I've been Banister Ryan ever since."

"How long have you been out here?" asked the Mouse.

Ryan paused long enough to do a quick mental computation. "Eighteen years. Bought the place seven years ago."

"The bar?"

"The whole damned town—all three buildings' worth."

"Well, Banister, that's an interesting story, but we're still thirsty."

"What'll you have?"

"I'll have a tall, cold beer," said the Mouse.

"The first one's on the house," said Ryan.

"You're kidding!"

He shook his head. "One thing I never kid about is money."

"Someday you must tell me how you stay in business."

"Someday I will," Ryan assured her.

"How about you?" said the Mouse to Penelope. "What'll you have?"

"A glass of water, please," said the girl.

"Right," said Ryan. "That'll be three hundred credits."

"*What?*" demanded the Mouse.

"Three hundred credits," repeated Ryan.

"For a glass of water?" said the Mouse incredulously.

"Nobody's holding a gun to your head," said Ryan cheerfully. "If you think you can get it cheaper somewhere else, go right ahead."

"Now I see how you make a living," said the Mouse irritably.

"Out here, water's worth a hell of a lot more than a bed," replied Ryan. "There's none on the surface for two hundred miles in any direction, and the miners use what little exists below the ground to extract their diamonds."

"Can't you recycle it?"

He shook his head. "Radioactive. Two glasses of it and you won't need a flashlight when you go out at night."

The Mouse pulled out a wad of credits and slapped them down on the table, and a moment later Ryan came out from behind the bar carrying a beer and a glass of water.

"I've sold water for a lot more than this from time to time," he explained pleasantly. "You wouldn't believe what a man with a pocketful of diamonds will pay to fill his canteen before he sets out for Haggard—especially if he hasn't told his partners that he's leaving."

The Mouse looked out a dusty window at the vast expanse of sand and rock. "Yes, I think I would."

"By the way, how long are you and the child going to be staying?"

"At three hundred credits for a glass of water, not as long as I thought."

"If you're short of money, there's work to be had," said Ryan.

"I don't know the first thing about mining."

Ryan shook his head. "I didn't mean that." He paused. "I've got a little enterprise going on the top floor. I can always use a healthy woman . . . and the little girl could earn a bundle."

"Not interested," said the Mouse.

"You'd be surprised how generous some of these miners can be."

"Forget it."

Ryan shrugged. "Well, if you change your mind, let me know."

The Mouse simply glared at him, and he walked back to his position behind the bar.

"Mind if I ask you a question?" he said as he watched her drain her beer.

"As long as it's not on the same subject."

"What are you and your daughter doing out here, anyway?"

"Maybe I'm married to one of the miners."

"Maybe I'm the Sultan of Sirius V," he shot back with a smile. "If you belonged to one of the miners, you'd have asked after him."

"I don't *belong* to anyone," said the Mouse, objecting to his choice of words.

"That's just what I meant," agreed Ryan. "So why are you here?"

"I like the desert."

"The police are after you, huh?" continued Ryan. "What'd you do back in Haggard?"

"Nothing."

"No one comes to Ophir for the climate and the view. If you tell me who's after you, maybe I can keep an eye out for them."

"We're looking for the man who robbed us," piped up Penelope. "Someone said he was in Ophir."

"I notice he left you enough money to rent a landcar and pay for your water," said Ryan, highly amused. "Nice try, kid."

"It's true," chimed in the Mouse. "My parents rented the car and loaned me the money."

"And they live in Haggard?"

"That's right."

"What's on the corner of Fourth and Quatermaine?" asked Ryan.

"The mayor's office."

"The Ophir Ballroom," said Ryan. "That's where we got the name for this place."

"Not any more," said the Mouse without missing a beat. "They tore it down three years ago."

"I don't believe you."

The Mouse shrugged. "Believe anything you want."

He stared at her for a minute, then matched her shrug with one of his own. "What the hell. It's none of my business."

"Right."

"I'm just making conversation, lady. It gets lonely around here until dark."

"Then the miners come?"

"That's right."

"How many of them?"

"It depends. Most of them have bubble modules out there, but you can't really relax or socialize in one. We might get two dozen or so."

"That many?"

"You look surprised."

"I didn't see any ships or landcars."

"They wouldn't leave 'em here and then walk six miles to the mines," replied Ryan. "Use your head, lady." He paused. "If you really *are* looking for some guy, you could be in for a long wait if you expect him to show up here. There are more than eighty miners out there. You'd be better off taking your landcar to the mines and looking for him when they knock off at sunset."

"Maybe I will," said the Mouse. "What direction are the mines from here?"

"Northwest. Just follow the tracks."

"Thanks," said the Mouse. "I'm too tired, and it's too damned hot to go out today. But if he doesn't show up, we'll head out there before sunrise and see if we can spot him."

"And then what?" asked Ryan.

"I'll go back to Haggard and get the police."

Ryan laughed.

"What's so funny?" asked the Mouse.

"They won't come to this hellhole for a thief. It'd probably take a mass murderer to get them out here."

"Then what will I do if I find him?" asked the Mouse, playing out her part and wishing that Penelope had kept her mouth shut.

"There's a guy upstairs right now who might be able to help you," said Ryan confidentially.

"I take it he's not a miner?" answered the Mouse sardonically.

"Ever hear of Three-Fisted Ollie?"

"Everyone has," said the Mouse uneasily. "Is *he* here?"

"Nope. This is the man who killed him a few months back."

"He's not dead," blurted Penelope.

"Isn't he, now?" said Ryan with a triumphant grin. "And how'd you come to know that, little lady?"

Penelope, flustered, looked helplessly toward the Mouse.

"What's this man's name?" said the Mouse coolly, ignoring the girl's gaffe.

"He claims his name is Bundy," said Ryan, "but I recognize him from his posters: he's the Forever Kid."

"The Forever Kid?" repeated the Mouse. "That's an odd name, even for the Frontier."

Ryan nodded. "It fits, though. He's some kind of sport or mutant. Grew up normal till he was eighteen or nineteen, and hasn't aged a day in the last couple of centuries."

"What is he—a bounty hunter?"

"Wouldn't do you much good if he was," answered Ryan. "Unless there's a price on your man's head. No, the Forever Kid's a killer. He hires out to anyone who can afford him."

"What's he doing here?"

"Some questions it just ain't politic to ask."

"But you brought him up."

"I don't mean you asking me," said Ryan with a grin. "I mean me asking *him*."

"When is he due downstairs?" asked the Mouse.

"Depends on how much fun he's having," answered Ryan. "But he's rooming at the hotel, so he'll be taking his meals here."

"And he's definitely a killer and not a bounty hunter?"

"Yep—not that it makes any difference to you. The child as much as said that you weren't robbed."

"Don't believe everything you hear," said the Mouse.

Ryan laughed again. "If I believed half of what I heard, I'd be dead and buried already."

"We're going to need a room," said the Mouse, getting up from the table and signaling Penelope to do the same.

Ryan looked at his computer, which was behind the bar. "Room 203," he said. "Two beds, with a view of the pool."

"You've got a swimming pool out here?" said the Mouse disbelievingly.

"Yep. Ain't got no water in it, but the pool's there. Breaks up the landscape, anyway." He paused. "You got a name?"

"You choose one," responded the Mouse.

Ryan nodded, as if this was a daily request, then typed a code into his computer. "Okay, Miz Mother and Miss Daughter. The stairway's off there to the left, behind the curtains, and the door's unlocked. Once you're inside, it'll flash the lock and unlock codes on a panel over one of the beds. Dinner's half an hour after sunset."

"Thanks," said the Mouse, leading Penelope to the curtain. "By the way, when did he get here?"

"The Kid? He showed up this morning." Ryan pointed out the window. "That's his vehicle a few yards to the left of yours." He paused. "Probably he's here on a job. Didn't seem my place to ask."

"It wasn't," said the Mouse, starting to climb the stairs.

They reached Room 203 a moment later. It was small and relatively clean, although even the sealed window couldn't keep all of the dust out of the room. There were two airbeds, a holographic video and a computer (neither of which could be operated without inserting a personal credit cube into them), a desk, two rather stark wooden chairs, and a bathroom containing a chemical toilet and a dryshower.

The Mouse sat on the edge of her bed, and Penelope, after propping Jennifer up against a pillow, seated herself on her own bed.

"I'm sorry," said the girl. "About Three-Fisted Ollie, I mean. I just blurted it out."

"No matter. He knew we were lying, anyway."

"Will he report us, do you think?"

"To whom?" asked the Mouse with no show of concern. "He's as close to being the law as you can get out here. Besides, he doesn't know who we are."

"He'll find out."

"You can see that in the future?"

Penelope shook her head. "No . . . but sooner or later they always find out."

"Maybe not this time," said the Mouse. "I want to have a little chat with the Forever Kid."

"But he's a killer!"

"But not a bounty hunter."

"What's the difference?" asked Penelope.

"There's a difference between capturing you and killing you," explained the Mouse. "Most of the men and women who are after you want you alive. This isn't the kind of man they'd hire to find you. His specialty is death."

"Maybe he was hired to kill whoever I'm with."

"It's a possibility," admitted the Mouse. "That's why I want to talk to him alone. If he's available, I want to hire him to protect us until we can hook up with Merlin again."

"What about me?"

"You're going to stay in the room. I'll bring your dinner back to you."

"But I can help you," protested Penelope. "If he wants to kill you, I'll know."

"Even if he wants to kill me, he won't do it until he knows where you are."

"The bartender will tell him."

"Not unless he tells the bartender who he's looking for, and why . . . and killers tend to be pretty closemouthed, especially when there's a reward for their victims." The Mouse paused. "It's a gamble, but we've got to take it."

"Why?"

"Because he's got to have a ship," she explained patiently. "If I can hire him to protect us until we can connect up again with Merlin, it means we won't have to drive out into the desert and try to steal a ship from one of the miners—and I've got a feeling they protect their ships as devoutly as they protect their diamonds."

Penelope frowned unhappily. "I thought we were supposed to be a team," she said.

"We are," the Mouse assured her. "But different members of a team have different duties. I don't perform Merlin's magic tricks, you know."

"What's *my* duty?" asked the girl.

"For the next few days, it's to warn me of danger," said the Mouse. "But only if showing yourself doesn't put us in even more danger."

"All right," said Penelope thoughtfully. "That seems fair."

"Good." The Mouse lay back on the bed. "I'm exhausted. That heat seems to have drained me. I'm going to take a nap." She reached into her pocket, withdrew a credit cube that she had appropriated on Westerly, and tossed it to Penelope. "Why don't you watch the video and wake me at twilight?"

"All right," said the girl.

Penelope shook the Mouse awake a moment later.

"What is it?"

"The cube doesn't work," said the girl.

"Hmm. I guess the owner reported that it was missing." The Mouse dug into her pocket and withdrew three more cubes. "Throw that one away and try these. One of them ought to work."

She lay back again, and a moment later heard Penelope giggling at something she saw on the holographic screen. Then she fell into a deep, exhausted sleep and didn't move a muscle until Penelope tapped her gently on the shoulder.

"Didn't any of the cubes work?" asked the Mouse, momentarily disoriented.

"It's almost dark out," responded the girl. "You've been asleep all afternoon."

The Mouse sat up, scratched her close-cropped hair vigorously, and then stretched her arms and looked out the window.

"I've got time for a dryshower," she announced, and went off to the bathroom to cleanse the dirt and dried sweat from her small, wiry body. She wished that she had some fresh clothes, but she settled for tossing her outfit into the dryshower for a few minutes. It came out wrinkled but clean, and a few minutes later she walked out into the hall and down the stairs, after warning Penelope not to let anyone else into the room.

A handful of miners were seated at the table nearest the door. They were hard, grizzled men who quaffed their beer as if it meant the difference between life and death, and complained long and loud to each other about everything from the weather to the price of industrial and investment-grade diamonds.

Then the Mouse looked toward the far end of the room, and there, sitting in the shadows, his back to the wall, an expression of boredom on his handsome face, sat a young man with a shock of unruly blond hair who seemed scarcely old enough to shave. His clothes were sporty without being ostentatious, and bulky enough to hide half a dozen weapons. There was a container of water on the table in front of him.

The Mouse walked around the miners' table, grateful that they were too absorbed in their conversation and their beer to offer any catcalls or whistles, and approached the young man.

"Good evening," she said pleasantly.

"Is it?" he replied, looking up at her, and she was suddenly struck by how bored and ancient his blue eyes seemed.

"It might be, if you'd invite me to sit down."

He nodded toward a chair opposite him. "Be my guest."

"What'll it be, Miz Mother?" Ryan called out from behind the bar. "Another glass of water?"

The Mouse shook her head. "Make it a beer."

"Coming right up."

"And a dinner menu," she added.

Ryan chuckled. "You make it sound like there's a choice."

"Isn't there?"

"Out here? We're lucky to have any food to serve at all. I'll bring you a plate when it's ready. Be another five minutes or so."

"Thanks."

"How about the little girl?"

"She's sleeping," replied the Mouse, studying the young man to see if he reacted to the news that she was traveling with a child. His face remained expressionless. "I'll bring a plate up to her when I'm done."

Ryan approached the table, handed a glass of beer to the Mouse, and retreated to his station.

"Well, that's over with," said the young man with the ancient eyes. "Now, what can I do for you?"

"That all depends," answered the Mouse.

"On what?"

"On who you are."

"My name's Bundy."

"I don't care what your name is."

The young man shrugged. "I don't much care what yours is, either. Why don't you just say what's on your mind?"

"I need protection," said the Mouse. "I think you can provide it."

"So you can live another fifty years?" he asked. "Take my word for it—it's not worth it."

"I want your protection, anyway."

"Do I look like the protective type?" asked the young man. "Hell, lady, I'm just a kid."

"A two-hundred-year-old kid," said the Mouse, staring into his clear blue eyes.

"Two hundred and twenty-three, to be exact," replied the Forever Kid, displaying neither surprise nor anger that she knew who he was.

"That's a long time to stay alive out here on the Frontier," said the Mouse. "Especially for a man in your line of work."

"Longevity is a greatly overrated virtue," replied the Kid.

"I'm thirty-seven," said the Mouse bluntly. "I stand a good chance of not reaching thirty-eight if I can't find someone to help me get away from here."

"You have my sympathy," said the Kid, his voice as bored as his eyes.

"I need more than your sympathy."

"My sympathy is freely given," said the Kid. "Everything else costs money."

"How much?"

"How far away do you want to go?"

"Very far."

"Then it'll cost very much."

"You haven't named a price," noted the Mouse.

The Forever Kid smiled for the first time. "You haven't named the opposition."

"I don't know who it is."

"Then I hardly see how I can help you."

"But I'm traveling with someone who *will* know."

"The little girl?"

"You know about her?"

The Kid nodded. "The bartender isn't exactly close-mouthed. Who are they after, you or her?"

"Right now, both of us."

"And you want my protection."

"And your ship," added the Mouse.

"That's going to cost more."

"I don't know how much you cost to begin with."

"I don't come cheap," said the Kid.

"I couldn't use someone who did."

He stared at her for a long moment. "One hundred thousand credits a week."

The Mouse took a deep breath. "That's awfully high."

"How highly do you value your life?"

"You'll go wherever I tell you to?"

The Kid nodded.

"I might have to pay in some other currency."

"New Stalin rubles or Maria Theresa dollars are acceptable. I won't take Far London pounds."

"Deal," said the Mouse, wondering where she could get the money and what the Forever Kid might do to her if she didn't come up with it.

"I'll want a week's pay in advance."

"That's out of the question."

"How do I know you can pay me?"

"You'll have to trust me."

"I trusted someone two centuries ago," said the Forever Kid, and suddenly his eyes briefly blazed to life. "She lied to me. I haven't trusted anyone since."

"But I haven't got the money now," protested the Mouse.

"Then you'll have to get it before I leave."

"When is that?"

"I have a little business to transact later tonight. I plan to leave in the morning."

"You're here on a contract?"

The Kid almost looked amused. "Nobody comes to Ophir for his health."

"A miner?"

"Why do you care?"

"Because you've been hired to kill someone, not rob him," said the Mouse. "Let me come along with you. If he's got a hundred thousand credits' worth of diamonds, we can still make a deal."

"What makes you think I won't appropriate his diamonds myself?" asked the Kid.

"You're a killer, not a thief," she said adamantly.

The Kid actually smiled at her. "What makes you think the two are mutually exclusive?"

"Because I *am* a thief, and if I was a killer, too, I wouldn't need you."

He stared at her for a long moment, and she shifted uncomfortably on her chair. "You amuse me," he said at last.

"I assume that means it's no deal?" said the Mouse dejectedly.

"I haven't met an amusing woman since before you were born," continued the Forever Kid. He paused and stared at her again, then nodded his head. "Okay, we've got a deal."

The Mouse extended her hand. "Shake."

The Kid stared at her outstretched hand. "I never shake hands."

"Have it your way," said the Mouse with a shrug. "When do we leave?"

"Another hour or so. I want to give them time to relax."

"*Them?*" said the Mouse.

The Kid nodded.

"Just how many miners do you plan to kill tonight?"

"Eight."

"*Eight?*" she repeated incredulously.

"Don't look so upset," said the Kid. "You'll have that much more opportunity to raise some capital."

"Eight," said the Mouse again. "That's awfully high odds."

"I charge awfully high prices."

"If you waited until midnight or so, you might be able to sneak up on them," suggested the Mouse.

"I doubt it."

"Why?"

"I sent them a message this afternoon that I was coming," said the Kid.

"You sent them a message? Why?"

"There's always a chance," he said almost wistfully.

"A chance they'll kill you?" she asked, not quite understanding.

He stared off into the distance for a long moment. "No," he said at last. "No, they won't be that lucky." He sighed. "And neither will I."

Ryan arrived just then with the Mouse's dinner. Suddenly she found that she no longer had an appetite.

7

Most deserts are cold at night, but this one, decided the Mouse as she and the Forever Kid drove across the sand in an open vehicle, was merely less hot.

"You've been very quiet since dinner," remarked the Kid. "Is anything wrong?"

"You're kidding, right?"

"I gave up kidding more than a century ago."

"Well, to tell you the truth, I was wondering if I'd be able to find my way back to Ophir in the dark, after they kill you."

"You won't have to," replied the Kid. "I'm not going to lose."

"Are you saying that you *can't* be killed?"

"I've been cut up pretty bad on occasion," he replied. "I can be killed, all right—but not tonight, not by these men."

"There are eight of them waiting for you out there," she said, waving a hand in the general direction they were headed. "They'll probably have taken up defensive positions all around the area. Hell, for all you know, one of them might be just a couple of hundred yards ahead of us, waiting to take a shot at you as you drive by."

The Kid shook his head. "They'll all be in their camp, taking comfort from each other's presence."

"How do you know that?"

He turned to her. "I've been doing this for two hundred years. I know how hunted men act."

"Maybe these men are different."

67

"I hope so," he said earnestly.

"Why?" she asked, honestly curious.

"Because it's been a long time since I've seen anything new."

"That's a hell of an answer."

"You think it's easy to be the Forever Kid?" he asked. "To know that when everyone now living in the whole galaxy has been dust for millennia, I'll still look the same? To eat the same meals, and fly to the same worlds, and do the same thing day in and month out, year in and century out?" He paused. "Everyone wants to be immortal, but let me tell you, lady, it's not really a consummation devoutly to be wished. Why do you think I got into this line of work? Because sooner or later someone will put me out of my—"

"Your misery?" she suggested.

He shook his head. "My boredom."

"Maybe it'll be tonight," said the Mouse. "That's why I'm wondering if I can find my way back."

"It won't be tonight," he replied with conviction.

"What makes you so sure?"

"I know how good I am."

"Maybe you exaggerate how good you are. You told the bartender that you killed Three-Fisted Ollie, but I know he's alive."

"I never said that I killed him," answered the Kid. "I said that I *could* kill him."

"Not from what I hear."

The Forever Kid shrugged. "Believe what you want."

They drove another two miles in silence, and then they saw the lights of a small camp off in the distance.

"That's it," said the Kid, nodding toward the lights.

"Then shouldn't we stop the landcar?"

"Soon," he said, starting to decelerate. "They don't have any weapons that are accurate at more than three hundred yards."

"You hope."

"I *know*," he replied, finally coming to a stop.

"I thought I saw some movement behind that boulder, to the left of the last bubble," whispered the Mouse.

"You did."

"Well, what are you going to do about it?"

The Kid got out of the vehicle and stretched lazily. "I'm going to go to work."

"What about me?"

"You stay here until it's over."

"A stationary target in a parked vehicle?" said the Mouse, getting out her side of the landcar. "No, thank you."

"You'd be safer in the car."

"You worry about your safety and I'll worry about mine," she shot back.

He shrugged. "As you wish."

He began walking off into the shadows.

"Let me follow you," said the Mouse, suddenly very uneasy about remaining behind.

"You'd just be in the way."

"There must be something I can do."

"There is."

"What?"

"Go into their camp under a white flag and tell them they've got five minutes to make their peace with whatever god they worship."

"Me?" repeated the Mouse incredulously.

The Forever Kid chuckled. "You see anyone else out here?"

"Not a chance," said the Mouse vehemently.

"It's up to you. I'll call to you when it's over."

"You know," said the Mouse, "there's a very fine line between confidence and madness."

There was no answer, and the Mouse realized that she was talking to herself. The Kid had gone.

She stood beside the vehicle, squinting into the darkness, trying to spot the other seven miners in the dim illumination three hundred yards ahead.

After a few minutes, she heard a single piercing scream, and then a number of rifle shots and the buzzing from laser pistols. She ducked down behind the vehicle, just in case the Kid had been wrong about the accuracy of the miners' weapons, but after a few moments of total silence she peeked around the side.

Three bodies, two of them grotesquely contorted, lay in the small pool of light beside the camp, and she could see the motionless bare foot of a fourth sticking out of the darkness.

Then came a high-pitched shriek, unmistakably feminine, and an instant later a woman staggered out of one of the survival bubbles, clutching her abdomen, and collapsed a few yards away from the men.

"Enough!" cried a man. "I give up."

"This isn't a child's game," replied the Kid from some distance. "You're not allowed to quit just because you're going to lose."

Three rifles—two projectile and one laser—tore into the spot where the Kid's voice had come from, and then all was silent again. After a tense moment, two women and a man emerged from their bubbles and cautiously approached the spot where the gunfire had converged. Suddenly one of the women screamed and fell to the ground, and the two remaining miners turned and began firing wildly into the darkness.

"Come out and face us, damn you!" hollered the man.

The Forever Kid stepped out of the shadows.

"Whoever paid you for this, I'll pay you more to go away," said the woman.

"I'm afraid that's not a viable option," said the Kid. There was a sudden movement of his right hand, and both miners keeled over.

The Kid spent the next few moments inspecting each of his victims, making sure they were dead. Then, satisfied, he turned toward the vehicle.

"You can come out now!" he shouted into the darkness.

The Mouse, still stunned by the ease with which he had dispatched his opponents, approached the camp gingerly.

"What the hell did you use on them?" she asked as she reached the first of the corpses.

"Something very small and very sharp," replied the Kid. "Eight somethings, actually."

"Amazing!" muttered the Mouse, stepping around two more bodies.

"Go gather your plunder and let's be going," said the Kid.

"You're not even breathing hard," noted the Mouse.

"Should I be?"

"Most people would work up a sweat after killing eight innocent miners," she replied caustically.

He stared curiously at her. "Innocent of what?"

"Whatever they did, they didn't deserve to die like this."

"Who knows?" said the Forever Kid with a shrug.

"You mean you don't even know why you killed them?" she demanded.

"Of course I do," answered the Kid. "I killed them because I was paid to kill them."

"But you don't know what they had done?"

He shrugged again. "That's none of my business."

"Don't you even care?"

"Not really," he answered. "Most people deserve killing for one reason or another."

"Have you always felt this way?"

Suddenly the Kid grinned. "Puberty must have made me cynical." He nodded toward the self-contained protective bubbles. "My business here is done. It's time you went about yours." He headed off toward the vehicle. "I'll get the landcar," he said, "while you pick up the spoils of conquest."

"You wouldn't be planning on leaving me behind, would you?" she said suspiciously.

He chuckled. "Not while you're here with all the money."

She began going through the bubbles, collecting uncut diamonds and rolls of credits, and a few minutes later she emerged from the last of the bubbles.

He was waiting there for her with the landcar, and fifteen minutes later she was shaking Penelope awake.

"Come on," she whispered. "It's time to go."

"Go where?" asked Penelope sleepily.

"I don't know," admitted the Mouse. "But away from here, anyway."

"Did you buy a ship?"

"Even better," said the Mouse. "I bought a man who owns a ship."

"What did you pay him with?" asked Penelope, sitting up and rubbing her eyes.

"Diamonds," said the Mouse, holding out a small bag filled with dull, uncut stones.

Penelope peeked into the bag.

"There's a gun there," she noted.

"I picked it up the same place where I got the diamonds," answered the Mouse.

"Why?"

"Just in case you decide that the Forever Kid wants to hurt us."

"How long will he stay with us?"

"Until we put down on a safe planet," said the Mouse. "Or until we run out of money. Whichever comes first."

"Are there any safe planets for us?"

"There's one," said the Mouse reluctantly. "I hadn't wanted to go there, but I don't think we have much of a choice. Word of our being here has got to leak out: this place is going to be crawling with killers by tomorrow night, or the next morning at the latest."

Penelope began getting dressed.

"What is the name of this world?" she asked.

"Last Chance."

"Have you ever been there before?"

The Mouse shook her head. "No, I haven't."

"Then why are you so sure that you don't want to go there?" persisted Penelope. "It might be very pleasant, with lakes and streams and green things."

"Because I don't like the man who runs it," replied the Mouse.

Penelope considered the Mouse's answer for a moment. "If you don't like him, why do you think we'll be safe there?"

"He owes me an awfully big favor."

"Has he agreed to pay you this favor?"

The Mouse grimaced. "I don't think he even knows I'm alive."

"How long has it been since you've seen him?" asked Penelope, picking up Jennifer and walking to the door.

"A very long time."

"He might not even remember you," suggested Penelope.

"He'll remember," said the Mouse grimly.

PART 2

The
Iceman's
Book

8

They called it Last Chance, and it had been well named. It was (currently, at least) the last populated planet on the way to the Galactic Core, the last source of nuclear fuel, the last place to fill up a ship's galleys, the last place (as far as anyone knew) to see another sentient being.

Last Chance, except for its location, was in all other respects unremarkable. It was small, but the gravity was within the normal range for human beings. It was hot, but not so hot that life couldn't exist. It was dry, but not so dry that water couldn't be coaxed up through the red clay that covered most of the surface. Its year was very long (4,623 Galactic Standard days), but its days and nights were within acceptable bounds: fourteen Galactic Standard hours each. Its seasons were mild, but distinguishable. Its native life, primarily avians and marsupials, was unique but not plentiful.

It boasted a single community, a rustic Tradertown known, also appropriately, as End of the Line. End of the Line consisted of two hotels, a rooming house for more permanent visitors, a series of small spaceship hangars, a post office, a whorehouse, three empty buildings whose purposes were long since forgotten, an assayer's office, a general store, and the End of the Line Tavern, which was also a restaurant, a book and tape store, a subspace transmitting station, a gambling parlor, and a weapons shop.

The End of the Line Tavern was the Iceman's, and he ruled it as completely as he ruled the rest of the planet. Not a ship landed without his permission. Not a ship took off without his knowledge. Not a man or woman entered the Tradertown without his consent. If, for reasons of his own, one of those men or women never left, there was no one to call him to task for it, nor would anyone who lacked a serious death wish have wanted to.

Nobody knew exactly why he was called the Iceman. His true name was Carlos Mendoza, but he hadn't used it in more than a decade, during which time he had had many other names, changing them to suit each new world the way some men changed their clothes. The Iceman wasn't even a name of his own devising, though it suited him well enough, and he elected to keep it.

He was physically nondescript. He lacked Undertaker McNair's terrifying gaze, or the awesome height and bulk of ManMountain Bates, or even the Forever Kid's shock of thick blond hair. He was an inch or two below normal height, and he had the beginning of a belly, and his brown hair was thinning on top and greying at the sides, but people tended to remember him, anyway. Especially people he didn't have much use for.

The Iceman's past was murky, his future not clearly defined, his present an intensely private matter. He was friendly enough: he'd talk to anyone who cared to pass the time of day, he'd tell an occasional joke, he'd sleep with an occasional woman, he'd play an occasional game of chance, when properly drunk he'd even read an occasional poem of his own creation—but even those people who thought they knew him or understood what motivated him were wrong. Only one person had ever gotten that close to him.

And now she was orbiting Last Chance, asking for permission to land.

9

The Mouse entered the End of the Line Tavern, spotted a table in the corner, and turned to the Forever Kid.

"Would you get a room for Penelope and me, and one for yourself?" she asked. "I'll be along in a little while."

The Kid looked around the enormous tavern and over at the gaming tables in the casino. "There's five bounty hunters here that I know of," he replied in low tones.

"I'll be all right," the Mouse assured him.

"You're paying me to protect you."

"I paid you to get me to Last Chance. I'm here now."

He shook his head. "You paid me for a week. You've still got four days coming to you."

"Just return half the money and we'll call it square."

"I don't make refunds."

"And you'd love to take on all five of them at once," said the Mouse with a knowing smile.

"I wouldn't be averse to it," he admitted, trying to keep the eagerness from his boyish face.

"Nobody's going to bother me here," said the Mouse.

"What makes you so sure?"

"Penelope would have warned me."

The Forever Kid stared down at the little girl. "Yeah?"

The Mouse smiled, reached out a hand, and tousled Penelope's hair. "She's my partner. You're just the hired help."

"That's right," said the little girl. "We're partners."

"How do you know who's likely to cause trouble?" the Kid asked her.

"Just be grateful that she *does* know," said the Mouse.

The Kid continued staring at Penelope. Finally he sighed. "Just my luck," he muttered.

"What are you talking about?" asked the Mouse.

"The last thing I need is an edge. Now it looks like I've got one whether I want it or not."

"Just for four more days," answered the Mouse. "Then you can take on three hundred killers all at once if that's what you want."

The Kid shrugged, took Penelope by the hand, walked back out into the dusty street, and headed over to the nearer of the two hotels. The Mouse noticed that, despite his obvious death wish, he nonetheless held Penelope with his left hand while his right swung to and fro just inches from his sonic pistol.

The Mouse walked over to the corner table, and a moment later a redheaded waitress approached her.

"What'll it be?" asked the girl.

"A beer," said the Mouse. It seemed foolish to ask for brand names; for a world this close to the Core to have *any* beer was accomplishment enough.

"Right," said the waitress, starting to turn away.

"And I want to see Carlos Mendoza."

"Who?"

"He's called the Iceman these days."

"You will."

"When?"

"When he's ready," said the waitress. "He knows you're here. Your drink's on the house. So's your room."

Yes, thought the Mouse grimly. *He knows I'm here, all right.*

"He'll stop by your table when he's ready," continued the waitress.

The waitress walked back to the bar, returned with her beer, then vanished through a doorway. The Mouse stared at her glass for a moment, then lifted it to her lips and took a long swallow. When she put it back down on the table, she found the Iceman sitting opposite her.

"It's been a long time," he said.

"Yes, it has."

"I thought you were dead. I'm glad to learn I was wrong."

There was a long, uncomfortable silence.

"How have you been?" he asked.

"Well. And you?"

"I'm getting by."

"When did you leave the service?" asked the Mouse.

"Nine years ago," replied the Iceman. "I figured fifteen years was enough for anyone."

"Yeah, I guess so."

Another silence.

"I wouldn't have thought you'd want to see me," he said at last. "I thought you'd be too bitter."

"I *am* bitter, Carlos. But I need a favor."

"Oh?"

She nodded. "I'm in a little bit of trouble."

"Judging from the way some people in here are staring at you," he said, indicating the bounty hunters, "I'd say you were in a *lot* of trouble."

"They say you run this world," she continued, ignoring his comment, "that nothing happens here without your permission. Is that true?"

"Essentially."

"I need a safe place to stay for a few weeks."

"Just a few weeks?"

"Within a month there'll be so many bounty hunters here you couldn't call them off even if you wanted to."

He smiled a humorless smile. "You'd be surprised what I can do on my world."

"Just the same, we'll be gone within a month, probably sooner. But I need some time to plan my next move without ducking at every shadow I see."

"What makes you think all these bounty hunters won't follow you?"

"If you can arrange for us to have a ten-hour head start when we leave, that's all we'll need."

"That can be arranged."

"Then we have your protection?"

"One of you doesn't need it," said the Iceman. "And from what I hear, he probably doesn't want it."

"So you know the Forever Kid?"

"I know *of* him." He paused. "Why is he traveling with you?"

"I hired him . . . but I can only afford him for a few more days."

"Who are you paying him to kill?"

"I don't know," said the Mouse. "Anyone who tries to kill me."

The Iceman paused thoughtfully, then spoke: "If that little girl is who I think she is, the job's too big for him."

"Who do you think she is?"

"Penelope Bailey."

The Mouse nodded.

"How did you . . . ah . . . *acquire* her?" asked the Iceman.

"I freed her from an alien who had her back on Wester-ly."

"You should have stolen a negatron bomb from the Navy," said the Iceman wryly. "You'd be in less trouble."

"I didn't know who she was," said the Mouse. "I just saw this little girl chained in an alien's room and decided I couldn't leave her there." She paused. "We've been on the run ever since. I think there may be as many as thirty or forty men out after us."

"Thirty or forty?" repeated the Iceman, amused.

"It's possible."

"You still don't know what you've done, do you?"

She frowned. "What do you mean?"

"There are three governments trying to find that little girl, and close to two hundred very motivated men and women are out to claim the reward."

The Mouse looked her surprise. "Three *governments*?" she repeated.

"At least."

She considered what he had said. "I didn't think there were two hundred bounty hunters on the whole Inner Frontier."

"There are now."

The Mouse shook her head in bewilderment. "All because of Penelope?"

"That's right," said the Iceman.

"And what about you?" she asked sharply.

"What *about* me?"

"Are you interested in the reward, too?"

He shook his head. "I've got enough money—and I've done enough favors for the Democracy, too."

She stared at him. "You're the last man I want to ask for a favor, but we need your protection."

"We?"

"Penelope and me."

"She doesn't need protection," said the Iceman. "*You* do, but not her."

"I'm not going to let anyone take her away and stick her in some laboratory somewhere."

"Most of them don't want to."

"A man called 32 does."

He stared at her intently. "What do you know about 32?"

"Just that he had her once and probably wants her back," replied the Mouse. "What do *you* know about him?"

"More than you," said the Iceman. He frowned. "How did he ever let her get away? He's the most careful, thorough man I know."

"How do you know him?"

"I've dealt with him in the past."

"During your master spy period?" she asked sardonically.

"A master spy is nothing but an employer of spy labor," replied the Iceman.

"I know. Like you hired me."

"Precisely."

"Did you hire *him*, too?"

The Iceman shook his head. "We worked for different agencies. Now and then our paths would cross." He paused. "He's the best I ever knew. I can't imagine that he could be so careless as to let the girl escape. She must be everything they say she is."

"What she mostly is is a lonely, frightened little girl who doesn't even know what world she was born on."

"She's also the most potentially powerful weapon in the galaxy," said the Iceman.

"She's just a little girl."

"Little girls grow up."

"And her abilities are very limited."

"Abilities can mature, too."

The Mouse shook her head. "All she can do is tell when someone is about to hurt her."

"And you don't think someone with precognition, whose abilities may very well be embryonic at the moment, poses a danger?"

"To who?" demanded the Mouse. "To bounty hunters who want to harm her?"

"To anyone or any world she decides she doesn't like."

"That's ridiculous!"

"Is it? From what I hear, you're traveling with a little child who can cause grown men to drop over dead."

"It doesn't work like that," said the Mouse.

"Are you saying she *can't* make people die?"

"It isn't that simple."

"It sounds precisely that simple to me."

The Mouse shook her head. "She possesses a form of precognition."

"So I've heard."

"She can see a number of possible futures, and sometimes, by her actions, she can affect which potential future becomes a reality."

"As I said, *you* need protection. *She* never did."

"She can't always choose a future in which she's safe. Sometimes there are no alternatives to being captured."

"Has it occurred to you that as she becomes more mature, more alternatives will manifest themselves to her?"

"I hope so," said the Mouse. "She's suffered enough for one lifetime."

The Iceman shook his head impatiently. "I don't mean that she'll see futures in which she's not threatened."

"Oh?"

"If there are an infinite number of possible futures, and she becomes more and more adept at visualizing and manipulating them, what makes you think that the day won't come when she can see a future in which she rules the entire galaxy with an iron hand—or that she won't be able to manipulate events to make that particular future come to pass?"

"My God, Carlos—she's just a frightened little girl! You make her sound like some kind of monster."

"I'm sure that Caligula and Adolf Hitler and Conrad Bland were once frightened little boys. They grew up." He paused. "Are you sure you want *her* to grow up?"

She glared at him furiously. "You really *are* a bastard. You didn't help me eleven years ago; I should have known better than to expect you to help me now."

"You knew the risk you were taking," said the Iceman.

"When I heard that you had been captured, I tried to work out an exchange, but they weren't interested."

"So you just wrote me off."

"Everyone was expendable." He stared at her dispassionately. "That's the nature of the game."

"It doesn't seem much like a game when you're stuck in a cell on an alien world."

"No, I suppose it doesn't."

Another silence followed, during which the Mouse stared at the Iceman and tried to reconcile what she saw with her memory of Carlos Mendoza.

"You chose your new name well," she said at last. "You were never the warmest or most demonstrative man, but you've become cold as ice."

"Being warm and demonstrative never solved anything," he replied. "In the long run it just brings you pain."

"I find it hard to believe I ever cared for you," she said. "It's like it was some other man."

"It was. His name was Carlos Mendoza, and he doesn't exist any longer."

"Probably just as well," said the Mouse, getting to her feet. "I guess we'll have to take our chances elsewhere. I'm sorry I bothered you."

"Shut up and sit down," said the Iceman. He didn't raise his voice, but his tone carried so much authority that the Mouse, to her surprise, found herself obeying him.

"That's better," he continued. "You and the girl are safe for as long as you remain on Last Chance. I owe you that much." He paused. "My protection doesn't extend to the Forever Kid. Now, go to the hotel and stay there for half an hour. That'll give me time to pass the word."

"What about the Kid?"

The Iceman shrugged. "He can stay or leave as he pleases—but if he's looking for someone to put a permanent end to his boredom, he's as likely to find him here as anywhere."

"You mean you?"

He shook his head. "He's got no reason to want to kill me, and I've got nothing to prove."

"If I'm still here in three weeks," said the Mouse, "someone will be joining me—an illusionist named Merlin. I want him protected, too."

He stared at her and finally nodded his assent.

She pushed her chair back from the table and got to her feet.

"I'll see you around," she said.

"I imagine you will."

"The waitress told me that I wasn't being charged for my room or my drink. Is that right?"

"Your meals are on the house, too."

"They'd damned well better be," she said. "It's a small enough price to pay to soothe a guilty conscience."

"I don't feel any guilt," he replied. "But I *do* feel a certain obligation."

"You may just overwhelm me with the force of your emotion," said the Mouse sardonically.

"I *am* glad you're still alive."

"Next you'll be telling me that you still love me," she replied sardonically.

"No, I don't."

"Or that you never did."

"I did, once." He paused. "It was a mistake. You can't send someone you love into danger."

"So you stopped sending people into danger?"

The Iceman shook his head sadly. "No. I stopped loving them."

10

That afternoon the Mouse stopped by the assayer's office and cashed in her diamonds for the standard 33 percent of market value. She walked out with 165,000 credits, and after she paid the Forever Kid for his entire week, she went to the room she was sharing with Penelope and hid the remaining money in the little girl's pillow, along with the 20,000 credits in cash she had removed from the miners' bodies.

"Is the money safe here?" she asked.

Penelope, who was playing with her doll, shrugged. "I suppose so."

"But you don't know for sure?"

"Nobody wants it right now."

"Will they want it tonight, when they think we're asleep?"

"Probably not," said Penelope.

"Why 'probably not'?" asked the Mouse. "Why not 'yes' or 'no' or 'I don't know'?"

"I can't see all the futures that far ahead. In the ones I can see, nobody tries to take the money away." She paused. "Well, all but one, anyway."

"And what happens in that one?"

"The man you call the Iceman kills the woman who tries to sneak up here to rob you."

"He'll actually kill her?"

"Only if she tries to come up here. In the other futures I can see, she doesn't stop by the assay office, or if she does, the man who works there doesn't tell her about your money."

85

"It must be very confusing for you sometimes, trying to separate the present from the future, or the real future from all the imaginary ones."

"They're *all* imaginary until one of them happens," answered Penelope, carefully straightening her doll's dress. "It used to be more confusing. I'm learning how to sort them out better."

"Do you ever see a future in which someone isn't trying to hurt or rob us?" asked the Mouse.

"Hardly ever."

"Well, I suppose there's a certain twisted logic to that," admitted the Mouse. "I have a feeling that half the galaxy wants to hurt us, and most of the other half would love to rob us." She sighed and eased herself onto her bed. "At least we're safe for the time being." She chuckled briefly. "Hell, with the Forever Kid and Mendoza both protecting us, it's probably the safest we've been since we met."

"Mouse?" said Penelope after a lengthy silence.

"What?"

"How long until dinner?"

"I thought you just had lunch an hour ago. Are you hungry again?"

"Not really," admitted Penelope. "But there's nothing to do here, and the Forever Kid told me I couldn't leave the room except to eat, and that when I did he had to come along."

"Well, that's what we're paying him for."

"I know . . . but I'm still bored."

"Play with Jennifer," said the Mouse, indicating the doll.

"*She's* bored, too."

"Then try watching a holo."

"There's only one frequency, and I've already seen what they're showing."

The Mouse sat up. "Okay. Find us a deck of cards and I'll teach you how to play Dubai gin."

The little girl pulled open two dresser drawers with no success, then walked over to the nondescript desk by the door, rummaged through it, and finally withdrew a deck of cards. When she took them out of their container, she found to her delight that each card sported some artist's holographic treatment of humanity's most famous mythic figures. There were Paul Bunyan and Billybuck Dancer, Tarzan and Santiago, Bigfoot and Geronimo, Saint Nicholas and Saint Ngani, all in heroic poses.

The Mouse briefly explained the rules of Dubai gin, then shuffled the deck and began dealing.

"Don't forget to deal to Jennifer, too," said Penelope, propping the doll up into a sitting position.

"I won't forget," said the Mouse, dealing nine cards facedown in front of the doll.

"These are lovely," commented Penelope as she began sorting the cards the Mouse had dealt her.

"You think so?" replied the Mouse. "When Merlin joins us, I'll have to have him show you a deck that he picked up on Sirius V. It has portraits of fifty-two extinct mammals from Earth, and he's got a matching deck with fifty-two extinct raptors."

"What's a raptor?"

"A bird that eats meat."

"Don't they all?"

"Hardly any of them do," answered the Mouse. Penelope fell silent, studying the holographs on the cards, and the Mouse waited another minute before speaking. "If you'd rather just look at the cards, we don't have to play."

"No," said Penelope. "I want to play, really I do."

"All right," said the Mouse. "You have to pick a card from the pile and then discard one over here." She indicated where the discard pile would be built.

Penelope did as she was told.

"Now it's Jennifer's turn," she announced.

She picked a card without looking at it, placed it in front of the doll, and discarded a four.

"Perhaps it might be better if you looked at Jennifer's cards before you played them," suggested the Mouse.

"That wouldn't be fair," said Penelope. "I should only look at my own cards."

"Then Jennifer's going to lose," said the Mouse.

"Oh?" said the little girl, looking concerned. "Why?"

"She discarded a very low card, a four. Sometimes that's a wise move, but in general you always want to rid yourself of the high cards first."

"Jennifer knows that."

"Evidently she doesn't, because she didn't do it."

"She was going to put the ten in the pile next time," explained Penelope.

"What ten?"

"The one she just picked." She reached over and held up the ten of hearts, which sported a holographic illustration of the goddess Pallas Athene. "It's so pretty she just wanted to keep it for a few minutes."

"How did you know that it was a ten?" asked the Mouse sharply. "I was watching you. You never looked at it."

"I knew that it had a picture of a pretty lady on it," said Penelope guiltily. "I didn't care that it was a ten."

"But you knew what it was," persisted the Mouse.

"I just wanted Jennifer to see the picture," said Penelope, who was close to tears now. "I wasn't trying to cheat, honest I wasn't."

"I know you weren't," said the Mouse soothingly.

"You're not mad at me?"

"How could I ever get mad at my partner?" said the Mouse, forcing a smile to her lips to mask her eagerness. "I wonder . . ." she said, allowing her voice to trail off.

"About what?"

"Was it just because you wanted to see this picture that you knew what the card would be, or could you do it again?"

"Promise you won't get mad if I tell you?"

"Cross my heart."

"The next card is a picture of a man dressed in black, with a black and red cloak."

"Can you see what value the card is?"

"Value?"

"Its number and suit."

"It's the king of spades."

The Mouse turned over the card. It was the king of spades, with a rather frightening representation of Count Dracula staring out at her.

"Do you know what's in my hand?" asked the Mouse.

Penelope described the holographs, then, with far less interest, identified the accompanying values and suits.

"Very good," said the Mouse.

"Will you still play cards with me, now that you know?" asked Penelope. "I can try to forget what they are when we're playing."

"I don't want you to forget a thing," said the Mouse.

"But if I don't, I'll win most of the time."

"Why not *all* the time?" asked the Mouse curiously. "Can't you choose a future in which you always get the best cards?"

The little girl shook her head. "In some of the futures, you don't shuffle them right. Besides, that would be cheating."

The Mouse considered this information for a moment, then shrugged. "What the hell—we don't want to win every hand, anyway. It would just frighten people off."

"We?" repeated Penelope. "I thought I was playing *against* you."

The Mouse shook her head impatiently. "We're through with that game."

"But you promised!" said Penelope, suddenly on the verge of tears again.

"We have a more important game to play," said the Mouse.

"What game?"

"A game in which we can be partners instead of opponents." The Mouse paused. "And you'll get to give me secret signals, too, just the way we talked about before."

"Really?" asked Penelope, her enthusiasm returning.

"Really."

"But won't we be cheating someone else? If I help you, I mean?"

"We won't be cheating anyone who doesn't deserve it," answered the Mouse. "And we're stuck here on Last Chance until Merlin shows up or I can put together enough money to buy a ship."

"Why can't we just tell the Forever Kid to take us with him?" asked Penelope.

"Because he doesn't *do* favors—he *sells* them. And I haven't got enough money to hire him for a second week."

"You're sure it's all right?" persisted Penelope, a worried expression on her face.

"I'm not only sure it's all right," answered the Mouse, "I'm sure it's the only way we're ever going to get off this dirtball." She paused, then added: "And it's not safe for us to stay on any one planet for more than a few days; too many people want to take you away from me."

"I know," said Penelope glumly. "I keep trying to choose

a future in which they all forget about me, but I don't know how."

"Just pick one in which we win lots of money at End of the Line's card table."

"I'll try," promised the girl.

"All right," said the Mouse. "Let's spend the next couple of hours making sure you know the rules. First comes a pair, then two pair, then three of a kind, then . . ."

11

The End of the Line was crowded. Its lights, glowing circular globes floating weightlessly near the ceiling, shone down on traders, prospectors, adventurers, bounty hunters, whores, gamblers, all the flotsam and jetsam of the Inner Frontier, as they gathered around the burnished chrome bar and the gaming tables. Here and there an occasional alien mingled with the mass of humanity, testing its luck at the tables, imbibing one of the special fluids that the Iceman supplied to his nonhuman customers, or selling black market commodities that weren't obtainable on the worlds of the Democracy.

The Mouse walked slowly through the mass of human and alien bodies, holding Penelope by the hand. The little girl drew some curious stares from brilliantly clad gamblers, some disapproving glances from provocatively dressed whores, some avaricious looks from the bounty hunters, but the Iceman's word had gone out, and nobody said a word or made a motion in their direction.

The Mouse was uncomfortably aware of the lean and hungry faces of the bounty hunters and was almost awed by the power the Iceman seemed to wield. These were cold, hard men, men who backed down from no one—and yet a single command from the Iceman had gone out on the grapevine, and none of them seemed willing to cross the line he had drawn.

"You going to be drinking or gambling?" asked a soft voice behind her, and she turned to find herself facing the Forever Kid.

"Gambling," she answered.

"You sure? There are a lot of pros here tonight."

"I'll be all right," she assured him. "And besides, if I'm going to be able to hire you for another week, I need to raise some money."

He shrugged. "That's up to you. Once you settle down at a table, I'll move to where I can keep an eye on you."

"Thanks," she said. "The Iceman has passed the word that no one is to bother us while we're on Last Chance, but there's always a chance that not everyone has heard." She felt a sudden surge of bitterness. "Besides, I counted on him once before and he failed me."

She walked past some of the alien games and the dice tables, and finally came to a hexagonal table where three men, two women, and a Lodinite were playing poker. The dealer stood out even in this crowd of bejeweled gamblers: the prismatic cloth of his garments changed colors with every motion he made, his fingers were covered with rings of bloodnight and sheerstone, his boots were made from the glowing skin of some alien reptile. He wore a monocle of plain glass, attached to his tunic by a gold chain, and on his shoulder perched a tiny alien bird, its orange eyes staring intently at his shining rings, as if it might leap to his hand and gobble them up at any instant.

The Mouse stood behind the player with the smallest pile of chips, a woman dressed in such worn, plain leather that she actually stood out more in this crowd of gamblers and gadflies than the dealer did. After a few moments the woman rose from her chair, gathered up her few remaining chips, and walked off.

"Is this a private game?" inquired the Mouse.

"No," replied the dealer. "But it's an expensive one."

"How much?"

"Ten thousand to buy in. A thousand is the minimum bet."

"Fine," said the Mouse, seating herself opposite the dealer and placing thirty thousand credits on the table. Once her money was on the table, the Forever Kid seated himself at an adjoining table that was not currently in use.

"I see you've come to play," said the dealer approvingly. "Bankers!" he called out. "Get the lady some chips!"

The casino banker walked over, picked up her money, and replaced it with thirty elegant chips carved from the pink-hued bone of some alien animal.

"What about the child?" asked the dealer as the banker answered a call at another table.

"She doesn't play," replied the Mouse.

"She also doesn't walk around looking at anyone's cards," explained the dealer.

"Are you accusing me of cheating before I've even played a hand?"

"Not at all," said the dealer. "I'm just making sure I won't have to accuse you later."

The Mouse turned to the little girl. "Penelope, go sit over there"—she pointed to the Forever Kid's table, which she could see without having to turn her head—"and wait for me."

"Can I have a deck of cards?" asked the girl. "So I can play solitaire?"

The dealer withdrew a sealed deck from his pocket and slid it across the table. "Give her these."

"Thank you," said the Mouse, picking up the deck and handing it to Penelope. "Now, go over there and wait for me."

Penelope thanked the dealer for the cards and walked over to the table.

"Got a name, ma'am?" asked the dealer.

"Lots of them," replied the Mouse.

"Any particular one I should call you?"

"Whatever you like."

The dealer smiled. "I've always been partial to Melisande, myself."

The Mouse considered it, then frowned. "My name is Mouse."

The dealer shrugged.

"What's yours?" she asked as she picked up her cards and studied them.

"Well, when I'm passing through Customs back in the Democracy, it's Valente, ma'am, Riccardo Valente. But out here, where I make my living by courting the goddess of chance, it's King Tout."

"Do I call you King or Tout?" asked the Mouse.

"Call me anything that suits your fancy, ma'am," replied King Tout.

"How about if we play some poker while I think about it?" said the Mouse, pushing two chips to the center of the table.

The Lodinite and the two men matched her bet, the woman dropped out, and King Tout surveyed his cards again.

"See you and raise you a thousand," he said, picking up three chips and placing them next to the others at the table's center.

The Mouse held her cards up, appeared to be studying them, and took a quick peek over the top of them at Penelope. The little girl rubbed her nose once, the sign that the Mouse was going to lose the hand, then went back to deciding which card to play in her solitaire game.

The Mouse considered tossing in her cards and minimizing her losses, but decided against it: having opened, it would look strange if she folded immediately, so she regretfully met King Tout's bet, drew two cards, and then refused to match the five thousand credits he bet after drawing a single card.

"Poor luck, ma'am," he said with a smile as he reached out and collected the pile of chips. He passed the deck to her. "I believe it's your deal."

"Same game," said the Mouse, pushing another chip to the center of the table.

She dealt out the cards, then picked up her hand. She had three queens, a five, and a four, and when none of the others chose to open, she was about to bet five thousand credits . . . but first she glanced at Penelope, whose hand seemed inadvertently to brush by her nose again as she looked down at the cards that were spread out before her.

The Mouse sighed, studied her cards for another moment, and then regretfully tossed her hand onto the table.

She won two small pots, dropped out of another one early on, and then it was King Tout's turn to deal again. As the Mouse picked up her hand, she took a quick peek at Penelope, who seemed to be paying absolutely no attention to her at all.

The Mouse held a deuce, a five, a six, a nine, and a queen, three of them red, two of them black, and she opened with a single chip. So did the next four players. King Tout pushed five chips to the center of the table.

The Mouse frowned and pretended to study her cards, again glancing surreptitiously at Penelope. As before, the child seemed immersed in her game of solitaire, and sat rigid and motionless.

"I'll see you," said the Mouse, matching King Tout's bet and hoping that Penelope's lack of a negative sign was purposeful and not merely neglectful.

"I'm out," said the Lodinite into its translating mechanism.

"Me, too," chimed in one of the men.

The remaining man stared at his hand for a long time, finally sighed and pushed a little pile of chips next to King Tout's.

"How many cards, ma'am?" asked King Tout pleasantly.

"Three," said the Mouse, tossing in the deuce, the five, and the six.

"One for me," said the man.

"Dealer stands pat," announced King Tout.

The Mouse slowly picked up her cards and found that she had drawn two nines and a queen.

"Check," she said.

"Same," said the other woman.

"Well," announced King Tout, "I'm afraid it's going to cost you five thousand credits to see what I've got."

The Mouse stared at him and resisted the urge to grin.

"I'll see you," she said at last, "and raise you five."

The man dropped out, and King Tout stared at his cards, fanning them so that he could see the edge of each in turn.

"You took three cards, right?"

"That's right," said the Mouse.

He looked at his hand once more and sighed deeply, as if he'd finally made his decision.

"See your five thousand," he said, pushing a large pile of chips to the center, "and raise you another five."

My God, thought the Mouse. *When I think of the walls I've climbed and the ventilation shafts I've wriggled through for a twentieth of this amount!*

"Right back at you," she said aloud, pushing ten chips of her own up against the rapidly growing pile between them.

Deep in his heart, King Tout had a feeling that he was beaten, that no one bluffed a pat hand to the tune of twenty thousand credits—but he'd invested so much money already that he felt he had to at least pay to see what the Mouse was holding, and so he did, tossing five more chips onto the table but declining to raise her again.

She laid out her full house—three nines and a pair of queens—and he folded his flush, tossed it facedown on the table, and with a nod indicated that she had won the hand.

"That was very bold of you, matching my opening bet while you were sitting there with just a pair of nines . . . or was it queens?" remarked King Tout.

The Mouse allowed herself the luxury of a smile. "Nice try, King Tout," she said. "But if you want to know what I bet with, it'll cost you another twenty thousand."

He matched her smile with his own grin. "I think I can live in ignorance."

She purposely lost five and seven thousand credits on the next two hands, then struck again and won a fifty-thousand-credit pot, most of the money coming from King Tout.

That set the pattern for the next ninety minutes. Within an hour the other players had all quit, and it was just her against King Tout. She never folded a poor hand at the beginning, but always lost just enough to encourage him to keep trying her . . . and then, when Penelope stared at her solitaire game, seemingly oblivious to the rest of the world, the Mouse would invariably win the larger pots.

Finally King Tout pushed his chair back.

"You're quitting?" asked the Mouse politely.

"I know when the cards are running against me," he said. "Will you be back here again tomorrow night?"

"I imagine so," she answered, deciding that whether she bought a ship or an extension of the Forever Kid's services or both, she was going to need more money.

"I'll be back," he promised, getting to his feet, offering her a low, courtly bow, and walking out the door.

"It won't do him much good, will it?" said a low voice at her side.

She turned and found herself staring at the Iceman, who had seated himself next to her. "I don't know what you mean."

"I mean that my protection doesn't extend to people who cheat my customers—not even you."

"It's hardly *my* fault if he doesn't know how to bet his cards," said the Mouse defensively.

"Would he have known how to bet them if the little girl had stayed in her room?" replied the Iceman. He paused. "You may not know it, but you've made yourself a powerful enemy tonight."

"I've had enemies before."

"Your courage does you no credit," said the Iceman. "It's the result of ignorance." He paused. "If I were you, I'd quit while I was ahead."

"I need the money if I'm ever going to get off this dirtball."

"If I were you, I'd find some other way to make it."

"I can get what I need in one more night," she said. "Will you extend your protection for forty more hours?"

He paused, considering her request.

"I'll let you know," he said, getting up and walking away.

As soon as he left the table, Penelope got up and approached the Mouse.

"Did I do good?" whispered the little girl.

"You did great," the Mouse assured her. "Do you think you can do it again tomorrow?"

"I suppose so," said Penelope.

"You *suppose* so?" repeated the Mouse. "What does that mean?"

"Just that I can't see that far ahead."

The Mouse relaxed. "You'll be just fine, partner," she said, tousling Penelope's blonde hair. "Now let me cash in my chips, and then let's go to bed."

She summoned the banker, converted her chips into cash, and then, taking Penelope by the hand, she began winding her way in and out of the tables and walking to the door, with the Forever Kid following a few paces behind.

"Had a good night, I see," said the Kid when they were out in the street.

"Yes, I did."

"Got enough money to leave now, or are we going to stick around?"

"I want to play one more night," answered the Mouse.

"Good."

She stopped and looked at him curiously. "Why should you care one way or the other?"

"Because that was King Tout you beat tonight," said the Forever Kid. "He'll be back."

"With more money, I hope," she said, trying to ignore a growing feeling of uneasiness.

"If you're lucky."

"And if I'm not?" asked the Mouse.

The Forever Kid's eyes brightened with anticipation.

"Then I've got a feeling *I'll* be lucky," he said.

12

The Mouse slept late the next morning and spent most of the day loafing in her room and watching the holovision with Penelope, who was willing to watch the umpteenth rerun of anything as long as she didn't have to do it alone.

She had their meals sent to their room, and at sunset she took a long shower, dressed in a new outfit she had bought during a brief tour of End of the Line's shops (and which was still dull in comparison to those she knew she would see at the casino), and spent a few minutes brushing Penelope's ragged hair and giving her some last-second instructions. Then, accompanied by the little girl, she descended to the street and walked the short distance to the tavern and casino.

The Iceman was waiting for her, as she had suspected he would be. He stopped her before she could walk across to the table where King Tout, dressed even more splendidly than the previous evening, his tiny alien bird again perched on his shoulder, was dealing cards to a trio of men whose blue-tinted skin proclaimed them to be some of the mutated colonists from Kakkab Kastu IV.

The Mouse spotted the Forever Kid sitting by himself at a table that was midway between the tavern and casino areas, then turned to Penelope. "Go and sit with the Kid," she said.

Penelope nodded, stopped by the bar to borrow a deck of cards, allowed the bartender to fill an elegant cocktail glass with fruit juice, then joined the Forever Kid at his table.

The Mouse turned to face the Iceman.

"What's your decision, Carlos?"

"If you insist on using the little girl, I'm withdrawing my protection."

"I've *got* to have more money," said the Mouse. "I'll have to count on my other protector."

"*Him?*" said the Iceman, jerking his head in the Forever Kid's direction. "Forget about it. He couldn't protect you for five seconds in here."

"He's managed to protect people for more than two centuries," said the Mouse.

The Iceman shook his head. "He's been *killing* people for more than two centuries. There's a difference. And the only reason he's still alive is because he protects himself first and his clients second." The Iceman looked around the bar and the casino. "There are six men and three women here, each of whom is pretty damned good at his job. Any of them would kill you and steal the child the second my protection was lifted. Even the Forever Kid can't save you from all of them."

The Mouse surveyed the interior of the building, trying to spot the nine people in question. Two or three she knew from their holographs, another from his weapons . . . but she realized that more than half of them were unknown to her.

"It's your decision," said the Iceman. "You do what you think best." He paused. "But remember what I said. If you use the little girl against King Tout, I'm—"

Just then a man and an alien entered the End of the Line, and the Iceman frowned.

"What is it?" asked the Mouse anxiously.

"Nothing," said the Iceman.

"Don't tell *me* it's nothing, Carlos," she admonished him. "I've seen that expression before."

He turned to her. "You know what I told you about not using the girl?"

"Yes."

"Forget it." He nodded his head almost imperceptibly toward the two newcomers. "Your friend just evened the odds."

She turned until she could just see them out of the corner of her eye.

"Who are they?" she asked.

"The man is called the Golden Duke. Ever hear of him?"

She shook her head.

"Well, take a good look at him," said the Iceman softly, "and if you ever see him anywhere but on Last Chance, run like hell."

"A killer?" she asked.

"A little bit of everything," replied the Iceman, staring at the tall, almost skeletal human. The Golden Duke obviously possessed some Oriental ancestry, which was apparent in the shape of his eyes, the tint of his skin, the prominence of his cheekbones, his straight black hair. He moved with the smooth grace of an athlete, as if he was prepared to change directions and speeds instantly. He carried no weapons, but his right arm ended in a prosthetic hand made entirely of gold, a hand that hid four lethal, retractable knives, one in each long, lean, golden finger.

"He's been known to run drugs back in the Democracy," continued the Iceman, "and he's also done a bit of arson."

The Golden Duke and his companion seated themselves at King Tout's table, and suddenly the other players all seemed to remember that they had pressing engagements elsewhere and made a mass exodus to neighboring tables or the long chrome bar.

"A gambler, too?" asked the Mouse.

"Not much of one," replied the Iceman.

"Then why is he sitting at the card table?"

"I imagine that King Tout has invited him to play cards with you."

"But you just said—"

"I said he wasn't a gambler." The Iceman paused. "If he helps King Tout cheat you, it isn't gambling, is it?"

"How do you think they'll try to cheat?" asked the Mouse.

"They'll probably whipsaw you," replied the Iceman.

"Whipsaw?" she repeated, puzzled.

"They'll have some way of signaling each other which of them has the best hand. The other two will drop out early, so if you win, it's a much smaller pot, but if you lose, you're going to have to pay just as much to see the winning hand, because the one holding it will keep raising like there's no tomorrow."

"I see," said the Mouse. She nodded to the alien. "Who's *that* one?"

"Her?" said the Iceman, looking at the humanoid alien with wide-set orange eyes, broad nostrils, a reddish wig that barely covered her gaping earholes, and a bodysuit that kept recirculating a clear fluid across her torso and legs. "They call her September Morn. She *is* a gambler, and a damned good one. She's King Tout's shill on alien worlds." He continued to stare at her. "She doesn't actually breathe the liquid through gills or anything like that, but she's got to keep her body moist. If that suit stops running water over her for more than a couple of minutes, she curls up and dies . . . or at least goes into some kind of catatonic state that's just about the same as being dead."

"How do you know?"

"I've seen the suit malfunction on a member of her race," answered the Iceman. "Not a pretty sight." He paused. "Not a pretty smell, for that matter."

They were both silent for a moment, and then the Mouse turned to him.

"What would happen if King Tout tried to kill me at the table? You're not even carrying a weapon."

"This is *my* world: I don't need one. And he won't try anything."

"But *if* he did."

"Then he'd have eleven holes in him before he could aim his pistol."

"You have eleven men watching him?"

"Twelve," answered the Iceman. "I assume one will miss."

"Where are they?"

"Around."

"They're very well hidden," said the Mouse, scanning the tavern and casino.

"They're supposed to be."

"How many are behind that mirror?" she continued, nodding her head toward the huge mirror behind the bar.

"A few."

"It's a one-way mirror, isn't it?"

The Iceman almost smiled. "They wouldn't be much use to me there if it wasn't, would they?"

"No, I suppose not," she answered. "Well," she added, looking across the room, "I suppose I'd better go over to the table and let King Tout and his friends do their worst."

"Just remember: they're not stupid."

She smiled with more confidence than she suddenly felt. "It's only money."

"You have something more valuable than money, and you're taking a chance on losing it," said the Iceman, glancing across the room at Penelope. "King Tout and his friends don't know who or what she is yet, but if either of you screws up, he'll figure it out pretty damned quick."

"We're still under your protection," she reminded him.

"I thought you were playing to raise money for a ship," he replied. "Once you take off from Last Chance, you're on your own."

She stared at him for a moment, looking for some sign of emotion—annoyance, jealousy, anything—but finding none. Then she turned and walked rapidly across the tavern into the casino, approached King Tout's table, and seated herself where she could watch Penelope without making it too obvious.

"Good evening, ma'am," said King Tout. "I trust you're ready to give me a chance to win some of my money back?"

"If you can," said the Mouse.

"It looks like a small game tonight," said King Tout. "Just the four of us."

"Suits me," said the Mouse.

"Fine. This gentleman on my left is called the Duke"—she smiled politely at the Golden Duke, who stared impassively at her—"and this charming lady is September." The alien called September Morn inclined her head slightly and briefly contorted her face into a smile.

"Same game as last night?" asked the Mouse.

"That'll be just fine, ma'am," said King Tout.

The Mouse signaled to the banker, who opened the safe and brought a number of thousand-credit chips to the table, placing them down in three neat stacks directly in front of her.

"Shall we raise the ante to two thousand tonight?" suggested King Tout.

"It sounds like you're in a hurry to get your money back," said the Mouse.

He shrugged. "If you'd rather not . . ."

She stared at him. "No, two thousand is fine—*if* you'll get an unopened deck from the bar."

"That shows a serious lack of trust, ma'am," said King Tout, though he looked unsurprised.

"We're playing for a serious amount of money," she answered.

He shrugged, then called for a fresh deck. He had the Mouse open it, then shoved two chips to the center of the table and shuffled the cards with an easy precision while the other three players placed their chips atop his.

The Mouse won the first hand, then lost three small pots in a row. The Golden Duke seemed totally uninterested in the game, dropping out of each hand early and never taking his dark, piercing eyes from her. September Morn played her hands with more skill and more subtlety, and won two of the pots.

Then the Mouse hit big, winning sixty thousand credits when her four jacks beat King Tout's full house. After that the whipsawing began, with the Golden Duke, King Tout, and September Morn taking turns riding out each hand; the one with the poorer cards always folded early, leaving the other to bet against the Mouse. The Mouse couldn't quite tell how they were signaling each other, nor did she particularly care.

The game went on for another hour, the Mouse gradually accumulating more money, until at last, as the deal came around to King Tout once more, he stopped shuffling and stared at her for a long moment.

"You're a very lucky card player, ma'am," he said at last.

"Maybe I'm just talented," she replied.

He shook his head. "No, I'd have to say that you're lucky."

She shrugged. "Have it your way: I'm lucky."

"*Very* lucky."

"Are you accusing me of cheating?" asked the Mouse.

"I would never accuse you of cheating without knowing how you did it."

"You know, it doesn't sound any better that way."

"How could you be cheating?" asked King Tout with an expression that belied his words. "Why, if my friend the Duke thought for a even a moment that you were cheating, he'd cut your heart out right here at the table. If there's one thing the Duke hates, it's a cheater."

"Yeah, well, your friend the Duke could use some lessons in poker," said the Mouse.

"Poker's not really his specialty," said King Tout meaningfully.

The Mouse looked briefly at the Golden Duke. "I can believe that." She pushed her chair back. "This is becoming rather unpleasant," she announced. "I think I've had enough for tonight."

"How much have you got in your pile there?" asked King Tout.

"I don't know," said the Mouse.

King Tout stared at her chips. "Looks to be about two hundred thousand."

"If you say so."

"I'll tell you what, ma'am," said King Tout. "I'll cut you for it."

"For the whole pot?"

He nodded.

The Mouse took a quick glance in Penelope's direction, but the little girl was seemingly involved in her solitaire game. Which makes sense, decided the Mouse; she can't tell me if I'll win or lose until I decide whether or not I'll even agree to play.

"What if I declined?" asked the Mouse. "Respectfully, of course."

"I think my friend the Duke would take it as a personal insult," answered King Tout.

The Mouse returned his smile. "My friend the Iceman might not like that."

"Then let's leave our friends out of it," said King Tout. "Let's make it just you and me. We'll cut for the whole pot." He pulled an unopened deck out of his pocket. "And we'll use a fresh deck."

"I kind of liked the one we were playing with."

"For this kind of money, we should use a brand-new deck."

The Mouse considered asking him to get a deck from the bar, but decided to look at Penelope first. She saw no negative signal, and she finally nodded her agreement.

"Okay," she said. "You match what I've got here and

we'll cut just once for it." She paused. "If you lose, you lose. We don't go double-or-nothing. You could keep that up all night until you finally won."

"Agreed," said King Tout. He broke open the deck and shuffled the cards, then placed them on the table.

"Be my guest," he said.

"You go first," she replied.

"I'd really prefer that you cut first."

She shook her head. "It's *my* money. If you want a chance at it, you cut first."

"As you wish," he said. His hand reached out, caressed the deck swiftly, and then cut to a king.

The Mouse looked at Penelope, who seemed oblivious to anything but her solitaire game. Finally Mouse cleared her throat, reached out, paused hesitantly for a moment, and placed her fingers carefully on the sides of the deck.

And then Penelope spilled her glass of fruit juice and made a distracting clatter as she jumped back from the table to avoid getting it on her clothes.

"Are you all right?" asked the Mouse, her hand once more poised above the deck.

"I'm sorry," said Penelope, starting to wipe her table with a napkin. "I was just clumsy. Are you mad at me?"

"No, of course not," said the Mouse.

"Ma'am," said King Tout impatiently. "We're waiting on you."

The Mouse stared at the deck, then took a deep breath and cut the cards—and came away with an ace.

"My congratulations, ma'am," said King Tout, getting to his feet and bowing deeply. "I guess tonight just wasn't my night."

September Morn also arose, but the Golden Duke remained seated, still staring impassively at her. Finally, when King Tout and the alien reached the door, he stood up and walked silently after them.

As she had the previous evening, Penelope walked over and joined the Mouse, while the Forever Kid remained at his table.

"Well, we did it!" whispered the Mouse, trying to control her excitement and elation. "What was that business with the spilled glass?"

"I saw that if you cut the cards, you'd draw a three, so

I tried to see how to change it," explained Penelope. "If I shrieked and you looked up, you'd draw a jack, and if I did other things you'd draw other cards . . . but I saw that if I spilled the juice, you'd draw an ace. It all depended on how startled you were and how much you moved your hand."

"Remarkable!" said the Mouse. "Just remarkable!" She summoned the banker, changed her chips into credits, and carried the cash over to the Forever Kid. "Here," she said, handing him the money. "You can probably protect this better than I can."

The Kid placed the wad of bills inside his tunic.

"Why the long face?" asked the Mouse. "I won. I can afford you for another week or two."

"They just walked out," said the Kid unhappily.

"What did you expect them to do?"

"I know what I *wanted* them to do," he replied. "I've heard about the Golden Duke. I never thought he'd walk away from a fight." He shook his head in abject disappointment.

"Look, I'm sorry you didn't get to die on this godforsaken planet," said the Mouse with false sympathy. "But look at the bright side: you'll have two more weeks of opportunities to toss your life away. In the meantime, do you mind taking Penelope back to the hotel?"

"I'm supposed to be keeping an eye on *both* of you," noted the Forever Kid.

"I'll be all right," said the Mouse. "Besides, everyone just saw me give you the money. Don't get your hopes up too high, but if anyone's going to be in danger, it'll be *you*."

That seemed to raise the Kid's spirits, but Penelope suddenly looked unhappy. "Can't I stay with you?" she asked.

The Mouse shook her head. "I have to talk to the Iceman."

"I'm not afraid of him."

"I know," said the Mouse with a smile. "But I have a feeling that he's afraid of *you*."

"Him?" said Penelope unbelievingly.

"Him," repeated the Mouse. "Now, go on over to the hotel. I'll join you in a few minutes."

The Kid got to his feet, took Penelope by the hand, and walked unhappily into the cool night air.

13

The Mouse saw the Iceman staring at her as he leaned against the long bar. She beckoned him to join her with a motion of her head, and he carried his drink past half a dozen gaudily dressed miners and traders, giving a wide berth to the huge alien Torqual who seemed to have no interest in drinking either whiskey or any of the exotic alien concoctions, but insisted on standing at the bar, anyway. A striking redheaded woman stopped the Iceman to whisper something to him; he looked across the tavern, seemed to consider whatever it was he had heard, then nodded his head and, without another look at the woman, walked the rest of the way to the Mouse's table.

"You won a lot of money tonight," he noted, seating himself and placing his drink in front of him. "Would you like me to keep it for you until you need it?"

"The Forever Kid won't let anyone take it away from him," she replied. "And I'm going to need it tomorrow morning."

"Oh?"

She nodded. "I need to buy a ship."

"I thought the Forever Kid had a ship."

"He does, but I can't keep paying him a hundred thousand credits a week. Sooner or later I'm going to need my own—probably sooner."

"How big?"

"Big enough for three people," said the Mouse. "No, make that four, in case the Kid's still with us when we join up with Merlin."

The Iceman arched an eyebrow at the mention of Merlin's name, but didn't ask any questions about him.

"Well?" said the Mouse.

"Well what?"

"Can I get a ship tomorrow?"

"Go over to the hangar. They usually have a few for sale, or, if not, they'll know where you can get one." The Iceman paused. "You're definitely leaving tomorrow?"

She nodded. "Too many people know she's here already. The longer I wait, the more of them we'll have chasing us when we finally leave. Now that I have the money, there's no reason to stay."

"She's in no danger," said the Iceman.

"Are you kidding?" she demanded. "Look around you. Not everyone is here just to drink your booze and play at your tables."

"*You're* in plenty of danger," replied the Iceman, gazing casually at a pair of bounty hunters who were pretending that they had no interest in the Mouse. "But you still don't seem to know what you're traveling with."

"I'm traveling with the best damned gambling partner anyone ever dreamed of."

The Iceman shrugged and took a sip of his drink. "Do what you want. It's none of my business."

"I don't know why you persist in thinking of her as dangerous," continued the Mouse. "I keep telling you: she's just a very tired, very frightened little girl."

"A little girl who has had two hundred professionals looking for her for the better part of a year, and who's still free," said the Iceman. "Doesn't that suggest something to you?"

The house banker caught the Iceman's eye, made some brief signal with his hand, and the Iceman shook his head. A moment later the banker was explaining to an annoyed customer that New Kenya shillings were not acceptable currency on Last Chance.

"She was an alien's prisoner when I found her," answered the Mouse. "I told you that."

"Is she an alien's prisoner now?"

"No. She's just damned lucky that I found her."

"Do you make a practice of entering the alien sections when you're looting a hotel?" asked the Iceman.

"No."

"How many rooms were there in that hotel?" he continued.

"I don't know."

"A few hundred?"

"Probably."

"Haven't you wondered how you wound up in the one alien room where she happened to be?"

"I *told* you how it happened," said the Mouse irritably.

"I know how it happened."

"You haven't changed at all, Carlos. You never trusted anyone or anything."

"Maybe that's why I'm still alive." He paused. "But let me give you one piece of advice."

"What?"

"Don't ever get her mad at you."

"I'm the only friend she's got."

"She didn't do that badly when she had no friends at all," he noted.

"What would you have me do?" demanded the Mouse. "Desert her? Return her to your friend 32?"

The Iceman stared at her for a long moment.

"If it was me," he said at last, "I think I'd kill her while I had the chance."

She stared at him for a long moment.

"No," she said distastefully, "you haven't changed."

She got up and walked out the door, then crossed the street and entered her hotel. She got on the airlift, ordered it to elevate her to her floor, then rode the corridor to her door. Just as she turned the corner leading to her room, she found herself face-to-face with the Golden Duke. He held a sonic weapon in his hand and silently directed her into a darkened room three doors down from her own.

"Lights," commanded a low voice, and suddenly the room was bathed in illumination.

"Good evening, ma'am," said King Tout as the Golden Duke stationed himself in front of the door. She looked around desperately, silently cursing her stupidity for not keeping Penelope with her, and saw September Morn smiling at her from her position by the room's only window.

"What do you want?" demanded the Mouse. "If it's money, I don't have it with me."

"Oh, we'll get around to talking money in a while, ma'am," said King Tout. "Right now I think I'd like to talk about luck."

"Luck?" repeated the Mouse.

"Luck." He stepped forward and pointed to a small scar above his temple. "Do you see this, ma'am?"

The Mouse nodded, but said nothing.

"Do you know what it is?"

"No."

"It's a surgical scar."

"Somebody you tried to whipsaw shot you in the head?"

He chuckled. "No, ma'am, I'm afraid not." Suddenly his smile vanished. "It's where I had a silicon bubble implanted. A Steinmetz/Harding 90347 bubble."

"Should that mean something to me?"

"It's the most powerful mathematics bubble ever invented," explained King Tout. "I can do eleven million calculations before the card you see registers on your retina." He paused. "Do you see my left eye, ma'am?"

"It looks just like the right one," answered the Mouse.

"It's supposed to. But it's artificial, ma'am. It can see into the infrared spectrum, just as this artificial digit"—he raised the index finger of his left hand—"can produce a mark that can only be seen by this eye." He paused again. "That's why I know you were lucky these last two nights, ma'am. Do you know *how* lucky?"

"Why don't you tell me?" said the Mouse.

"Well, in the beginning, I had a nine to one chance of winning, just because of the bubble. But when I started losing, I started cheating. By the end of the evening, you'd beaten odds of more than six thousand to one. That was impressive enough. But *tonight*," he continued, "tonight I was dealing seconds *and* we were whipsawing you *and* I knew I was going to cut to a king, because I marked it when I opened the deck. The precise odds of your coming out ahead tonight, ma'am, were 53,024 to one." He paused again. "That's so lucky it's almost unbelievable . . . so you'll have to forgive me if I don't believe it."

The Mouse made no reply, and King Tout continued speaking.

"You know, ma'am, for almost two nights I couldn't figure out how you were doing it. I know you couldn't read the cards, because you don't have an eye that can see into the infrared spectrum, and even if you did, you couldn't have broken my code. I knew you didn't have a collaborator, because there was no one else at the table, and I knew there was no way you could know what was in my hand, because on two occasions I didn't even look myself."

"Get to the point," said the Mouse.

"The point?" repeated King Tout. "The point is that I couldn't figure out how you were cheating me, so I decided to make you cut the deck with me, and I decided to pick a king, and then I watched to see what happened next."

"What happened was that I drew an ace, in case it's slipped your memory."

"Oh, I knew you'd draw the ace, ma'am," said King Tout. "It never crossed my mind that you might not. No, I was looking to see what happened *before* you drew it."

"Nothing happened."

"Not quite nothing," he corrected her. "The little girl happened." He paused. "At first I thought she must be a telepath, but then I got to thinking, and I realized that a telepath couldn't know where the ace was, or read my hand when I myself hadn't looked at it and didn't know what was in it. And then I remembered hearing stories about a little girl that everyone seems to want." He stared at the Mouse. "She's the Bailey girl, isn't she?"

"Don't be ridiculous," said the Mouse. "She's my daughter."

"Duke?" said King Tout, and four thin blades slid out of the fingers of the Golden Duke's prosthetic right hand.

"Now, ma'am, I'm going to ask you one more time, and if you lie to me, my friend is going to gut you like a fish. Do you understand?"

"You go to hell," said the Mouse.

"I'm sure that's where we're all going, ma'am," said King Tout. "Now, is she the Bailey girl or not?"

"*Don't!*" yelled a small voice on the other side of the door.

King Tout and the Golden Duke froze for a moment. Then the gambler motioned the Golden Duke to pull the Mouse into a corner, took a small laser pistol out of his pocket, and ordered the door to open.

"Don't hurt her!" said Penelope. "She's my best friend."

"Do come in, young lady," said King Tout, stepping aside and allowing the girl to run to the Mouse's side.

"You shouldn't have done that," said the Mouse. "He was bluffing."

Penelope shook her head. "In every future I could see, you didn't tell him and the Golden Duke killed you."

"So that's how it works!" said King Tout with a smile. "Just as easy as that? You see a million futures and choose the one you like best?"

"It's not that easy," answered Penelope.

"If it worked like that, you'd never have surprised me here," said the Mouse.

"Ah, but she was in her room, far away from you, ma'am, or I've no doubt you'd be back at the tavern, begging the Iceman for help."

"He's watching you right this minute," said the Mouse.

"Oh, I very much doubt it," said King Tout. "My friend September managed to find all of his holo feedlines—it's one of her talents: she's attracted to power, any kind of power . . . electrical, conductive, nuclear—and my friend the Duke cut the lines."

"Then he'll know that something's going on here that you don't want him to see."

"Just how clumsy do you think I am, ma'am?" asked King Tout. "Right now his security people are watching holos of an empty room, which my friend September rigged before the Duke went to work."

"He'll find out."

"Oh, I'm sure he will," agreed King Tout, "but not before we're all long gone."

"I wouldn't be too sure of that if I were you," said a youthful voice from the still-open doorway, and they all turned to see the Forever Kid standing there, his fingertips poised lightly on the holster of his sonic pistol.

"I know who you are," said King Tout.

"I know who you are, too," said the Forever Kid.

"This doesn't concern you. Just be on your way and no one will get hurt."

"Just follow your two friends out into the hall, or a lot of people are going to get hurt," responded the Kid, his eyes alive with excitement for the first time since the Mouse had known him.

"We're not looking for a fight," said King Tout.

"Sometimes you can't always have what you want," replied the Kid.

"Let me take him," said the Golden Duke, his face absolutely expressionless as he stared at his antagonist.

"You can try," said the Kid, his hand tensing.

"*No!*" screamed Penelope suddenly.

All the participants froze for an instant.

"What is it?" asked the Mouse.

"I don't want you to die!" sobbed Penelope.

"I'm not going to die."

"If the Forever Kid draws his gun, no matter what happens, you'll die and I can't change it!" wept the girl.

"Well?" said King Tout, still looking at the Kid.

"Kid, you'd better leave," said the Mouse at last.

"But I can take these three," he protested.

"Nobody said you couldn't," answered the Mouse, trying to steady her voice. "But even if you do, I'm going to catch a laser beam or a sonic blast." She stared at him. "Please, Kid?"

The Kid stared at the Golden Duke for another moment, then slowly backed out of the room and rode the corridor to the end of the hall, where he disappeared around a corner.

"Very wise of you, ma'am," said King Tout.

"I'm not ready to die yet," said the Mouse.

"Nobody's ever really ready to die," he agreed.

"Then release us and the Iceman won't kill you," said the Mouse. "He's not like the Forever Kid. I can't call *him* off."

"Why don't you let *me* worry about the Iceman?" said King Tout. "He hasn't left the planet in five years. He's not about to start now." He paused. "However, you and the girl are."

"You'll never live to collect the reward for her," said the Mouse.

"I know this may come as a shock to you," said King Tout, "but I have absolutely no interest in any reward."

"Sure you don't."

"Really. The reward is a single finite amount, whereas the possibilities involved in using this little girl are infinite. Do you know how much I can win at some of the Democracy's larger casinos with her help?"

"I'll never help you," said Penelope.

"Of course you will, my dear," said King Tout pleasantly.

"You can't make me, no matter what you do to me!"

"You're a rare treasure, my dear," said King Tout. "I would never dream of hurting you." He suddenly put an arm around the Mouse. "But I have absolutely no objection to hurting *her*."

"No!" said Penelope. "She's my only friend! Leave her alone and I'll go with you."

"Oh, I couldn't do that, my dear. Now that I understand what you are, I would never dream of taking you without some means of controlling you. Sooner or later you'd find some way to escape or perhaps even kill me. But if you know that I'll have the Duke kill your friend the first time you disobey me, then I think we can have a long and happy relationship." He smiled. "You're very young, my child. When you're older, I'm sure you'll be able to appreciate my point of view."

"Let's go," said the Golden Duke, holding his claws to the Mouse's throat and preparing to step out into the hall.

"Not just yet," said King Tout.

"What now?" demanded the Golden Duke.

"Blindfold and gag the little girl."

"Why? She's no problem."

King Tout sighed. "I'm glad at least one of us is using his head in this endeavor." He signaled September Morn to begin binding Penelope's eyes. "You may have forgotten it already, but there happens to be a very disgruntled killer out there in the corridors waiting for us. As long as the Mouse thinks she will be killed, she won't order him to attack. Now, what do you suppose will happen if the little girl can see a future in which only we three will be killed?"

A light of dawning comprehension spread across the Golden Duke's features.

"Right," continued King Tout. "So if she can't tell them, they won't take the chance." He checked Penelope's blindfold. "Good. Now the gag."

The alien placed a crumpled handkerchief into the girl's mouth, then bound it shut.

"All right," said King Tout, surveying his captives. "I do believe we're ready to go." He turned to the Mouse.

"Ma'am, if you'd be so kind, tell your friend not to molest us."

"Kid!" yelled the Mouse. "If you're still out there, let us pass." She paused. "Remember, you're still working for me. That's an order."

There was no answer.

"Kid," said the Mouse. "I mean it!"

Then the little party entered the corridor, the Golden Duke's blades resting gently on the Mouse's throat. She half expected to run into the Forever Kid at every turn of the corridor, or perhaps in the lobby, or even at the hangar, but within ten minutes they were aboard the gambler's ship, and in another five Last Chance was so far behind them that it didn't even register on the viewscreen.

14

The End of the Line Tavern was closed for the night when the Forever Kid arrived. He pounded on the door, and a moment later the interior of the building was bathed in light and the Iceman spoke the seven-digit code that unlocked the ornate door.

"I've been looking for you," said the Forever Kid ominously.

"You found me."

"Why can't I get clearance to take off from Last Chance?" demanded the Kid, walking into the tavern.

"I wanted to talk to you first," said the Iceman. "Care for a drink?"

"I'm in a hurry."

"They'll keep," said the Iceman. "If King Tout had wanted his money back, he'd have sent the Golden Duke after you. He wanted the little girl." He paused. "She and the Mouse are safe for the time being."

"You know they're gone?"

The Iceman almost smiled. "Not much happens on my world that I don't know about."

"Why didn't you stop them?" asked the Kid. "I seem to remember that they were under your protection."

"And I seemed to remember that you were being paid to protect them," responded the Iceman. "It looks like neither of us did a very good job." He walked across the empty room to the bar, where he pulled out an oddly shaped bottle and two glasses. "You sure I can't offer you a drink?"

The Kid shook his head. "Just give me clearance to leave: I'm still working for them."

This time the Iceman actually smiled. "You couldn't care less about them," he said bluntly. The Kid made no answer, and he continued: "You just want to take on the Golden Duke."

The Kid considered the Iceman's statement for a moment, then shrugged. "What difference does it make?" he replied, not bothering to deny it. "The result will be the same. I'll kill him and free them."

"I have no objection to that," said the Iceman, filling his glass with a blue liquid.

"Then why haven't I been cleared to leave?"

"Because I thought you might like to come with me."

"You thought wrong."

The Iceman downed his drink. "My ship's faster and more comfortable than yours."

"I work alone."

"I know where King Tout will be going."

The Kid was unimpressed. "I'll find him. A man like that doesn't stay hidden for long."

"You're only on salary for a day or two more," continued the Iceman. He paused. "Come to work for me and I'll double whatever the Mouse was paying you."

The Forever Kid returned his stare and paused before speaking. "What's *your* interest in this?" he finally asked. "You don't exactly strike me as the philanthropic type."

"I own this world," answered the Iceman. "I rule it as surely as any king ever ruled his domain back on Earth. I passed the word that they were to be left alone, and King Tout disobeyed me." He poured another drink and downed it in a single swallow. "If I let him get away with it, I won't even rule this barroom next year."

"And that's it?" asked the Kid.

"Most of it," replied the Iceman. "You look amused."

"That's because you don't care any more about them than I do," said the Kid. "You're going to protect your reputation, and I'm going because I want to take on the Golden Duke." He paused. "I find that amusing."

"Ah, well, heroes are hard to come by these days," said the Iceman with fine irony. "Out here you take what you can get. And what they've got is us."

"How many of your men are you taking along?"

"None."

The Forever Kid arched an eyebrow, but said nothing.

"I'll hire anyone I need once we get to where we're going," added the Iceman.

"They say you used to be quite a killer yourself," said the Kid.

"They say a lot of things," replied the Iceman. "Not all of them are true."

"Not all of them are lies, either."

The Iceman stared out the door into the night for a moment.

"It was true once," he said at last. "Then I found that it was easier to hire people who were more eager than I was."

"Eager to kill?"

The Iceman shook his head. "Eager to die." He placed the bottle back behind the bar. "Ready to go?"

"What about my ship?" asked the Kid.

"Leave it here. If you come back in one piece, I'll waive the storage charges. If you don't, you won't need it anyway."

"And the Mouse's money?" continued the Kid, patting the wad of bills beneath his shirt.

"Take it along. She won't be coming back here, whatever happens to you or the girl."

It took the Kid less than five minutes to gather his belongings and stuff them into a single small bag that he slung over his shoulder, and five minutes after that he and the Iceman were aboard the latter's ship, breaking out of orbit and heading toward the more populated worlds of the Inner Frontier, on the outskirts of mankind's sprawling Democracy.

They slept as the ship's computer kept them on course, then awoke some time later and ate breakfast in total silence. As the Iceman poured himself a cup of coffee, he looked at the youthful figure sitting across the galley from him.

"You're not the most talkative man I've ever met," he said dryly.

"*You* live for a couple of centuries and you'll find out that *you've* said just about everything you want to say," answered the Kid.

"I suppose so," said the Iceman, nodding thoughtfully.

"I do have a question or two for you," said the Forever Kid. "But they can wait."

"Ask away."

"Might be better not to. We're going to be stuck on this ship for a few days. No sense getting mad at each other."

"I don't get mad anymore," said the Iceman.

"You ain't chasing King Tout just for the fun of it," observed the Kid.

"I'm chasing him to teach him an object lesson: that no one can disobey me on Last Chance. But I'm not angry. This is simply business."

"And of course you wouldn't mind too much if he kills the little girl, would you?"

"What makes you think so?"

"I got eyes and ears. I use 'em."

The Iceman paused. "He won't kill her," he said at last, ignoring the Forever Kid's question.

"When he wins enough, or someone figures out what he's doing, he might."

"Not a chance."

"You think not?" said the Kid. "He and the Golden Duke never struck me as compassionate."

"It's got nothing to do with compassion," answered the Iceman.

"Then why do you think he won't kill her?"

The Iceman paused. "Because she won't let him," he said at last.

The Kid paused thoughtfully. "She's really got you worried, doesn't she?"

"No," replied the Iceman. "Just concerned."

"Well, don't get *too* concerned," said the Kid. "I'm still being paid to defend her."

"*I'm* paying you now," said the Iceman. "You'll do what I tell you to."

"Not for two more days," said the Kid. "And I wouldn't give too many orders if I were you. I don't kill children."

"Hired killers kill whoever they're paid to kill," said the Iceman. "However," he added, "no one is going to kill this child—not King Tout, not the Golden Duke, not you, not anyone." He paused again. "Penelope Bailey doesn't need your help. I'm paying you to help me free the Mouse, and to make sure everyone understands what happens when someone disobeys my orders on my world."

"Mind if I ask another question?" said the Kid after a momentary silence.

"Go ahead."

"Why *are* you so hot to rescue the Mouse? According to her, the last time she needed help you left her to rot in a jail on Msalli IV."

"The situation's different this time. When I sent her to Msalli IV, we were both working for the government on a secret mission. She could have turned the assignment down. She knew the odds, and she knew that if she was caught, the political and military situation there meant there could be no rescue attempt." He paused. "Once they caught her, that was that. I was under orders not to mount a rescue mission."

"I got the impression you two were pretty close back then."

"We were."

"But not close enough to disobey orders, I guess?"

"We were nearing a political solution to our problems. If I'd tried to break her out, I'd have lost a lot of good men and women, and probably precipitated a war."

"You got your war, anyway," said the Forever Kid. "I showed up just a little too late to hire out as a mercenary."

"Yeah, we got our war, anyway," acknowledged the Iceman with a sigh. "But at least I wasn't the cause of it."

The Kid refilled his coffee cup and stirred it idly. "Why did she agree to take the assignment, if the odds were stacked against her?" he asked.

"For the same reason she's King Tout's prisoner right now."

The Kid frowned. "I don't think I follow you."

"The Mouse was the best thief I ever knew," said the Iceman. "There was no building she couldn't scale, no room she couldn't break into, no situation she couldn't bluff her way out of. Cool head, quick mind, nerves of steel. That's why I recruited her." He paused. "But she had a flaw. She still has it, for that matter."

The Kid seemed to consider this, then finally shrugged. "What is it?"

"To borrow a line from Shakespeare, she loves not wisely but too well. She didn't go to Msalli IV because she thought she could do the job; she went because she loved me, and I asked her to. And now she's decided to be a mother to the Bailey girl, and she's in the throes of another kind of love, and she's in trouble again." He shook his head sadly. "She lets her emotions cloud her judgment. It's going to get her killed one of these days."

"We'll get her out of this in one piece," said the Forever Kid confidently. "We may not be in the hero business, but we're sure as hell in the rescue business."

"First things first," replied the Iceman. "We're in the *punishing* business."

"But you don't mind if we rescue her somewhere along the way?" asked the Kid, amused.

"I'm not even sure who she most needs rescuing *from*," said the Iceman grimly.

They fell silent then—the Iceman immersed in his own thoughts and memories, the Forever Kid simply tired of talking—as the ship continued to speed through the Inner Frontier.

15

Suddenly Penelope sat up in her bunk

"He's coming!" she whispered, frightened.

"Who's coming?" asked the Mouse apprehensively, staring at the locked door to their quarters.

"The Iceman."

"He's here on this ship?"

Penelope shook her head. "But he's coming."

"You must be mistaken," said the Mouse. "He never leaves Last Chance."

"He's coming to kill King Tout and the Golden Duke," said Penelope with absolute conviction. "And maybe me."

"You think the Iceman will kill you?"

"He thinks I'm a bad person," said Penelope. She turned to the Mouse. "Why does he hate me?"

The Mouse climbed down from the upper bunk, sat down next to the little girl, and put a reassuring arm around her. "He doesn't love or hate anyone," she explained. "He's too detached to feel anything for anybody."

"The Forever Kid is with him," said Penelope. "Maybe *he'll* save us from the Iceman."

"You've got it all wrong, Penelope," said the Mouse. "If they're together, they're coming to save us from King Tout and his friends."

Penelope saw the Iceman's cold, remote face in her mind's eye, and shuddered. "I'd rather stay with King Tout."

"The Iceman won't hurt you," said the Mouse soothingly. "I promise you."

"You're wrong," said the little girl. "Of all the men who are hunting me, he's the one who *can* hurt me."

"How do you know?"

"I just *know*." Suddenly a tear rolled down her face. "I miss Jennifer. I wish we hadn't left her behind."

"We didn't have any choice," said the Mouse.

"But she's all alone there, back at the hotel."

"If she was with us, she'd be a prisoner," the Mouse pointed out. "She's better off where she is."

"But she was my first friend, and now I'll never see her again."

"She'll never really be gone as long as you remember her," said the Mouse.

"I want her to be with me, though," said Penelope.

"Sometimes you have to say good-bye to someone you love," answered the Mouse. "It's part of growing up."

"Does everybody leave someone they love behind when they grow up?" asked the little girl.

"Almost everybody." She paused. "Sometimes they get left behind themselves. I suppose it comes to the same thing in the end."

"But Jennifer likes to be talked to," persisted Penelope. "What if the maids just put her in a closet?"

"I'm sure they'll give Jennifer to some lonely little girl who needs a first friend," said the Mouse.

"Really?" asked Penelope, brightening somewhat.

"I'm sure of it."

"I hope so."

Suddenly the Mouse smiled. "How would you like to sleep in the upper bunk?"

"Do you mean it?" asked Penelope.

"Sure."

"I'd like it very much."

The Mouse hugged the little girl, then lifted her to the higher bunk, and began examining her surroundings for the hundredth time. The walls, ceiling, and floor of their small cabin were composed of a titanium alloy and were a dull battleship grey. The two bunks were bolted to the bulkhead. The cabin's computer lock had been disabled, and the door was now bolted from the outside. The tiny lavatory consisted of a dryshower, a chemical toilet, and a drysink. The ventilation shafts were far too small for any human, even the Mouse, to crawl through. There was no viewport, no vidscreen, no intercom.

The Mouse paced the floor for a few moments, looking for a weak spot, but to no avail. If there was a means of escape, even a remote possibility of escape, she was sure she'd have spotted it by now. Still, she went over every inch of the cabin methodically, pretending she hadn't already done so two dozen times already, and finally she returned to the lower bunk.

A few minutes later she heard the bolt move, and then September Morn entered their cabin with two trays.

"Dinner," said the alien, handing a tray to each of her prisoners.

"How much longer before we arrive?" asked the Mouse.

The alien's face contorted in its grotesque parody of a human smile. "If I tell you that, you might guess where we're going."

"What difference does it make?" said the Mouse. "Who do you think we're going to tell?"

"You? No one." She glanced at Penelope. "Her? Who knows?"

"She's not a telepath."

"You say she reads the future. I say she reads our minds. What's the difference?"

"The difference is that she can't communicate telepathically with anyone, so you might as well tell us where we're going."

September Morn smiled again. "If I don't tell you, there's no difference. If I do tell you and she *is* a telepath, there might be a very big difference."

"But I can't read minds or send messages," protested Penelope.

"You would say that regardless," replied September Morn.

And with that, she walked out of the room and bolted the door again as it slid shut behind her.

"I don't like the sound of that," said the Mouse.

"Of what?" asked Penelope.

"If they think you're a telepath, they might demand that you read a mind or send a thought for them, and if you explain that you can't do it and they don't believe you, we could be in for a lot of trouble."

"We're already in a lot of trouble," said Penelope, picking unenthusiastically at her food.

"As jails go, I've seen worse," said the Mouse, inspecting her own tray and starting to eat an exotic salad made of vegetables from half a dozen different alien worlds.

"What was the alien one like?" asked Penelope. "The one where the Iceman deserted you?"

"Not very pleasant."

"Was it cold and dark and damp?" asked Penelope with a child's innocent enthusiasm.

The Mouse paused, as if remembering.

"It was dark," she said, "but not cold. Actually, it felt more like an oven. Msalli IV is a very warm world."

"Did they torture you?"

The Mouse shook her head. "Not so you'd notice it. They just threw me in a cell and left me there. Sometimes they remembered to feed me, sometimes they didn't."

"How long were you sentenced for?"

The Mouse smiled wryly. "The Klai—that's the race that lives there—don't operate like that. When you're found guilty of something, they toss you into jail, and when you die, they bury you." She paused. "I almost died from their water a couple of times. Diseases aren't supposed to be cross-species, but I guess enough filth will make anyone sick—and that was the filthiest water I ever saw."

"Did they give you a doctor to make you well?"

"Eventually. That was how I escaped."

"Tell me about it!" said Penelope eagerly. "Did you kill the doctor with one of his surgical instruments?"

The Mouse smiled. "You've never seen a Klai, have you? They're about eight feet tall, and perhaps six hundred pounds, with skin like armor. Stabbing or shooting one of them would just make him angry."

"Then what did you do?" persisted the girl.

"I pretended to be sicker and weaker than I was, and after a couple of days, when I felt strong enough and they weren't watching as closely as they should have, I sneaked out of my room and found an air shaft leading to the subbasement. I spent three days hiding there, following various passages, until I found a sewage tunnel that led to a drainage ditch almost half a mile beyond the prison."

"How did you get off the planet?"

"Two days after I escaped, the Democracy invaded it, and I just presented myself to one of our military units. They transferred me to the flagship, questioned me until they were convinced that I was who I said I was, and then transported me to the nearest human world."

Penelope shifted her position on her bunk so that she could see the Mouse better. "Why didn't the Iceman try to rescue you?"

"I used to wonder a lot about that," admitted the Mouse. "I couldn't figure out why he cared more about his orders than he cared about me." She shrugged. "Then one day I realized that he would never send someone he cared for into that situation, and finally it made sense."

Penelope's eyes narrowed. "I don't like him."

"Well, there are people I'm more fond of, myself," agreed the Mouse dryly.

"Why is he coming after us?" asked Penelope, deciding she didn't like her meal and pushing her tray aside. "He doesn't like you, and he hates me."

"He has a reason for everything he does," answered the Mouse. "My guess is that he's going to let the Forever Kid kill King Tout and his friends, just to prove that no one can get away with disobeying his orders on Last Chance." She paused. "*Can* the Kid beat all three of them?"

Penelope shrugged. "I don't know."

"He was about to try at our hotel. What did you see then?"

"In some futures he won, in some he didn't—but in all of them you were killed."

"The Golden Duke must be pretty good at his trade."

"Oh, he always killed the Golden Duke," said Penelope. "But in some futures September Morn killed him."

"I didn't even notice her carrying a weapon," said the Mouse. "What does she use, and where does she hide it?"

"There were so many futures, and everything happened so fast," said Penelope helplessly. "I can't remember."

"But *she's* the dangerous one?"

"I don't know. Maybe it was because the Forever Kid was concentrating on the Golden Duke."

"Oh, well," sighed the Mouse. "We'll just have to hope that the Kid is up to it."

"What if he isn't?"

"Then Carlos will find another way to kill them."

"Can he?"

"He was one of the best in his day, but that's not the way he operates anymore. Still," she concluded, "once he sets his mind on something, he usually gets what he wants."

"What if he wants me dead?" asked Penelope.

"Then he'll have to kill me first," promised the Mouse. "And he won't do that."

"Why not, if he doesn't care about you?"

"Because I know how his mind works. He hates waste, and killing me would serve no purpose."

"It would if you were protecting me."

"He'd try to find a way around me," said the Mouse. "Take my word for it."

"How would he do that?"

"I don't know." The Mouse noted the genuine fear on Penelope's face and reached up to hold the child's hand. "Don't worry. It's a moot point. He's coming to rescue us, not harm us."

"I hope you're right."

"Don't you know?"

Penelope shook her head. "Not yet. It's too far off."

"Well, believe me: I'm not going to let anyone harm you."

Penelope suddenly climbed down from her own bunk to the Mouse's and threw her arms around her.

"You're my best friend. My *only* friend," she amended. "I want us to be together always."

"You're *my* best friend, too," said the Mouse.

Suddenly Penelope straightened up.

"What is it?" asked the Mouse.

"We just changed course."

"I didn't feel anything. How can you tell?"

"I just know."

"Do you know where we're heading?"

Penelope squinted and peered into space, as if trying to read a sign within her mind.

"The Starboat," she said at last.

"The Starboat?" repeated the Mouse. "What is it?"

"It's a huge ship that's orbiting a red world."

"How huge?"

"It's got lots of cabins, and big rooms like the one the Iceman owned."

"You mean taverns?"

"Those, too."

"Casinos?"

Penelope nodded. "Rooms where they play cards and games like that."

"Do you know the name of the red world?"

"No." Suddenly Penelope smiled. "But I know something else."

"What?"

"I know that there's a man on the Starboat who can help us."

"Who?"

"I don't know his name, but he's dressed in very bright colors, and he's very tall, and he has a beard."

"Is he a killer?" asked the Mouse. "A bounty hunter?"

"I don't think so."

"How will he help us?"

"I don't know yet," said Penelope. "But once we're at the Starboat, I'll know how."

"If he figures out you're helping to cheat him, he might kill us all."

Penelope shook her head firmly. "No. I don't know what he'll do, but I know he won't hurt us."

"He'll help *both* of us, not just you?"

"Yes."

"You're absolutely sure?"

"I would never leave without you," Penelope assured her.

"Can Carlos catch up with us before we reach the Starboat?"

"No."

"Then we've got a decision to make," said the Mouse.

"This man will *help* us," insisted Penelope.

"Will he kill King Tout or the others?"

"I don't know."

"Can you see if King Tout will come after us again?"

"No."

"No he won't, or no you can't see?"

"I can't see that far."

The Mouse sighed deeply. "I just don't know," she said. "At least if Carlos and the Kid catch up with us, we know they won't leave until King Tout and his friends are dead."

"I don't want the Iceman to catch up with us," said Penelope, her fear reflected on her face once again.

The Mouse studied the little girl's face intently. "And you're sure this man will help us?" she asked at last. "Not just try, but succeed?"

"I think so."

"But you're not sure?"

"I will be, before I let him know that we need his help."

"Once he knows, he'd better act fast," said the Mouse, "or you're going to be minus a best friend."

"King Tout will only hurt you if I disobey him," said Penelope with absolute conviction. "Once I find someone to help me, he'll be much more worried about his own skin."

"You can see that, too?"

Penelope smiled. "Not in the future. I know it, because King Tout is so simple to understand."

"He is?"

The little girl nodded. "He's no smarter than Jennifer was," she said, and the Mouse noted a certain contempt in her voice that had never been there previously.

"He was smart enough to capture us," replied the Mouse, watching Penelope closely for a reaction.

"I couldn't see far enough ahead. Next week or next month I'll be able to." She hugged the Mouse again. "They think they can hurt you, but I won't let them." She paused thoughtfully, then added, "They're very foolish men, King Tout and the Golden Duke." Suddenly a look of childish fury crossed her face. "And they'll be sorry they made me leave Jennifer behind."

The Mouse looked at her for a moment, startled—and then, just as quickly as it had appeared, the almost alien expression of rage vanished from Penelope's face.

"I love you, Mouse," she said.

The Mouse embraced her. "And I love you, too, Penelope."

"And if they try to hurt you," she continued, "something bad will happen to them."

"Like what?" asked the Mouse.

"Oh, I don't know," said Penelope with a shrug. "Just something."

16

The Starboat was the most impressive and elegant space station on the Inner Frontier.

Hundreds of ships, some small, some incredibly large, were docked along its sleek, shining hull. In fact, the hull itself was the first thing to capture a visitor's attention, for it proclaimed the station's name in two-hundred-foot-high letters that blazed like a million tiny suns, and it was visible to approaching ships that were still thousands of miles away.

The interior lived up to the hull's glittering promise. There were restaurants, bars, nightclubs, and a dozen immense public gambling rooms, as well as some very private rooms for high-stakes games, games that even King Tout couldn't afford. Men in formal dress, women in very little dress at all, aliens in exotic attire, all moved discreetly from table to table, from game to game, offering drinks, drugs, an assortment of alien tobaccos, and gaming chips.

The tables themselves were divided almost evenly between human and alien games, and, not surprisingly, the jaded human customers clustered around the more popular alien games, losing tens of thousands of credits at a time at games such as *jabob*, so complex that it took years to learn, while the score or more of alien races—Canphorites, Domarians, Lodinites, even a pair of methane-breathing Atrians in their frigid protective suits—lost just as heavily at poker, blackjack, and roulette.

There was no form of wager one couldn't make aboard the Starboat. One huge room, housing hundreds of computer and video screens, offered up-to-the-minute news and odds on sporting events all across the Democracy, while another posted odds and results of the tens of thousands of elections that occurred daily for major and minor political offices on the Democracy's fifty thousand worlds. A third room was devoted to an endless series of trivia games, which were making their hundredth or so reappearance in a galaxy where Man had grown out of touch with his origins and constantly sought to relearn them.

The Golden Duke had been left behind to keep an eye on the Mouse—or, more specifically, to punish her if Penelope refused to make her talents available to her captors—and King Tout had taken September Morn and the little girl with him aboard the Starboat.

They were scanned very briefly and very thoroughly at one entrance. Then King Tout walked up to one of the many cashiers' windows, established a line of credit, and took a quick tour of the gaming rooms. Finally he found a table, no different than any other, that seemed to appeal to him, and he gestured September Morn to take one of the empty seats at it.

Then he leaned over and whispered to Penelope.

"You remember the signals we talked about?"

She nodded. "I touch my left ear when you're going to win, and my right ear when September has the best hand."

"That's right, my child," he said. "And do you remember what will happen to your friend if you give me the wrong signal even once?"

"I remember," said Penelope. She looked around the room. "Where do you want me to sit?"

"Come with me," said King Tout, leading her to a long bar that lined the back wall. He lifted her up onto an exotic-looking stool and summoned the bartender, an orange-skinned Belonian.

"Do you have something nonalcoholic for the young lady to drink?" he asked pleasantly.

"We have a wide selection," said the Belonian into its translating device.

King Tout slipped a wad of New Stalin rubles out of his pocket and laid them on the bar.

"Give her whatever she wants, and make sure that nobody bothers her."

The Belonian flashed its purple teeth in its version of a happy smile and picked up the money.

"It will be my pleasure, sir," it replied.

King Tout turned to Penelope. "I don't want you moving away from here, do you understand?"

"I understand," said the girl.

"I hope so, my child, or it will go very hard on your friend."

Penelope stared at him, but said nothing, and a moment later he walked back to the table and seated himself where he had a clear view of the girl.

The Belonian brought Penelope a selection of three fruit-flavored drinks, and she chose the one in the most elaborate container, a sparkling crystal that was shaped like the horn of some ancient animal. A moment later the first hand was dealt, and she casually raised her hand to her right ear. King Tout smiled—his opponents thought he was smiling at some remark one of them had made—and kept betting and raising until everyone except September Morn had dropped out, then tossed his cards in without showing them when she displayed a full house of aces and jacks.

Her captors lost the next two hands, and then Penelope touched her left ear, signaling a win by King Tout. This time it was September Morn who kept betting and raising until all but one player was driven out, and then she folded and allowed King Tout to continue betting on his own.

They continued in this manner for another half hour. They didn't always raise each other when King Tout knew they were holding winning hands, and they didn't always drop out early when he knew they were destined to lose, but they gradually accumulated most of the money at the table. A couple of the players—a Canphorite and a human—decided that they'd had enough, and were replaced by two others, both human this time.

And as King Tout and September Morn accumulated their winnings, Penelope sat almost motionless at the bar, her blue eyes scanning the room, her mind sorting out different possibilities, different futures, different means to the end she desired.

Finally she found what she had been looking for. It was a tall, stunningly dressed man, his glowing garments changing colors constantly, his hair and beard a rainbow of hues, his boots made from the phosphorescent blue fur of the now-extinct Icedemon of Belloq IV. He seemed to be wandering aimlessly through the room, pausing now at one table for a moment, now at another, his dark eyes missing no detail. Finally he stopped in front of a huge roulette wheel, summoned one of the many waiter-cashiers, and ordered a handful of chips. Penelope didn't know his name, or why he was aboard the Starboat, but she knew that this was the man she sought.

Penelope observed the man for a few moments, as he wagered on four successive turns of the wheel and lost each time. So intent was she on studying him that she almost forgot to signal King Tout that he had another winning hand, and tried to ignore his glare as she informed him only after the initial series of bets.

Then the opportunity she had known would occur came to pass. A thin young man walked up to the bar, and she managed to spill her drink, splashing some of it on him.

"I'm so sorry!" she said apologetically.

"No problem," said the man, signaling for a bar towel and wiping his sleeve off. "But you should really be a little more careful, young lady."

Penelope waited until the alien bartender was out of earshot.

"I spilled it on purpose," she said very softly.

The man stared at her and said nothing.

"I need help," she continued.

"If you go around spilling drinks on strangers just to amuse yourself, you need more than help," he said. "You need some manners, young lady."

He turned and started to walk away.

"If you go away," she whispered intently, "I won't tell you what number will win next at the roulette wheel."

"And if I stay here, you'll give me the winner and I'll win a million credits?" he asked, highly amused.

"How much you win depends on how much you bet."

The young man glanced over at the roulette table. "The wheel's spinning now," he said. "Why don't you tell me the winning number, just as a show of good faith?"

"27," said Penelope without hesitation.

"You're sure?"

"Yes."

He grinned at her. "What do I get if you're wrong?"

"Nothing," she replied, freezing suddenly as King Tout, who had just been dealt a losing hand, looked across the room at her. "But because you didn't believe me, you won't get anything, anyway."

"Didn't anyone ever teach you how to speak to adults?" said the man. "Because—"

"27 on the black!" announced the croupier.

Penelope resisted the urge to smile smugly at the young man.

"Luck," he said.

"If you believe that, I won't give you the next number."

"Why are you giving me any numbers at all?"

She waited until two men who were passing the bar momentarily obscured her from King Tout's line of vision. "I told you: I need help."

He frowned. "You want me to bet for you?"

"No. I want you to rescue my friend and me—and don't look at me when we talk," she added.

"What friend?" he asked, gazing around the crowded room.

"She's not here. She's on a ship that's docked outside."

"I'm not in the rescuing business, little lady," said the man.

"The next number will be 8," she said suddenly.

The man waited until the ball had come to rest, and the croupier confirmed that the winning number was indeed an 8.

"*Now* do you believe I can tell you the winning numbers?" whispered Penelope, glancing at King Tout out of the corner of her eye, and finding that the gambler was too involved in the play of his hand to pay much attention to her.

"Very interesting," he said, the grin gone from his face. "I would have sworn that was an honest wheel."

"It is."

"I don't believe it."

"What difference does it make?" said Penelope. "Whether it's honest or not, I can tell you the winning numbers."

He stared at her. "Every time?"

"Yes." She glanced again at King Tout's table. "And stop looking at me."

"Why?"

"I don't want anyone to know we're talking to each other."

"Why *are* you talking to me?" he asked, quickly averting his gaze.

"I keep telling you: I need help."

"Why did you choose me?"

"I don't want you," said Penelope. "I want the man you work for."

"What makes you think I work for anyone?"

"I haven't got time to explain," said Penelope. "But if I walked over and talked to *him*, they'd hurt my friend. Nobody knows who you are, so I'm talking to you instead."

"You seem to know an awful lot about things that are none of your business, young lady," said the man, frowning. He paused briefly. "Who do you think I work for?"

"The man with the fur boots."

"And if you were right, why do you think he'd want to help you?"

"He doesn't want to now, but he will when you give him my message."

"Why should I give him a message from a little girl who knows too many things?"

"Because if you don't, I'll find someone else to do it, and then he'll be mad at you."

The young man looked over at the roulette table, then back at Penelope.

"What kind of message do you want me to give him?"

"After the fat woman with the white hair leaves the table, the next three winners will be 31, then 9, then 11."

"31, 9, and 11?"

"Yes."

"Then what?"

"Then come back to the bar and I'll tell you where my friend is. I can't let them see me talking to him."

"Them? Who is *them*?"

Penelope touched her right ear as September Morn picked up a winning hand and King Tout stared across the room at her.

"Go away now," she whispered. "I've talked to you too long already."

The young man looked around the room once more,

trying to spot whoever it was that the little girl was afraid of, then walked casually to the roulette table. A moment later an overweight, white-haired woman got up and left, and he watched in silence as the wheel spun and the ball landed on 31. Finally he edged his way closer to the colorfully dressed man and whispered something to him. The larger man stared at him curiously for a moment, then shrugged and placed a large bet on number 9.

He collected his winnings, then put another pile of chips on number 11. When the ball landed there, he whispered something to the young man, who made his way back to the bar, pausing to briefly observe a couple of poker games and a *jabob* table along the way.

He stopped about eight feet away from Penelope, leaned against the bar, and spoke softly while staring at the store of liquor bottles directly in front of him.

"Okay, little lady," he said softly, "you've got yourself a deal." He paused. "One condition, though."

Penelope knew what the condition was, but asked anyway.

"He wants two more winners."

"After he rescues my friend."

"Uh-uh," said the man. "We blast our way into a ship, we may have to leave in one hell of a hurry. He wants the numbers now."

"There's a man with a gold tooth sitting at the table. After he wins, the next two numbers will be 2 and 29."

"I'll be right back."

The young man relayed the information to his employer, then returned to his position at the bar.

"All right," he said. "If they're winners, we're in business." He paused. "Tell me about your friend."

"Her name is Mouse," said Penelope.

"Mouse?" repeated the young man. "I hate to think of what she looks like."

"She's very pretty," said Penelope defensively.

"Where is she?"

"On King Tout's ship."

"King Tout? Who is he?"

"He's playing cards in the middle of the room."

"Before I turn to look, tell me how I can recognize him. It's a damned crowded room."

"September Morn's with him."

"That doesn't help."

"She's an alien. There's water in her suit."

"A water-breather? I didn't see one when I walked through the room."

"She doesn't breathe it, but she has to run it all over her body."

"Okay, that should do it."

The young man turned slowly, his eyes scanning the room, then went back to his original position, staring at the back of the bar.

"All right. Is there anyone else in on this besides King Tout and the alien?"

"There's a man on the ship."

"And that's it—just the three of them?"

"And my friend."

"Has the ship got a name?" asked the man as the first of the two numbers Penelope had given him came up.

"I don't know its name."

"Registration number?"

"I don't know."

"I hope you don't expect us to force our way into every damned ship that's docked out there."

"I can describe it to you and tell you where it's docked," said Penelope.

"Why don't you just come along and point it out to me?"

"Because if I leave with you, the Golden Duke will kill my friend before we get there."

"The Golden Duke?" repeated the man. "I've heard of him."

The second number won.

"All right," said the man. "Tell me how to find the ship."

Penelope described its shape, size, and location.

"Next time you see me, walk out of here through that doorway down by the dice tables," said the man.

"Don't take too long," said Penelope.

"We're rescuing you and your friend," answered the man irritably. "Isn't that enough?"

"There's someone else after us," said Penelope. "They'll be here before long."

"What the hell did you two do—rob the Treasury on Deluros VIII?"

"We didn't do anything," said Penelope heatedly.

The colorfully clad man picked up his winnings from the roulette table, stopped at a cashier's window, and walked out of the room without glancing in their direction.

"Time to go to work," said the man. "I'll be back in a few minutes."

"Please be careful," said Penelope.

The man smiled sardonically. "It's thoughtful of you to worry about me."

"Be careful that the Golden Duke doesn't hurt my friend."

"He may be a killer, but he's not crazy," said the man. "When he knows what he's up against, he'll release her without a fight."

"Sometimes he will, sometimes he won't," said Penelope.

"What are you talking about? We're only going to rescue her once."

"Just make sure that my friend doesn't get hurt."

"We'll do our best."

"You'd better."

He chuckled. "Or what?"

"Or you'll be very sorry," said Penelope with such conviction that the man's smile vanished. He stared at her for another moment, wondering uneasily what he was getting into, then shrugged and left the casino.

17

King Tout's ship was still docked at the Starboat when the communications system was activated.

"Request permission to come aboard," said the Iceman's dispassionate voice.

"You?" said King Tout, surprised. "You came this far—after *them*?"

"Me," said the Iceman.

"Go away," said King Tout into his speaker. "I don't even have them anymore."

"*Demand* permission to come aboard."

"Permission denied."

There was a ten-minute silence. Then the Iceman's voice echoed through the ship again.

"I've just placed a small explosive device in one of your ship's exhaust vents. I'm holding the triggering mechanism in my hand. Now, one way or another, I'm coming onto that ship. Whether anyone's alive when I get there is a matter of complete indifference to me."

"I don't believe you," said King Tout.

"That's your privilege. You've got thirty seconds to open your hatch."

The gambler took twenty-three seconds, then reluctantly ordered his ship's computer to open the hatch, and a moment later the Iceman and the Forever Kid stepped into the small ship.

The interior had been modified so that there were no walls between the cockpit, the galley, and one of the cabins, and

the Iceman found himself facing King Tout in an area perhaps fifteen feet on a side. September Morn, no longer in her
special protective suit, sat nude in a narrow vat of tinted liquid and stared at them through alien eyes. The Golden Duke,
a laser pistol at his side, paid no attention to the Iceman at
all, but stared, tense and unblinking, at the Forever Kid.

"*Is* there a bomb?" asked King Tout.

"Quite possibly," said the Iceman.

"That's hardly a definitive answer," said the gambler
wryly.

"You noticed."

King Tout shrugged. "It makes no difference, anyway.
The people you want are gone."

"The people I want are right here," said the Iceman.

The gambler shook his head. "They're gone," he repeated. "That little girl made fools of us."

"How?"

"Have you ever heard of the Yankee Clipper?"

"No."

"He calls himself a trader, but he's nothing but a pirate.
He's got a quite a fleet, and he works the area around the
Quinellus Cluster. No cargo comes or goes that he doesn't
get a piece of, no ship of any kind moves in or out unless
they pay a tribute. He's the worst kind of thief."

"The worst kind of thief steals people, not money," said
the Iceman.

"I resent that remark!"

"Resent it all you like," said the Iceman. "Now, what
about the Yankee Clipper?"

"He was on the Starboat tonight, at the roulette wheel.
Somehow, and I still don't know how, the Bailey girl got
him to take her away with him. I didn't even know it until
after they were gone."

"And the Mouse?" said the Iceman. "Where is she?"

"They took her, too," said King Tout. "That's when I
found out—when the Duke told me she was gone."

The Forever Kid looked amused. "You let them steal the
Mouse from you?"

"There were forty of them," growled the Golden Duke
defensively. "What would *you* have done?"

"Stopped them," said the Kid.

"I don't blame my associate," continued King Tout. "It

was the child's doing. I didn't realize it at the time, but if she can see the future, she can *change* it—and that's just what she did, even though I was watching her every minute." He shrugged. "I'm well rid of the little monster. I won a tidy little sum tonight, and if she could manipulate events the way she did, then sooner or later she could have managed to kill my friends and me."

"Sooner, I should think," remarked the Iceman.

"She's a positive menace," said King Tout.

"It's a distinct possibility."

King Tout stared curiously at the Iceman. "You never had any intention of rescuing her!" he said at last.

"What I intend to do about her is my own business."

"You came after us to kill her!" continued the gambler.

"I haven't said that."

"But I can tell, I can see it written all over your face," said the gambler. "Look, we no longer have her. Let's call a truce and we'll throw in with you. I owe her something for the way she made fools of us tonight."

"You still don't understand, do you?" said the Iceman.

"Understand what?"

"I didn't come after her at all."

"The Mouse, then?"

The Iceman shook his head. "I gave an order back on Last Chance. You disobeyed it. Now it's time to face the consequences of your actions."

King Tout's eyes went wide with surprise. "Then you were never after *them* at all!"

"This isn't a rescue mission," said the Forever Kid, smiling at the Golden Duke. "It's a punishment party."

"But this is ridiculous!" protested King Tout. "*We're* not the enemy. The enemy is out there—it's the Bailey girl."

"You broke the law," said the Iceman.

"What law, for God's sake?"

"*My* law." He turned to the Forever Kid. "Let's see if you're as good as you think you are."

"Better," said the Kid, reaching for his sonic weapon.

The Golden Duke's fingers closed around his laser pistol, but he was dead before he could pull it out and aim it. Then slowly, almost casually, the Kid turned his weapon on King Tout and dispatched the gambler.

"Damn!" muttered the Forever Kid.

"Don't feel bad," said the Iceman. "It was execution, not murder."

"I don't feel bad about killing them," replied the Kid. "I was just hoping that the Golden Duke would be more of a challenge." He shrugged. "I don't know where the hell he built his reputation." His gaze fell on September Morn, who had watched the entire proceeding, motionless and silent. "What about this one?"

"Kill her."

The Kid looked at the naked alien, crouched down and defenseless in her tub of life-giving solution. "Now, *that* seems like murder," he said.

"I have a projectile pistol tucked in my belt," replied the Iceman. "Either you put her out of her misery fast, or I'll blow a couple of holes in her tub and you can watch her die slowly as the liquid drains out."

"You *are* a relentless bastard, aren't you?" said the Kid. Suddenly he smiled. "I admire your professionalism."

"What I am is your employer," said the Iceman. "Kill her."

He turned away and set off to explore the rest of the ship, hoping to find some hint of where the pirate had taken Penelope and the Mouse. When he returned, September Morn was dead.

"What now?" asked the Forever Kid.

"I'm going after the Yankee Clipper," said the Iceman. "You take these three back to Last Chance."

"What's the sense in that?" said the Kid. "They're already dead."

"I want everybody on Last Chance to know it."

"Send them a holograph."

"A makeup artist can work a lot of magic with a holograph," replied the Iceman. "When you get back to Last Chance, string them up where everyone can see them."

The Kid paused in thought for a long moment. "I don't think so," he said at last.

"You're working for me, remember?"

The Kid shook his head. "I'm holding more than two hundred thousand credits' worth of the Mouse's money," he replied. "The way I see it, it won't do her any good while she's a prisoner, so she and the little girl just bought me for two more weeks."

"The little girl doesn't need your help," said the Iceman. "That ought to be apparent by now."

"That's *your* opinion."

"That's a fact."

"There's another reason, too."

"Oh?"

The Kid's face came alive with excitement. "I'd like to face forty men at once."

The Iceman paused for a moment, then shrugged. "Well, if you really want to die in glorious battle, you might as well come along," he said. "Just let me make arrangements for someone to take these three back to Last Chance and we'll be on our way."

"Just a minute," said the Kid.

"What is it?"

"I know why *I'm* going," he said. "Why are *you*?"

"What difference does it make?"

"None until we get there," said the Kid.

"And then?"

"I'm going there to save the little girl, not kill her." He paused. "If you want to kill her, you've got to get past me to do it."

"Would you really shoot your employer?" asked the Iceman.

The Forever Kid couldn't tell if he was angry or curious or merely amused.

"No, I wouldn't," answered the Kid.

"That settles that."

"Not quite," said the Kid. "I quit. I'm not working for you anymore."

The Iceman smiled. "I admire your professionalism." He paused. "Of course, I could just be interested in rescuing the Mouse. I haven't said otherwise."

"I doubt it."

"Why?"

"Because I know you better now than I did before."

"I haven't said that I plan to kill anyone, either," noted the Iceman.

"What you say doesn't matter," replied the Kid adamantly. "Just remember: if you try to kill the little girl before the Mouse's money runs out, you're going to have to get past *me* first."

"You do what you think you have to do," said the Iceman, totally unperturbed.

"I plan to," said the Kid. Suddenly a boyish smile crossed his face. "It could prove very interesting."

"It could at that," conceded the Iceman.

They stared at each other in silence for an uneasy moment. Then the Iceman turned to the hatch door.

"Come on," he said at last. "Let's hire someone to cart these bodies back to Last Chance."

He walked through the hatch, and a moment later the Kid fell into step behind him.

The Iceman made his arrangements for the corpses, and twenty minutes later he and the Forever Kid had formed an uneasy truce and were racing toward the distant Quinellus Cluster in pursuit of the Yankee Clipper and his human cargo.

PART 3

The Yankee Clipper's Book

18

"Actually, I dislike the word 'pirate' and its connotations," said the Yankee Clipper, leaning back in his chair and sipping an Altairian brandy. "I consider myself to be a simple, hardworking businessman."

The Mouse and Penelope were sitting in a luxurious lounge aboard the pirate ship. There were tables, chairs, couches, picture frames, all of shining, polished chrome. The carpeting—the first the Mouse had ever seen on a ship—was formal and muted in color. The bulkheads were covered with paintings and holographs—both naturalistic and abstract—from a hundred worlds, and all about the lounge were *objets d'art*, each plundered from a different planet.

"Simple businessmen don't own spacecraft like this," answered the Mouse. "This room alone is larger than most ships I've been on."

"I've been very fortunate," replied the Yankee Clipper. "And of course, I've been quite aggressive in my pursuit of financial security." He uttered a brief command to his computer, and suddenly the room was filled with the sound of Beethoven's Ninth Symphony.

"Well, I'll give you this much," said the Mouse: "you're not at all like any other pirate I've known."

He smiled. "I take that as a compliment." The Yankee Clipper withdrew a large cigar from a pocket, held it lovingly in his hand for a moment, and finally lit it. "Excellent!" he said. "Anyone who doubts the wisdom of subjugating alien races need only smoke a single Antarean cigar and he'll become an instant convert to the somewhat hazy principles upon which our beloved Democracy was founded."

"A Democracy that *you* loot and plunder," noted the Mouse.

"Well, I *do* have my disagreements with them," he replied easily, "but I'm glad to say that we do see eye-to-eye on the subject of fine tobaccos." He paused. "Would you believe that I used to work for them?"

"Them?" repeated the Mouse. "You mean the Antarean tobacco farms?"

He chuckled. "No—the Democracy. I spent more than a decade as a part of its bureaucracy."

"In the Navy?"

"Why should you think so?"

"Well, you *do* command a ship," answered the Mouse.

"Anyone can command this ship," he replied. "You just activate the captain's computer and say, 'Go here' or 'Go there' or 'Destroy such and such a vessel.' One hardly needs any training to be a ship's captain." He paused and smiled again. "I prefer to own the entire fleet and let my subordinates worry about how to get it from one point to another."

"What kind of job prepared you for that?" asked the Mouse.

"None," answered the Yankee Clipper, noticing that his cigar had gone out and relighting it. "Actually, I was a tax collector. I worked my way up through the ranks until I was in charge of the entire Taxation Bureau on Nilander IV. Then I decided that I'd much rather be an entrepreneur than a wage slave, so I appropriated a few million credits and began contemplating various new enterprises." He took a sip of his brandy, then turned to Penelope, who had been sitting perfectly still. "I'm sure we must be boring you. You're at liberty to inspect the entire ship, as long as you ask permission before touching anything."

"I'll stay with my friend," said Penelope, reaching out and holding the Mouse's hand.

The Yankee Clipper shrugged. "As you wish." He turned back to the Mouse. "It took them almost two years to discover what I had done, during which time I had ample opportunity to consider my options."

"They took that long to find out you had robbed the treasury?" asked the Mouse.

"I'm surprised they found out so quickly," he replied. "I was quite good at fixing the records, and they were trying to administer some fifty thousand worlds from Deluros VIII, which was half a galaxy away." He put his cigar down in a crystal ashtray and picked up his brandy glass. "At first I simply planned to rob the planetary treasury on a regular basis, but Nilander IV is a poor planet when all is said and done, and I decided that I could never satisfy my financial ambitions in such a situation. So I purchased a ship—not this one, to be sure—and took my leave of the Nilander System." He paused, smiling pleasantly at the recollection. "I was in a totally liquid financial position, so I began to look around to see where I might receive the best return on my investment. My, ah, shall we say, questionable status seemed to dictate a profession beyond the physical limits of the Democracy. I've never liked the Outer Frontier— the Rim was always such a desolate place—and the Spiral Arm is too sparsely populated, so I decided upon the Inner Frontier. I spent some time in the Binder system, reviewing my options, and I finally decided to become what you refer to as a pirate. After careful consideration I even acquired a piratical name, as seemed to be the custom out here." He paused. "I took it right after that unfortunate incident near New Botswana."

"You were the one who destroyed the Navy convoy?"

"Most regrettable," he said with obvious insincerity. "But they *had* posted a reward for me. I viewed it as an object lesson."

"An object lesson during which more than four thousand men lost their lives," she said.

"Oh, I very much doubt that the total came to much more than twenty-five hundred," he said, dismissing it with a wave of his hand. "Still," he added thoughtfully, "that was the day I officially became a pirate in the eyes of the Democracy. Prior to that I was merely a thief."

"You must admit they had some justification for the term," said the Mouse.

"I suppose so," sighed the Yankee Clipper. "But there's such an unsavory connotation to it. Most pirates are such low, vulgar types. I decided from the start to run my enterprise like a business, to assess each risk coldly and rationally, to never allow pride or emotion to influence me." He paused and took another puff of his cigar. "And I must admit that I'm wealthier than even *I* had anticipated."

"I thought *all* pirates were rich," remarked the Mouse. "Or dead."

The Yankee Clipper shook his head. "Most of them are destitute on any given day." A note of contempt came into his voice. "They waste what they plunder and then have to go out and do it all over again. I decided that there had to be a better way. So I assembled my crew, hiring ex-Navy men whenever I could—men who understood discipline and could execute orders without arguing—and paid them exorbitantly. Half of the profits from our little ventures are divided among my crew and myself, and the other half goes into what I think I shall term capital expansion."

"More ships?" suggested the Mouse.

"And more men."

"It sounds very businesslike."

"It is. I run it more efficiently than the Democracy runs its government or Navy, and we have an exceptionally high return on investment, all things considered." He paused as an officer entered the room, presented him with a pair of papers requiring his signature, and then saluted and departed. "I realize that this does not fit your preconceptions about piracy, but it's the wave of the future. Even my competitors—those who are still alive and at large—are borrowing my methods."

"When you describe it like that, it makes it very hard for me to remember that your business is killing and looting," said the Mouse.

"Only when absolutely necessary," said the Clipper. "We much prefer to sell our protection to isolated worlds on the Frontier. After all," he added, "once you've killed a man, you can never make a profit from him again. But if you enter into a long-term business relationship . . ." He smiled and let his voice trail off.

"And just what kind of business relationship do you think you've entered into with *us*?" asked the Mouse as an intercom light began pulsating on the pirate's wrist radio and he deactivated it without paying it any apparent attention.

"The very best kind," answered the Yankee Clipper. "A profitable one."

"You freed me from that ship, and you helped Penelope

and me get away from King Tout and his friends, and we're very grateful," said the Mouse. "But as I see it, you were paid in advance."

"Have I asked for more money?" said the Yankee Clipper.

"No," said the Mouse. She paused and stared at him. "That's what puzzles me."

"Well, put your mind at ease," said the Yankee Clipper. "You are my guests, not my prisoners, and you have free run of the ship. Your quarters are spacious and luxurious, and contain all the amenities. We possess a galley equal to that of any cruise ship, and there is even a small fitness room filled with the very finest equipment."

"And that's it?" said the Mouse suspiciously. "Now we're even?"

"Certainly. You are free agents, and you will not be charged a single credit during your stay here as my personal guests." He paused. "We have a small commissary on the fourth level. Select anything you like from it, *gratis.*"

"Gratis?" repeated the Mouse suspiciously.

"I repeat: you are my guests."

"Where are we bound for?" asked the Mouse.

"The Quinellus Cluster," said Penelope.

The Yankee Clipper looked down at the little girl and smiled. "You're absolutely right, my dear." He turned his attention back to the Mouse. "The Quinellus Cluster is my base of operations, and we'll all be much safer back there. I've made some discreet inquiries since we left the Starboat, and it seems that quite a lot of people have an interest in your lovely little traveling companion." He smiled at Penelope. "You haven't a thing to worry about, my dear. You're perfectly safe as long as you remain with me."

"We appreciate your hospitality," said the Mouse, "but I think we'd like to be let off on the first colony planet we come to as soon as you reach the Cluster. We have arrangements to make, and a friend to contact."

"I won't hear of it," said the Yankee Clipper. "My subspace radio is at your disposal. Contact your friend right from the ship."

"I think as long as all our accounts are even, we'd rather not trouble you any further."

"It's no trouble at all," insisted the pirate.

"Just the same, we'd rather be let off as soon as you reach the Cluster."

"Well, of course, if you insist," said the Yankee Clipper with an eloquent shrug.

"Let's say that we strongly request it," answered the Mouse.

"Your wish is my command," said the Yankee Clipper. He paused. "Five million."

"Five million what?"

"Five million credits, of course."

"All right," said the Mouse. "What *about* five million credits?"

"That's my fee for letting you off the ship."

"You said we didn't owe you anything."

"You don't."

"And that we were your guests."

"Indeed you are," he replied, finally draining his brandy glass and setting it down on a polished chrome surface. "But of course, once you decline my hospitality and leave the comfort and safety of my ship, you're no longer my guests, are you?" He smiled. "You know and I know that young Penelope here is worth millions to various interested parties. I'm perfectly willing to play host to you so long as her value continues to appreciate—but if I'm to part with that potential profit, then I'll have to charge you a minimum fee of five million credits."

The Mouse stared at him without speaking. Suddenly she felt Penelope's hand squeezing her own.

"It's all right," said the little girl.

The Mouse looked down at her. "You knew he was going to do this, didn't you?"

"We needed him," said Penelope, ignoring the question.

"But we're virtually prisoners on his ship."

"It's all right," repeated Penelope. "At least the Iceman didn't catch us."

"The Iceman?" interrupted the Yankee Clipper. "Who's the Iceman?"

"A very bad man," said Penelope. "He wants to hurt me."

"Then you've made a very wise choice, my dear," said the pirate. "I wouldn't dream of hurting you, or indeed of letting any harm come to you from any source whatsoever."

"I know."

"I am, after all, not without compassion for a child in your situation," continued the Yankee Clipper. He paused thoughtfully. "Also, I suspect your value would decrease if you were harmed."

The Mouse glared at him. "So we're just going to fly around the Quinellus Cluster with you until you decide that she's worth enough to part with?" she demanded.

"Essentially," answered the Yankee Clipper. "I've already sent discreet messages to various interested parties."

"They'll blow your ship apart," said the Mouse.

The pirate smiled. "Not while she's aboard it, they won't." He paused. "But before I deny myself the pleasure of your company, it seems only reasonable that we establish a fair market value for the little girl. I could hardly do that without informing everyone that she's . . . ah . . . available for the right price."

"Unless we come up with five million credits first," said the Mouse.

"Certainly," agreed the Yankee Clipper. "I'm not an unreasonable man, and a bird in the hand is worth two in the bush. This lovely child could contract a fatal disease, or attempt to kill herself, or simply lose her remarkable ability." He paused and smiled. "Of course, I don't see how you can possibly produce such a sum, given your present situation, but I'm always willing to admit I'm wrong."

"If you'd play cards or roulette, I could help you win five million credits," said Penelope.

"I hardly think so, my dear," answered the Yankee Clipper easily. "Everyone knows who and what you are." He sighed. "And that *does* make it difficult to find volunteers for a game of chance while you're aboard the ship."

Penelope frowned. "You're no better than King Tout was."

"On the contrary, I'm *much* better," he corrected her. "For one thing, I'm providing you with every comfort at my disposal. For another, I've already given you my word that no physical harm will come to you. But mostly, I'm better than King Tout because I learn from other people's mistakes."

"What are you talking about?" demanded the Mouse.

"I should think that would be obvious. The reason you're

here instead of back at the Starboat is because lovely little Penelope here somehow manipulated events so that I would rescue you." He stared at the little girl, and though his voice remained cordial and conversational, there was a sudden hardness about his eyes. "I must warn you, my dear child, that if I notice any irregularity aboard my ship, any irregularity at all—if I should trip and break a leg, or flinch while shaving, or if this mysterious Iceman should approach too closely—then I will take you to the Deepsleep Chamber and freeze you cryogenically until such time as I have completed my transaction with whoever wants you the most desperately. Deepsleep is absolutely painless—we use it for extended voyages in deep space—but I rather suspect that when your brain is sound asleep and your metabolism is slowed to a crawl, you will be in no position to influence events as you did with King Tout."

Suddenly the Yankee Clipper got to his feet. "But enough about business. You are my honored guests, and I look forward to your company at dinner this evening. In the meantime"—he shot them a final smile as he walked to the door, which slid into a bulkhead—"please do make yourselves comfortable. I expect you'll be staying with me for quite some time."

Then he was gone, and Penelope and the Mouse were left alone in the huge, empty lounge.

"Did you see this coming, back at the Starboat?" asked the Mouse.

"Not exactly," answered Penelope. "I knew he would rescue us, and I knew that he wouldn't hurt us."

"But you didn't know that he'd sell you to the highest bidder?" she continued.

"It doesn't matter," said the little girl. "He's taking us in the right direction. That's all that matters."

"The right direction?" repeated the Mouse.

Penelope nodded.

"The right direction for what?"

"I don't know yet," replied Penelope. "But I know it's the right direction." She tightened her grip on the Mouse's hand. "Don't worry. I won't let anyone hurt you."

The Mouse suddenly realized that she believed her—and that realization made her more uneasy than the thought of being at the Yankee Clipper's mercy.

19

The Mouse led Penelope through the small commissary, past the meager supply of clothing and toiletries and the even smaller stock of books and tapes, until she came to the area that, had it borne a label, would have been marked "Miscellaneous."

"But what are we looking for?" asked the little girl.

"You'll see," said the Mouse with a smile.

She began rummaging through what were obviously the unwanted spoils of conquest, and finally she found what she had been looking for.

"Oh, they're beautiful!" exclaimed Penelope as the Mouse stepped aside and revealed four exquisite dolls, each dressed in colorful robes and bright jewelry.

"I think they're from New Kenya," said the Mouse, "but I could be wrong. I'm sure someone can tell us."

"They're very large," said Penelope. "Much bigger than Jennifer was."

"Well, they were made to be displayed, not played with," replied the Mouse. "That's why they're so stiff. My guess is that they were part of a collection. Perhaps the others were destroyed, or maybe they had real jewelry and they're in some crewman's quarters."

"I love their necklaces," said Penelope, gingerly fingering a beaded necklace on one of the dolls.

"I would imagine each of them represents some nation or religion," said the Mouse.

"And their robes are so pretty!" continued the little girl.

155

Then her gaze fell on something else that lay half buried
beneath a neatly folded length of silk.

"Well," said the Mouse, "take your choice. You can have
any of them you want—or all four, if you like."

"I want *this* one," said Penelope, reaching beneath the silk
and withdrawing a small rag doll that had a tiny scrap of red
cloth wrapped around it.

"I didn't even see that one," said the Mouse.

"*I* did."

"It's not as pretty as the others."

"I know."

"Why don't you take them all?" suggested the Mouse.

"This is the one I want," said Penelope firmly. "The
others are for grown-ups. This one is for little girls."

"And it reminds you of Jennifer?" asked the Mouse with
a smile.

Penelope nodded.

"All right, it's yours." She looked around. "I wonder
where we pay for it?"

"We don't," said Penelope. "Remember what the Yankee
Clipper said? We can have anything we want for free."

"I know. But I'd still like to find a shopkeeper or a cashier
or something and explain it to him, so we don't get shot for
robbing the store."

"We won't," said Penelope.

The Mouse shrugged. "Oh, well—you haven't been wrong
yet." She paused. "What are you going to call her? Jennifer?"

Penelope shook her head. "Jennifer's gone. I need a new
name for this one." She frowned, concentrating on the doll,
then looked up at the Mouse. "What's your name?"

"Mouse."

"I mean your *real* name."

"Oh, it's not a very special name at all," replied the
Mouse. "I got rid of it the day I arrived on the Inner
Frontier."

"I'd still like to know."

The Mouse shrugged. "Maryanne," she said distastefully.

"Maryanne," repeated Penelope thoughtfully. "Maryanne." She nodded her head approvingly. "That's what
I'll call her."

"You're sure?"

"Yes. That way even when you're not with me, Maryanne will remind me of you."

"What's this talk of not being with you?" said the Mouse. "We're a team, remember?"

"But you told me about how sometimes you have to leave someone you love behind, the way I had to leave Jennifer." The little girl paused. "You left Merlin. Someday maybe you'll leave me behind, too."

"Not a chance," said the Mouse reassuringly. She put her arms around Penelope. "I didn't love Merlin. And besides, we'll be rejoining him soon."

"I don't think so," said Penelope. "He's not in any of the futures I can see."

"But you can only see a little way ahead," noted the Mouse.

"Sometimes I can see longer."

"Oh?"

"Not always, but sometimes."

"More often than you used to be able to?" asked the Mouse.

"Yes." Penelope paused. "I wonder why?"

"It's just a sign that you're growing up, I suppose," said the Mouse. "You can run faster and eat more food and say bigger words that you used to, so why shouldn't you be able to see further ahead, too?"

Penelope shrugged. "I don't know."

"That was a rhetorical question," said the Mouse with a smile.

"I don't know what that means."

"It means you don't have to answer it." She looked at the other four dolls again. "You're sure you don't want anything else?"

"All I want is Maryanne," answered Penelope, cradling the doll in her arms.

The Mouse winced. "God, I hate that name!"

"It's a pretty name, and since you don't want it, it should go to a pretty doll."

"You're the boss," said the Mouse with a sigh of defeat.

"Am I really?" asked Penelope.

"Well, you're the boss about which doll you get to keep and what you want to name it," said the Mouse. She paused. "And if Carlos were here, he'd probably try to convince me that you could become the boss of the whole galaxy if you wanted to."

"That's silly," said Penelope.

"I agree." The Mouse looked around the commissary one last time. "All right, let's go back to our cabin."

"You go ahead," said Penelope. "I want to show Maryanne around the ship."

"I'll come with you," volunteered the Mouse.

"It's not necessary," said Penelope. "I won't get lost, and the Yankee Clipper has told everyone that we're his guests."

"I don't mind coming with you," said the Mouse. "It's no trouble."

"It's really not necessary," repeated Penelope firmly.

"You're sure you'll be all right?" asked the Mouse in concerned tones.

"I'll be all right."

The Mouse stared at the little girl for a moment and then shrugged.

"Well, I suppose everyone deserves a little time to themselves," she said at last. "Maybe I'll go back to our room and take a nap."

The Mouse hugged Penelope and headed off in the direction of their cabin, while the little girl, still holding the doll as if it were made of crystal and might be expected to shatter at any moment, began going the opposite direction. She passed the infirmary, then rode an airlift to the top deck and turned to her left. There was much more activity here, for this was the operations level, and crewmen were continuously moving purposefully from one area to another, paying no attention to her at all.

Penelope, moving with equal purpose, walked down the corridor that led to the observation deck, a relatively large room filled with some fifteen viewscreens, each displaying a section of space that an external holocamera transmitted, all of them together showing the ship's surroundings for more than a parsec in every direction.

Standing alone in the middle of the room was the slender man that she had approached aboard the Starboat.

"Good afternoon," he said when he noticed that she had joined him.

"Good afternoon," she replied formally.

"That looks like a new doll."

"Her name's Maryanne," said Penelope, holding up the doll for the man to see.

"You know, I've never asked you what *your* name was."

"Penelope."

"Welcome to the ship, Penelope," said the man. "My name's Potemkin—Mischa Potemkin."

"That sounds like a real name," she said, surprised.

"It is."

"I thought hardly anyone out here used their real name—except for me and Maryanne, anyway."

"That's precisely why I choose to," said Potemkin with a smile. "I think it makes me very distinctive."

"It does," agreed Penelope.

"Well, Penelope, what are you doing here all by yourself?"

"I'm not by myself," answered the girl. "Maryanne's with me."

"I apologize," said Potemkin. "Where are you and Maryanne doing here?"

"I'm talking to you, and Maryanne is looking at all the viewscreens."

Potemkin chuckled. "That isn't what I meant."

Penelope stared at him politely, waiting for him to explain himself.

"I mean," he said at last, "why are you on the observation deck at all?"

"I saw you here, and everyone else seems so busy, so I thought I'd talk to you."

"What do you want to talk about?" asked Potemkin.

"Oh, I don't know," said Penelope, looking around the room. Her gaze fell on a viewscreen. "How does this work?" she asked, pointing to the screen. "I mean, it can't be a window, because we're in the middle of the ship."

"It's just like a holograph projection screen in your home," explained Potemkin. "We have cameras outside the ship, and they transmit what they see to the various screens."

"But you can't change the channels."

He smiled. "That's why we have so many screens."

"How do you fix a camera when it breaks?"

"We don't," said Potemkin. "We just cast it off and attach a new one."

"Do *you* attach it?"

Potemkin looked amused. "That's not my job."

"What *is* your job?" asked Penelope. "Everyone else seems to be working very hard, and you're just standing around looking at the screens. Are you the man who warns the captain when we're approaching a meteor swarm?"

"No, the ship does that automatically."

"Then what do you do?"

"Nothing, for the moment."

"Are you a passenger, then?" she persisted.

"No," said Potemkin. "I'm the War Chief."

"War Chief?"

He smiled. "Back in the Democracy, I suppose they'd call me a military advisor. I don't work until we're attacking someone, or under attack ourselves—but when that happens, I work very hard indeed."

"So if you tell the Yankee Clipper to attack someone, he does it—and if you say not to, he doesn't?"

"Usually."

"That makes you very important," she said admiringly.

"From time to time."

She paused, staring at him. "What happens if you give him the wrong advice?"

"Then we lose."

"Lose?" she repeated.

"Die."

"And do you make lots of money?"

"I hardly see that that's any of your business, young lady," said Potemkin.

"Not yet," agreed Penelope.

"What is *that* supposed to mean?" demanded Potemkin.

Penelope looked down solicitously at her doll. "I think she's hungry," she announced.

"She can wait," said Potemkin. "What did you mean—'not yet'?"

"You know what I meant," said Penelope, still looking at her doll.

"Suppose you tell me, anyway."

"Sometimes you could give him the wrong advice."

"It's possible," admitted Potemkin. "Nobody's right all the time."

"*I* am," said Penelope with no trace of smugness.

"Bunk."

"I feel very sorry for you, Mr. Potemkin," she said sincerely.

"Oh? Why?"

"Because one day soon—maybe tomorrow, maybe even tonight—the Yankee Clipper will remember what I did in the casino, and he'll realize that I would be a better War Chief than you."

Potemkin laughed harshly. "You don't know the first thing about military tactics."

"But I know all about the future," she pointed out. "If he can win a battle, I'll know how. And if he can't, I'll know that, too."

Potemkin stared at her through narrowed eyes for a long moment.

"You didn't just find me here by accident, did you?" he said at last.

"No, I didn't," admitted the little girl. "I knew you'd be here."

"And you knew we'd have this conversation?"

"Sort of," answered Penelope. "I didn't know what the words would be, but I knew we'd talk if I wanted us to."

"Do you know that I've killed people who have threatened my position?"

"No," she replied. "But I believe it. You have good manners, but you're not a very nice man."

"If I decide you're right," continued Potemkin, "what makes you think that I won't kill you, too?"

"You're not nice," repeated Penelope, "but you're smart. If you kill me, you know that the Yankee Clipper will figure out why you did it and then he'll kill you, because you'll have killed someone who could have made sure he never lost a battle."

"I might take my chances on that," said Potemkin ominously. "It's better than going back to being a common crewman."

"You don't have to kill me *or* be a crewman," said Penelope.

"Oh?"

"All you have to do is let me and my friends off on a planet."

"Friends?"

"Mouse and Maryanne," she replied, indicating the doll.

Potemkin shook his head. "I don't think I'm inclined to do that," he said. "You're worth a couple of million credits, maybe more. For all I know, the Clipper has already contacted some of the people who are looking for you."

"Is money that important to you?" asked Penelope.

"It's one of my favorite things."

She stared into his eyes. "In one of the futures I can see, you put us down on a planet along with the Yankee Clipper, and you become the captain of the ship and take over all *his* money."

"Do you see if I live out the day after I do that?" he asked sardonically.

She shook her head. "I can't see your future once I leave you." She paused. "But I can see lots of futures in which I become the War Chief, and lots more in which the Yankee Clipper kills you because you hurt me."

"Do you see any in which we just stay the way we are and finally sell you to the highest bidder?"

"No."

"Why not?"

"Because I'm not looking for them."

"Well, you'd better *start* looking," said Potemkin. "Because that's the way it's going to be."

"I don't think so," said Penelope seriously. "Very soon now the Yankee Clipper will decide I would be a better War Chief than you." She paused. "Long before you have a chance to sell me." She looked at the doll again. "I really have to go and feed her," she said apologetically, and began walking toward the doorway through which she had entered.

Potemkin watched her walk away. Then, just before she stepped into the corridor, he called out:

"Not that I believe any of this for an instant—but if I did, which planet do you think I'd let you off on?"

She re-entered the room and walked to the viewscreen at which she had originally been staring. She peered intently at it for a moment, then pointed to a yellow star.

"There are eleven planets circling this star," she said. "We want the fourth one."

"Have you been there before?" he asked.

"No."

"Then why did you pick it out from all the rest?"

She smiled at him. "It looks very pretty."

"It looks like every other Class G star in the Cluster." He stared at her. "Are you sure you don't have any friends there?"

"I'm sure."

"But you'll find some?" he continued.

"One, maybe."

"Just one?" he said disbelievingly.

"Sometimes one is enough," said Penelope. She cuddled the doll again. "I really have to go now, or Maryanne is going to be mad at me."

She left the room as Potemkin stared silently after her, and a few minutes later she was back in her own spacious quarters. The Mouse, who had been napping on her bed, sat up abruptly at the sound of the door sliding into the wall.

"I'm sorry," said Penelope. "I didn't mean to wake you."

"It's just as well," replied the Mouse, throwing back her tufted satin comforter. "If you hadn't, I'd never have been able to get to sleep tonight."

"It's always night in space," Penelope pointed out.

"This is a military ship. It runs on Galactic Standard time." The Mouse rubbed her eyes. "How are you and Maryanne getting along?"

"She needs some new clothes," said Penelope. "She can't go around just wearing part of a blanket."

"Then we'll make some for her."

"Could we?" asked the little girl eagerly.

"I don't know why not," said the Mouse, looking around the room. "You know, if we could find some of the fabric they used for our furniture, she'd be better dressed than anyone else on the ship."

"That would be nice," agreed Penelope.

"How did Maryanne enjoy her tour of the ship?"

"I don't think she likes it here very much," said Penelope.

"I'm sorry to hear that, because I've got a feeling she's stuck here for a while."

"Maybe not," said the little girl.

The Mouse stared at her. "Oh?"

"There's a very pretty planet not far away," continued Penelope. "I think that Maryanne would be much happier there."

"Who do you think is going to let Maryanne off on this

very pretty planet?" asked the Mouse cautiously.

"Oh, I don't know," answered the little girl. "Someone."

"Someone like the Yankee Clipper?" persisted the Mouse.

Penelope shook her head. "No. I don't think so."

"I know he seems pleasant, Penelope, but he's a very dangerous man."

"He won't hurt you," said Penelope. "You're my only friend." She suddenly remembered Maryanne. "Well, my best friend, anyway. I'd never let anyone hurt you."

The Mouse smiled ruefully. "That's what *I'm* supposed to say to *you*."

"I'm sorry," said Penelope, flustered. "I didn't mean to be bossy. Not with you."

The Mouse got up, walked across the wide expanse of floor separating them, and hugged her warmly. "You're not being bossy, Penelope. You're being caring, and that's a good thing to be. I just don't want you endangering yourself. You have a marvelous gift, but you're still a little girl, and you don't know what some of these people can be like when you make them mad."

"Yes, I do," said Penelope. "I can see what they're like." She placed a finger to her temple. "In here."

"Then you know better than to cross them."

"But we have to get to the planet."

"What's so important about this planet?"

Penelope shrugged. "I don't know yet."

"But you're sure we should go there?" persisted the Mouse.

The girl nodded her head. "Yes."

"When do you think you'll know why?"

"Soon," said Penelope with total conviction. "Very soon."

Then she remembered Maryanne, and as the Mouse watched her with a puzzled expression on her face, she spent the next few minutes cleaning the doll and readjusting its tiny robe, to all outward appearances a little blonde girl without a care in the world, rather than a valuable prisoner aboard the most powerful pirate ship in the Quinellus Cluster.

20

Penelope was sound asleep when a hand reached out and shook her gently by the shoulder. She moaned and turned away, but the hand continued shaking her.

"Go away!" she muttered.

"Wake up, kid," whispered a masculine voice.

"Leave me alone!"

"We've got to talk."

The Mouse awoke, sat up, looked across the relatively spacious cabin, and saw the slender man sitting on the edge of Penelope's bed.

"What do you want?" she demanded.

"This doesn't concern you," answered Potemkin.

"Anything to do with her concerns me."

"I'm not going to hurt her, lady," said Potemkin. "But I've got to talk to her."

"Go away," said Penelope again.

"Kid, you can wake up peacefully, or I can turn the lights on and throw a bucket of cold water over you," said Potemkin. "It's up to you."

Penelope slowly sat up in her bed, rubbing her eyes.

"Oh," she said, upon recognizing Potemkin. "It's you."

"Penelope, if you don't want to talk to him, I can call for help," said the Mouse.

"He *is* help," said Penelope, leaving the Mouse totally confused.

"Maybe I am, maybe I'm not," said Potemkin. "First I've got a couple of questions to ask."

165

"You expected him?" asked the Mouse.

"Not this soon, but yes," said Penelope.

"Does this have something to do with that walk around the ship you took this afternoon?" persisted the Mouse.

"Ask your questions later, lady," said Potemkin. "I'm in a hurry."

"It's all right, Mouse," said Penelope reassuringly. "Really it is. He won't hurt us."

"Don't be too sure of that," said Potemkin.

"If you were going to hurt us, I'd know," said Penelope with no trace of fear or apprehension. "You're here to talk."

"I could change my mind."

"You're a smart man, and that would be a stupid thing to do," said the little girl, staring at him unblinking.

He met her gaze for a moment, then lowered his eyes briefly.

"All right," he said. "I need some answers, and I need them fast."

"I'll answer anything I can," said Penelope.

"Don't answer anything yet," said the Mouse. She turned to Potemkin. "I've already found three spy devices, and I've probably missed some."

"No problem," said Potemkin. "My own man will be monitoring us during this watch." He turned to Penelope. "I'm not ready to take on the Clipper yet. He's got too many people loyal to him. I don't think I can pull it off."

"Are you sure?" said the girl.

"Damn it—we're talking about mutiny against the most successful pirate in the Cluster! It's not worth the risk, unless you can guarantee that I'll succeed."

"I told you—I can't see what will happen after I'm not with you any longer."

"I know . . . but I came up with another way to get you to your planet."

"Whose planet?" interjected the Mouse.

"Shut up, lady—I'm talking to the girl!" Potemkin turned back to Penelope. "What if I arrange for the auction to take place on the planet?" He paused. "The Clipper would have to take you there to deliver you."

"He wouldn't take us alone," said Penelope. "He'd have lots of guards."

Potemkin laughed mirthlessly. "Are you trying to convince me at this late date that you can't get away from a bunch of guards if you want to? Hell, you've gotten away from bounty hunters all across the Democracy and the Inner Frontier."

"I just said that he'd have a lot of guards with him."

"What will happen to him on the planet?"

Penelope shrugged. "I don't know."

"I don't believe that for a second," said Potemkin. "Will he live or die?"

"In some futures he lives, in some he dies. In some I can't tell."

"In how many of these futures does he figure out that he's on the planet because I don't want you on the ship?"

"Very few," said Penelope.

"And in those very few, what kind of action does he take against me?"

"Once he leaves me, I can't see what he'll do."

"If he dies, how will you kill him?" demanded Potemkin. "Is there any way it can be connected to me?"

"I won't kill him at all," said Penelope. "I'm just a little girl."

He jerked a thumb in the Mouse's direction. "Does *she* do it?"

"No."

"You're sure?"

"I'm sure."

"So if he dies on the planet, it can't be blamed on me?" continued Potemkin.

"If he dies on the planet, it can't be blamed on you," agreed Penelope.

"And if he doesn't die and you get away, it still won't be blamed on me?"

"I don't know. But if he doesn't know that you chose the planet, if he thinks the others did . . ."

"Okay," said Potemkin. "That's what I needed to know."

"Will you arrange to set us down there?" asked Penelope.

"I'll have to think about it."

"You really don't want us to stay on the ship."

"I know."

"And you don't want to hurt us."

"I said I'd think about it," said Potemkin irritably. He got to his feet and walked to the door. "You'll know when I've made up my mind."

Then he was out in the corridor and the door slid shut behind him, and the Mouse was staring at Penelope, a puzzled expression on her face.

"Do you want to tell me about that?" she asked at last.

"We have to get to the planet I told you about," answered Penelope. "Potemkin will see to it that we do."

"Potemkin? Is that his name?"

Penelope nodded. "Mischa Potemkin. Isn't that a funny name?"

"You're sure he'll set us down on this planet that you're so anxious to reach?"

"Pretty sure," said Penelope with a shrug, as she picked up Maryanne and began straightening her tiny red blanket.

The Mouse frowned again. "You're the Yankee Clipper's prisoner, and Potemkin works for the Clipper. They stand to make millions of credits by selling you to any of the people who are trying to find you. Why should he suddenly be willing to put you off on a planet and never see you again?"

"I explained to him why it would be a smart thing to do," said Penelope, smoothing Maryanne's hair. "When can we get Maryanne some new outfits?"

"I don't know," said the Mouse distractedly. "We can look around the ship tomorrow and see if there's any material we can use."

"Will it hurt her if I wash her in the dryshower?"

"No, I don't suppose so. Can we go back to talking about Potemkin for a minute?"

Penelope sighed. "If you want." She held Maryanne up and stared at her. "But I want to wash her soon. She needs a bath every day, or she might get sick."

"Try to pay attention, Penelope," said the Mouse, keeping her voice calm and soothing with some effort. "A very dangerous man is willing to cost his even more dangerous boss millions of credits and set us down on a strange planet." She paused briefly. "Can you tell me why he would do such a thing?"

"If I told you, you'd laugh," said Penelope.

"Not even if I thought it was funny," the Mouse assured her.

"You promise?"

"I promise."

"He's afraid of me," said Penelope. She giggled. "Isn't that funny—a pirate being afraid of a little girl?"

"*Why* is he afraid of you?" asked the Mouse sharply. "What did you two talk about this afternoon?"

"Oh, lots of things." Penelope seemed to lose interest. "I really have to wash Maryanne now, Mouse." She walked to the bathroom compartment and paused at the door. "Do you want to come into the dryshower with us?"

The Mouse shook her head. "No, you go ahead."

"You'll still be here when I get out?"

"Where would I go?" asked the Mouse ironically.

"I don't know," said the little girl. "But sometimes I think you're upset with me, and I'm afraid you'll leave me and I'll be alone again."

"I'll never leave you, Penelope," said the Mouse sincerely. "If you can see the future, you know that."

"I can hardly ever see the good things," explained Penelope. "Just the bad ones."

"Well, if leaving you is a bad thing, you should be able to see it if I was going to do it."

Penelope's face brightened suddenly. "That's right!" she exclaimed happily. She ran over to the Mouse and threw her arms around her. "I love you, Mouse!"

"I love you, Penelope," said the Mouse, returning her hug. "Now go take your dryshower, and then maybe we'll talk some more."

Penelope emerged from the dryshower a few minutes later, dressed in a fresh outfit.

"Where's Maryanne?" asked the Mouse.

"I left her there."

"There? Where?"

"In the bathroom."

"Why?"

"Because if you're going to talk about Potemkin and the Yankee Clipper, I don't want her to hear what you say. It might frighten her."

"It doesn't frighten you, though, does it?" asked the Mouse.

"No."

"Why not?"

"Because they're not going to hurt us."

The Mouse frowned, trying to find the best way to keep Penelope's interest from flagging. "Well, it frightens *me*," she said at last. "Maybe you can explain to me why I shouldn't be frightened."

"The Yankee Clipper won't hurt us because we're worth so much money," said the girl.

"He can hurt us without killing us."

"He won't, though," said Penelope. Then she added thoughtfully, "At least, not while we're on the ship. I can't see much further ahead."

"What about Potemkin?"

"He'd *like* to hurt us, but he's afraid to."

"Why?"

"Why does he want to hurt us, or why is he afraid to?" asked Penelope.

"Both."

"He wants to hurt us, because I explained to him that I would be a better War Chief than he is."

"I see," said the Mouse. She paused for a moment. "Did he believe you?"

"Why shouldn't he?" replied Penelope. "It's the truth."

"Then why is he afraid to hurt you?"

"Because the Yankee Clipper knows that I can see the future. He hasn't figured out yet that I'd be a good War Chief, but if Potemkin hurts me, he'll try to think of why, and then pretty soon he'll know."

"That must have been some conversation you had with Potemkin this afternoon," said the Mouse.

"He was very upset," said Penelope, smiling at the memory. Suddenly she giggled again. "You should have seen his face! It got all red."

"I'll just bet it did," said the Mouse with a smile. "So you convinced him the best way to get rid of you was to put you on a planet?"

"To put *us* on one," Penelope corrected her. "I wouldn't ever leave you behind, Mouse."

"I appreciate that," said the Mouse. "Did you suggest that he take over the ship and put the Yankee Clipper down with us as well?"

Penelope shook her head. "That was his idea, but it wasn't a very good one. It makes more sense to let the Yankee

Clipper take us there to deliver us to whoever wants to buy me."

"You're not worried about that?" asked the Mouse.

"No," answered the little girl.

"Why not?" persisted the Mouse. "He'll probably take twenty or thirty of his men down with him to guard us."

"That's all right," said Penelope with no show of concern.

"*Why* is it all right?"

"Because I'll find a friend there."

"But you don't know who?"

"No."

"Then how do you know this friend will be able to help us?"

Penelope shrugged. "I just know."

"You're putting an awfully big burden on a friend you've never met," said the Mouse.

"Oh, he's not the only one who can help us," said Penelope with a shrug.

"He isn't?" said the Mouse, surprised. "Who else is there?"

"There's the Forever Kid."

"He's on this planet?"

"He will be, once his ship tells him we've landed."

"You didn't mention Carlos Mendoza," noted the Mouse. "Isn't he still with the Kid?"

Penelope frowned. "Yes, he is—but he doesn't want to help me."

"I've told you before: I won't let him hurt you."

"You can't stop him," said the girl. She sighed. "Maybe my new friend will be able to."

"Don't worry about Carlos," said the Mouse firmly. "Trust me: he does a lot of things I disapprove of, but killing children isn't one of them."

"He frightens me."

"I can't figure out why," said the Mouse. "You've seen Three-Fisted Ollie and Cemetery Smith and the Golden Duke and all these other killers. Why does a small, middle-aged man frighten you worse than they do?"

"Because none of the others wanted to kill me," explained Penelope. "They were just doing their jobs."

"The Golden Duke would have killed you if King Tout had ordered him to."

"That's different," said Penelope.

"How?"

"He didn't hate me. Neither did any of the others, not even 32." She paused. "But the Iceman doesn't want to kill me for money, or because someone tells him to." A tear trickled down her cheek. "He doesn't even *know* me, and he wants me dead." Two more tears followed the first one. "I don't know why. I've never done anything to him."

"You're wrong," said the Mouse soothingly. "He really doesn't want to hurt you."

"I'm *not* wrong," insisted Penelope.

"Then he's destined to be disappointed," said the Mouse earnestly.

"Why did you ever like him, Mouse?" asked Penelope.

"I was lonely," said the Mouse with a sigh, "and sometimes lonely people make poor choices."

"Were you lonely when you found me?"

"No," said the Mouse, hugging her. "You were the best choice I ever made."

"Really?" asked Penelope, brightening somewhat.

"Really."

"And we'll always be together?"

"Always," promised the Mouse.

Then Penelope remembered Maryanne, and brought her out of the bathroom and began playing with her. The Mouse watched her for almost an hour as the little girl lavished her love and attention upon the rag doll. Then the Mouse fell asleep, and a few moments later Penelope followed suit.

It was early morning when the door slid into the wall and the Yankee Clipper entered their compartment.

"Doesn't anyone ever knock?" demanded the Mouse irritably.

"Wake up and pay attention," announced the pirate, walking over to a chair and seating himself. "There's been a change of plans: it seems that some of the parties who are interested in the girl have decided that they wouldn't feel comfortable transacting their business aboard what they consider to be the flagship of a pirate fleet." He smiled wryly. "I suppose I'd feel much the same way if I were in their place." He paused. "So we'll be transferring the two of you to a nearby planet, and we'll complete our business there."

"Could you identify these parties?" asked the Mouse.

"Why bother yourselves with details?" he replied. "You'll know who makes the high bid for her, and the rest doesn't really matter."

"So it's to be an auction?"

The Yankee Clipper laughed. "She won't be placed on a block, with an auctioneer showing off her teeth, if that's what you mean. I'll allow the various interested parties to ascertain that she's in my possession, and then I'll determine which reward I choose to accept."

"The highest one, no doubt," said the Mouse dryly.

"Not necessarily," said the Yankee Clipper seriously. "The Democracy wants her, as does the Canphorite Confederation. I've had certain, shall we say, disagreements with both governments; a blanket pardon from either one, in addition to money, might weigh heavily in my consideration of the various rewards."

"Why?" asked the Mouse, curious. "Do you plan to stop being a pirate?"

"Certainly not," he answered. "But at the moment, I cannot invest my money within the Democracy or the Confederation without putting it at risk. Furthermore," he added, "I would like to think that if worse came to worst, there would be a government somewhere that would allow me sanctuary."

"Seems like a defeatist attitude to me," said the Mouse.

"Does it?" asked the Yankee Clipper. "It seems like a fiscally and politically sound attitude to me. After all, who knows what tomorrow may bring"—suddenly he grinned—"other than a certain little girl, that is?"

"When do we leave?" asked Penelope.

"Eleven hundred hours, ship's time," answered the pirate. "This ship is too large to land, so we'll transfer to a shuttlecraft."

" 'We'?" repeated the Mouse.

"Absolutely," said the Yankee Clipper. "I'm coming with you." He smiled. "I know it's irregular for a captain to leave his vessel in unsecured territory, but I think unusual situations call for unusual responses." He turned to Penelope. "I have no idea what you can do to me if I stay aboard the ship. Probably I have nothing to worry about, but I try never to deal in probabilities when I can deal in certainties. And it's certain that you won't cause the shuttlecraft to crash if you're in it, so I plan to be in it, too." He paused. "We're going to become great friends, Penelope, my child. I don't plan to let you out of my sight until the transaction is complete, and I'll always have at least half a dozen armed men surrounding us." He smiled at her again. "If I choke on a meal, if I have a stroke, if anything at all untoward befalls me, they will have orders to kill you instantly. Do you understand?"

"I understand," said Penelope.

"Good," said the Yankee Clipper. "Then we might as well make the best of the circumstances." He paused. "At least we shouldn't be bored. We'll be transacting our business on one of the most interesting planets in the Cluster."

"Oh?" said the Mouse.

He nodded. "It's a world I've always meant to visit, but I simply haven't found the time until now."

"What's its name?" asked the Mouse.

"Calliope," replied the Yankee Clipper.

21

Calliope was known throughout the Quinellus Cluster as a pleasure planet, and, to be sure, it had more than its share of whorehouses and drug dens and perverse amusements— but that is a very narrow definition of the word "pleasure," and Calliope was, after all, not just a small section of a jaded city, but an entire planet.

In the western hemisphere it boasted a dinosaur park, a 22,000-square-mile reserve housing some 80,000 gargantuan, warm-blooded reptiles from the primeval planet of Quantos VIII. An inland ocean was filled with imported predators and prey from Pinnipes II, and each of the hundreds of hotels lining the beaches supplied not only a fleet of fishing boats but also a number of small but comfortable submarines for their clientele's viewing pleasure.

There were enormous ranches on which the customers could participate in real cattle drives, huge rings where the matadors would face the brave bulls (and whatever other brave but doomed animals were released in them), a dazzling array of safari excursions, and golf courses by the thousands.

Just beyond the 19,000-hectare amusement park near the eastern hemisphere's spaceport was a racetrack that could accommodate any of the seventeen species of animals from as many oxygen worlds upon which pari-mutuel betting was permitted. There were even clones of the now-extinct horse of Earth, and Man o' War, Citation, Secretariat, and Seattle Slew met one another and their most famous competitors on a regular basis.

Fully one-third of the Great Eastern Continent was set aside as a hunting reserve for safari enthusiasts, and so well known was it among the *aficionados* of blood sports that, far from bragging about the trophies that had been taken, the government actually boasted about the number of hunters who had been killed by the animals they were stalking.

Mount Ramsey boasted the second-longest continuous ski slope in the galaxy, and it was said that an enthusiast could begin his descent before dawn and still be racing downhill when nightfall occurred.

There were daily vehicle races on the salt flats, daily boat races down the River Jordan, daily sporting championships of a thousand different types in the dozen huge stadiums that had been erected across the planet. There were nine cities, of which Xanadu was the largest. Each city supplied an endless array of round-the-clock entertainment, restaurants, and shopping; two of the nine catered almost exclusively to aliens, while a third, which bore the name of New Gomorrah, possessed seven different multi-environment hotels as well as an enclosed amusement park for chlorine-breathers.

Though it was within the Quinellus Cluster and hence officially a part of the Inner Frontier, Calliope was actually run by a number of cartels from the Spiral Arm and the Galactic Rim, and was patronized, in increasing numbers, by vacationers and sightseers from within the Democracy itself.

The Yankee Clipper's party, consisting of himself, the Mouse, Penelope Bailey, and eighteen armed guards, landed at the spaceport near Xanadu, and soon checked into a very exclusive, very private hotel on the outskirts of the city, not too far from one of the smaller amusement parks. The Mouse and Penelope shared the pirate's palatial suite, but the doors and windows were under constant surveillance by his men, who worked their jobs in six-man shifts. Food, drink, and even new clothing for Maryanne were brought to the suite, but neither Penelope nor the Mouse was allowed to leave it, and whenever the Yankee Clipper found it necessary to leave, one of his men entered and kept his weapon trained on the Mouse until the pirate returned.

On the morning of their second day there, the Yankee Clipper, his beard newly trimmed, his clothes even more brilliant than usual, entered the parlor of their suite and seated himself on a large leather sofa.

"Well, another day or two and you'll be on your way, young lady," he said to Penelope.

"Who's bidding for her?" asked the Mouse.

The pirate chuckled. "You might better ask who *isn't*. This is a very popular little girl we've got here. The Democracy wants her, the Confederation wants her, two scientific institutions want her, a religious foundation wants her, and nine private parties want her." He paused, lit a cigar, and balanced it on the edge of an exquisite crystal ashtray. "Potemkin tells me that they should all have arrived here by tomorrow night. We'll have a nice dinner, exchange a few pleasantries, and transact our business—and *then*," he added, "I can finally stop worrying about what you might do to me."

"I can't do anything to you," said Penelope, standing before a huge window that overlooked the city center. "I'm your prisoner."

"You've been other people's prisoner in the past," said the pirate. "Most of them aren't around to tell what happened to them, but I'll wager that it wasn't pleasant."

"They were bad men," said Penelope with a shrug.

"I hope you'll remember just how well I'm treating you," said the Yankee Clipper.

"You're the worst of them all."

"Nonsense. I saved you from King Tout, didn't I?"

"That doesn't make you a good man," replied the girl. "Just a greedy one."

"I'm also a very untrusting one," shot back the Yankee Clipper, picking up his cigar and taking a puff of it. "If anything happens to me while I'm on the planet, my men have orders to kill your friend here."

"If anything happens to you, Mouse will have nothing to do with it," said Penelope, unable to hide a worried expression from her face.

"Oh, they'll try to kill you, too," said the pirate. "But I don't know if it can be done. On the other hand, I'm sure they can kill the Mouse, and she'll be the one they shoot first." He smiled at her. "I hope you'll remember that."

"You're a bad man," said Penelope. "You're going to be very sorry you treated us like this."

"Nonsense," scoffed the Yankee Clipper. "I've treated you like visiting royalty." He gestured vaguely with a hand. "Look at this parlor. Elegant furniture, beautiful views, original oil paintings on the walls, room service to cater to your every whim. I even had the bar stocked with fruit juice and soft drinks, just for you."

"You know what I mean," said Penelope seriously. "I may just be a little girl, but I have a good memory. Someday you'll be sorry."

"Someday I'll be dead of old age, too," said the pirate with a shrug. "In the meantime, though, I suggest you think about what will happen to your friend if any harm befalls me."

He walked out of the parlor, and the door closed behind him.

"You've got one Standard day to find your unknown friend," remarked the Mouse. "Or, more to the point, *he* has one Standard day to find *us*, since it doesn't seem very likely that we're going to get out of this suite unless someone kills all of the Clipper's guards."

"We'll get out," said Penelope with certainty.

"How?"

The little girl shrugged. "I'm not sure yet. There are a lot of futures."

"There always are," said the Mouse. "The question is: can you influence some of them enough to get us out of here?"

Penelope made no reply, and since she seemed to be concentrating on something that only she could see or fathom, the Mouse slipped a disk into the holo player and watched a selection of three-dimensional advertisements of the local entertainments. She learned that she had just missed a Wild West pageant, re-created from Earth's ancient past, as well as a much-ballyhooed match for the freehand middleweight championship of the Inner Frontier. Upcoming attractions included a visit from the Cluster's most famous circus, the conclusion of a relay race around Calliope's equator that had begun eighty-two days previously, and a re-creation of the decisive battle of the Sett War, which would take place on the sprawling savannah some fifteen miles to the west of Xanadu.

"Damn!" muttered the Mouse. "It just isn't fair!"

"What isn't?" asked Penelope.

"All my life I've dreamed of a world like this, teeming with fat men and fatter wallets," said the Mouse, "and now that I'm finally here, I'm locked away in a hotel so close to all that money I can almost taste it." A wistful expression came over her face. "Do you know what Merlin and I could do here, how much money we could make?"

"I thought *I* was your partner," said Penelope in hurt tones.

"You are," the Mouse assured her.

"Then why are you talking about Merlin?"

"Because Merlin is my partner, too—and he had the deftest fingers I ever saw," answered the Mouse. "You and I are good at other things—but Merlin could have started at one side of this hotel's lobby, walked to the other side, and picked up twenty wallets by the time he got there." She smiled. "And oh, what he could have done circulating in the crowd at the racetrack!"

"I can make you more money than he could," said Penelope.

"I don't doubt it."

"We don't need him."

"We need all the help we can get, from anyone who will give it to us," said the Mouse.

"Not from Merlin."

"Why are you suddenly so concerned with Merlin?" asked the Mouse. "You haven't mentioned him in weeks."

"We were happy without him," said Penelope.

The Mouse sighed. "You have to understand that you don't stop liking a friend, or being loyal to him, just because you've found someone you like better."

Penelope stared at her.

"Do you really like me better?"

"Yes," said the Mouse. "But don't forget—Merlin has been leading Three-Fisted Ollie and Cemetery Smith and some other bounty hunters away from us for weeks now." She paused. "What kind of friends would we be if we didn't want him back after he risked his life for us?"

"You're right," said Penelope after some consideration. "I'm sorry."

"It's all right," said the Mouse soothingly. "You don't have to apologize."

"I just worry about being alone again."

"*I* worry about how we're going to get out of here," responded the Mouse. She started making another round of the parlor—her fourteenth since arriving—testing the walls, the windows, the floors, the ventilation system, looking for weak points and finding none.

"There are lots of ways," said Penelope as the Mouse continued walking around the parlor, probing for possible means of escape. "I just don't know which one I can make happen yet."

"Do they concern your friend?"

Penelope shook her head. "He doesn't even know who we are."

"Then how can he be your friend?"

The little girl shrugged helplessly. "I don't know."

"Are you certain you're right?"

"I *think* so," said Penelope. "Picking the right future isn't as easy as it used to be. I see more things now, things I don't always understand."

"What kind of things?" asked the Mouse, finally completing her latest inspection of the premises and turning back to the little girl.

"I don't know," said Penelope. "Just things."

"Pictures? Images? Whole scenes?"

"I can't explain it," answered the girl. "It's just much more complicated than it was." She paused, frowning. "You'd think it would get easier now that I'm getting bigger."

"Maybe you're getting more powerful," suggested the Mouse. "Maybe you see more things and can influence more things."

"Do you really think so?"

"It's possible."

"Then why can't I always understand what I see?" asked Penelope.

"Because you're still a little girl, and you don't have enough experience to know all the things that you're seeing, all the permutations of each choice you make."

"I don't know what you mean."

The Mouse smiled. "When you do, then perhaps you'll also know what you're seeing."

"I hope so," said Penelope earnestly. "It's very confusing. I used to see everything so very clearly. Now there are some things that I don't see at all, that I just seem to *know*, and other things that I don't understand."

"I'm sure someday it will all make sense," said the Mouse.

"I'm glad you can't see what I see, Mouse," said Penelope. "Sometimes it can be very confusing—and scary."

"Scary?"

Penelope nodded. "I can see the Iceman and the Forever Kid finding us, and I can see the Yankee Clipper killing you when he finds out."

"Oh?" said the Mouse apprehensively.

"I won't let it happen," said Penelope. "There are lots of other futures."

"I certainly hope so."

"But I don't understand all of them."

"Just pick one in which I don't get killed, and I'll settle for it," said the Mouse.

"You won't get killed," Penelope assured her.

"Are Carlos and the Kid on Calliope already?" asked the Mouse.

"I don't know," said the girl. "But I know they'll find this room by tonight, so if they're not here, they're very close." Suddenly she tensed.

"What is it?"

"In some of the futures they die, and in some they don't."

"Let's hope for one in which they don't," said the Mouse.

"That's what I'm seeing now," said Penelope.

"Then why do you look so upset?"

"Because if they both come into this room, they're going to try to kill each other."

"Why?" asked the Mouse, puzzled.

"Because of me."

"You're absolutely sure?"

Penelope frowned. "No. The Iceman hasn't made up his mind yet."

"About what?"

"About whether to kill me or not."

"Well, if he tries, the Kid won't let him."

Penelope closed her eyes and seemed to concentrate. Finally she opened them, visibly shaken.

"I don't know. I can't see who wins."

"Carlos is a middle-aged man who probably hasn't fought anyone in years," said the Mouse. "The Kid is a professional killer. I've seen him in action. There's no way that Carlos can beat him."

"I still can't see," repeated Penelope. Suddenly she started trembling. "We have to get away from here, Mouse."

"That's what I keep saying."

"You don't understand," said the girl urgently. "I don't want to be here when the Iceman gets here. If he wants me dead, and he can kill the Forever Kid, I'm not strong enough to stop him yet."

"Yet?" repeated the Mouse.

"Someday I may be, but not yet." Penelope's face was ashen white. "Don't let him kill me, Mouse!"

"I won't," said the Mouse, putting her arms around the frightened little girl, and wondering how strong Penelope planned to become if she lived long enough.

22

The door slid open and the Yankee Clipper stepped into the parlor.

"I'm sorry to trouble you lovely ladies," he said. "We'll be just a minute."

He was followed by a pair of bounty hunters Mouse recognized from Westerly. One of them took a couple of steps toward Penelope, who stared at him curiously but without any trace of fear, then nodded to the pirate. A moment later both bounty hunters left.

"The interested parties are beginning to arrive," explained the Yankee Clipper. "Each, of course, wants to make sure that I can really deliver Penelope Bailey, so I'm afraid we'll be intruding upon your privacy from time to time."

"I can tell how it upsets you," said the Mouse sardonically.

"Believe it or not, I take no pleasure in selling human beings," said the pirate. "But we're talking about a great deal of money here—and frankly, I'll feel much safer once she's halfway across the galaxy." He paused. "And of course, she's not being sold into slavery. Given the price that she commands, I'm sure she'll be treated with the utmost consideration and kept in luxury." He smiled again. "At least, it comforts me to think so."

He left the parlor, and one of his guards entered a moment later.

Penelope busied herself dressing Maryanne with the new clothes she had ordered earlier in the day, while the Mouse activated the holovision and tried to concentrate on the results of the day's seemingly endless procession of sporting events. Twice more the Yankee Clipper brought people up to the suite—once it was a member of the Democracy's military, once a nondescript woman who might have been anything from a bureaucrat to a bounty hunter—and finally the Mouse ordered lunch for herself and Penelope.

A waiter from room service arrived about ten minutes later, guiding a small aircart that held their meals. He waited patiently while the guard searched him, then walked across the room to the polished hardwood table where the Mouse was sitting.

"Your lunch, madam," said the waiter.

The moment she heard his voice the Mouse turned from the holoscreen to look at his face.

The waiter, his back to the guard, winked at her and smiled, and suddenly the Mouse felt an enormous sense of relief.

"Where will the young lady be taking her lunch?" asked the waiter.

"Right here," answered the Mouse, hoping that her voice didn't reflect her excitement.

"As you wish," said the waiter, arranging a place setting for Penelope, who was still playing with Maryanne and seemed oblivious to his presence.

"Excuse me," said the waiter, turning to the guard, "but there seems to be an extra dessert here. Would you care for it?" He smiled ingratiatingly. "There will, of course, be no additional charge."

The guard shrugged. "Why not?"

The waiter placed a covered dish at the far end of the table.

"Bring it over," said the guard.

"Certainly," said the waiter. He picked up the dish and walked across the room, stopping in front of the guard.

"What is it?" asked the guard.

"One moment, sir," said the waiter, removing the lid from the dish and handing it to the guard.

The guard leaned forward to take the dish, and suddenly found himself staring down the barrel of a small laser pistol.

"Where the hell did you get that?" he demanded.

"The hand is quicker than the eye," replied the waiter. He reached over his head with his free hand and suddenly pulled a bouquet of flowers out of the air. "Take a sniff," he said, holding them up to the guard's nose. "I know they're not roses, but this is less painful and less permanent than forcing me to use the gun."

"What are you—?" began the guard, who collapsed before he could complete his question.

The waiter looked at the unconscious body for a moment, then tossed the bouquet on top of it and turned to face the Mouse and Penelope.

"Hi, Merlin," said Penelope.

"Am I ever glad to see you!" said the Mouse, getting to her feet. "What are you doing here?"

"Save your questions for later," said Merlin. "We've got to move fast. I shorted out the monitoring device just before I entered the suite, but it'll only take them a couple of minutes to figure out that it's not an electronic failure."

"Are the other guards still outside in the corridor?" asked the Mouse.

Merlin nodded. "Mean-looking bunch. There's no way we can get out past them."

He walked to the window and examined it. "Is it rigged?" he asked the Mouse.

"Of course not," she answered. "We're seventeen floors up. Who is going to break in?"

"You've got a point," admitted Merlin.

As they were speaking, Merlin examined the huge picture window, then made a fist and pressed his ring up against the glass, very near the bottom. "I just love magician's props," he said with a grin.

The Mouse could hear the whirring of a tiny motor inside the ring, and it cut through the glass with no difficulty. Merlin completed about 320 degrees of a large circle, perhaps thirty inches in diameter, then reached into his pocket for a small suction device, which he attached to the glass. He then cut the remainder of the circle and used the device to pull the glass into the room.

"Even if the building has enough handholds, someone's bound to see me before I climb down to the ground," said the Mouse. "And even if no one saw me, there's no way the two of you could follow me down the side of a building."

"You're not going down, you're going *up*," said Merlin.

"Up?" she repeated.

He nodded. "This is the penthouse. The roof's about eight feet above the window."

"And what about you and Penelope?"

Merlin took off his timepiece and pressed a hidden release.

"Here," he said, withdrawing a thin, incredibly strong wire from the band and attaching it to the Mouse's waist. "It's a titanium alloy with a tight molecular bonding; it'll hold more than a ton before it snaps. Once you get to the roof, tie your end to something secure, and then Penelope and I will climb up."

"You can't climb hand over hand on that thing," said the Mouse. "It'll cut right through your fingers."

Merlin smiled. "I won't have to. There's a little pulley mechanism in there that'll reel the wire in."

"It'll dislocate your arm."

He smiled. "I'm wearing a harness beneath my waiter's jacket. I'll be fine."

The Mouse looked unconvinced. "Have you ever tried this stunt before?"

"No . . . but I got the wristband from a friend who does it every night in the circus."

"Why did he part with it?"

"He was in hospital getting a pair of prosthetic legs," answered Merlin. "He hadn't any use for it." He saw her worried expression. "He was there because of a different trick, not this one."

"I don't know . . ." said the Mouse.

"Please, Mouse," said Penelope. "We have to hurry!"

"All right," said the Mouse instantly.

She ducked her head, stepped through the hole in the window onto the ledge, quickly and expertly found some handholds and footholds, and began making her way up the outer wall of the building.

"Careful," whispered Merlin, more to himself than to the Mouse, who was now halfway to the roof. "Careful."

"It's all right," said Penelope, picking up Maryanne from the floor, where she had been playing with her before Merlin arrived. "She's not going to fall."

"I wish I was as sure as you," said Merlin, craning his neck to watch the Mouse.

Penelope walked over to the table and calmly ate one of the sandwiches that Merlin had delivered in his guise as a hotel waiter.

"Don't you give a damn what happens to her?" he demanded irritably when he saw what she was doing.

"I told you—she's not going to fall."

"You'd better be right," he said. "Because if you're not, I'm not only going to lose a partner, but you and I are still stuck in this room."

Penelope held a final bite of the sandwich up to Mary-anne's mouth, then placed it on the table and carefully dabbed at the doll's lips with a linen napkin. Then she tucked the doll under her arm and walked to the window.

"She should be there now," she announced.

"She is," said Merlin with a sigh of relief. He turned to Penelope. "Let's figure out the logistics here. We can't both fit through the hole together, and if we break the glass and it crashes down to the street, we'll give ourselves away." He examined the window again. "Grab a couple of napkins from the table."

Penelope smiled and held up the napkins she had brought with her.

"So you figured it out, too?" he said. "Smart kid." He attached the wire to his harness. "Be very careful going through the hole here. Then, once you're on the ledge, wrap your hands in the napkins and hold on to the edge of the glass while I climb through." His gaze went from the girl to the ledge to the roof and back again. "I don't suppose you're strong enough to hold on to my back?"

"I don't think so," answered Penelope.

"All right," he continued after a moment's thought. "Once I get out on the ledge, too, I'll lift you up until you can wrap your arms around my neck and your legs around my waist. That way I'll be able to keep an arm around you as well." He paused. "Try not to worry. It won't take us very long once the pulley mechanism starts working."

"I'm not worried at all," said Penelope.

"I wish I could say the same," muttered Merlin. "Every-thing *should* work, but this is the Mouse's specialty. I've never done anything like this."

"We'll be fine."

He felt the cord jerk against his harness; the Mouse was signaling him that she had secured her end on the roof.

"I hope so," he said. "Put the doll down and I'll lift you through the hole."

"Maryanne goes where I go," said Penelope.

"It's just a doll," said Merlin. "I'll buy you another."

"I don't want another. I want *her*."

He stared at her for a moment, then shrugged and sighed. "Okay, give her to me and I'll put her in a pocket."

"No, you won't," said Penelope. "You'll leave her behind."

"All right—carry her yourself," said Merlin irritably. "See if I give a damn."

He guided Penelope through the hole in the window while she clutched Maryanne to her chest. Then he maneuvered her until she was balanced on the narrow window ledge. She grasped the edge of the glass with a napkin-wrapped hand while the other held the doll.

A moment later Merlin was standing on the ledge beside her, and then, with the Mouse guiding them, they began their ascent. For a moment they got caught at the edge of the roof, and Merlin was absolutely certain the titanium cord would break or the pulley mechanism would fail, but eventually, with the Mouse's help, they reached the temporary safety of the roof.

"Follow me," said the Mouse as Merlin stood, hands on knees, gasping for breath, and Penelope inspected Maryanne for abrasions.

Merlin nodded and forced himself to follow the Mouse and Penelope across the rooftop. When they reached the edge, they looked down some sixty feet at the rooftop of an adjacent building.

"We can't chance taking the fire stairs here," explained the Mouse, "because we might run into the Yankee Clipper's men in the lobby. I think our best bet is to get to the building next door and leave through *its* lobby. How long is that cord of yours, Merlin?"

"Long enough to reach that rooftop, anyway."

The Mouse smiled. "Don't look so worried. Going down is much easier than going up."

"Faster, anyway," he muttered.

They were both right: it was easier and it was faster, and five minutes later the three of them walked down the fire stairs to the ground floor.

23

The stairwell let them out in the bustling lobby of an office building. Most of the shopping arcade seemed to consist of local travel agencies, but there was also a small branch bank and a clothing store that specialized in safari outfits.

"How did you find us?" asked the Mouse as they walked to the main exit. "In fact, how did you even know we were on Calliope?"

"Later," said Merlin, looking around. "Let's put a little distance between us and your pirate friend first."

He summoned a groundcab, asked the driver to recommend an inexpensive family hotel near one of the smaller entertainment complexes at the south end of town, and they rode in silence until they reached the hotel some fifteen minutes later.

Merlin walked up to the desk, explained that there had been a mix-up at the spaceport and that their luggage would be arriving that evening or the next morning, and booked two adjoining bedrooms. No comment was made: misplaced luggage was a common occurrence, given the quantity of luggage that had to move through the spaceport, and certainly the three of them appeared to be a typical family, operating on a budget but still determined to enjoy those features of Calliope that they could afford.

When they reached their rooms and opened the connecting door between them, Penelope approached the Mouse. "I saw some little girls outside on the play equipment," she said. "Can I go play with them?"

The Mouse shook her head. "I'm afraid not."

"Why not?"

"Because those little girls don't have eighteen pirates and half the bounty hunters in the Cluster looking for them, and you do. We can't take a chance that someone might identify you."

"No one will," said Penelope. "Not today."

"You're sure?" said the Mouse.

"Yes."

"You're taking *her* word for it?" demanded Merlin.

"Of course," said the Mouse.

"If she's spotted, we're all in trouble," continued the magician, and suddenly the Mouse remembered that he was unaware of her extraordinary power, that they had parted before Penelope had demonstrated it for the first time.

"She won't be spotted," said the Mouse. "If you won't trust her, then trust *me*."

Merlin placed a hand on Penelope's shoulder and waited until she turned to face him.

"You be very careful, now," he said. "And if you see anyone staring at you, you come right back here and let me know."

"Nobody will stare at me," replied Penelope.

"I'm sure they won't," said the Mouse, before Merlin could protest. "Go on out and play."

"Will you watch Maryanne for me?" asked the little girl. "I don't want her new clothes to get dirty."

"I'd be happy to," answered the Mouse, taking the doll from her.

"Thank you," said Penelope. "I guess I'll go now."

"Have a good time," said the Mouse.

Penelope paused at the door, a worried expression on her face.

"What's the matter?" asked the Mouse.

"I don't know any games," said Penelope. "I haven't seen another little girl since I was five years old."

"Then they'll teach you."

"What if they don't like me?"

"Nonsense," said the Mouse. "You're a very likable little girl."

"But *if* they don't?"

"They will," the Mouse assured her.

Penelope stared at the doll. "Maybe I should bring Maryanne, after all. If they don't like me, maybe they'll like *her*."

"Don't worry so," said the Mouse soothingly. "Who wouldn't like a sweet little girl like you?"

"Lots of people," said Penelope seriously. "Like the Iceman."

"You'll be fine," the Mouse assured her. "Just introduce yourself and I'm sure they'll be happy to meet you."

"I hope so," said Penelope uncertainly. Then she ordered the door to open, stepped out into the corridor, waved a very nervous good-bye to the Mouse and Merlin, and began walking away as the door closed behind her.

"Who's the Iceman?" asked Merlin, finally inspecting the inexpensively furnished room with an expression of distaste. "Kind of a personal boogeyman?"

"Not exactly," said the Mouse, seating herself on a large chair and tucking her feet beneath her. "I used to work for him, a long time ago."

"I never heard you mention him."

"He had a different name then," said the Mouse. "Enough about the Iceman. How did you ever find us?"

"It's a long story." He stared at a holographic print of an alien landscape that hung above the bed. "God, that's ugly!"

"Maybe you should begin at the beginning," said the Mouse. "How did you get away from all those bounty hunters after you dropped us off on Binder X?"

"I didn't."

The Mouse frowned. "What are you talking about?"

"I didn't get away from them all," repeated Merlin. "I thought I had lost them, but Three-Fisted Ollie caught up with me on a little hellhole called Feathergill." He sighed. "Six billion birds, fifty billion fish, and one ugly little Tradertown with two run-down hotels. I'll swear every other person on the planet was an ornithologist or an ichthyologist. If there was one place in the whole galaxy I could have sworn no one would look for me, it was Feathergill."

"Obviously you were wrong."

"I spent almost a month there," replied the magician. "Three-Fisted Ollie found me a few days ago."

"Obviously he didn't kill you."

Merlin chuckled. "Obviously."

"So what happened?"

"He wanted the little girl. He and Cemetery Smith had gotten word that the Yankee Clipper was putting her up for auction to the highest bidder, and their employer wanted her pretty badly. But they had a problem: neither of them had ever seen Penelope close up. Ollie knew I had, and he wanted to make sure no one was selling a ringer, so he and Smith offered me a deal—half a million credits if I could make a positive identification, whether their employer is the high bidder or not."

"So that's how you knew where the Yankee Clipper was keeping us!"

"Of course that's how I knew," replied Merlin with a smile. "I'm an illusionist, not a magician." He walked across the faded carpet to a plain wooden chair and sat down on it, grimacing in discomfort. "All interested parties were allowed to make sure the girl was as advertised. In fact, I almost bumped into a pair of mean-looking bounty hunters coming out before I got into my waiter's outfit."

The Mouse looked amused. "You're a man of many talents, no question about it," she said. "Today you were a waiter, and tomorrow you can go back to being an illusionist—but for tonight, you're a hero for rescuing Penelope and me."

"I rescued *you*," Merlin corrected her. "I just *borrowed* Penelope."

"What do you mean?" asked the Mouse warily.

"If she's worth half a million credits just to identify, think of how much the Yankee Clipper will pay to get her back." He paused. "Or if we can find a safe enough place to hide her, maybe we'll even conduct the auction ourselves."

"What are you talking about?"

"You're being awfully dense, Mouse," said Merlin. "We're sitting on a gold mine. We could make a big enough killing so both of us could retire. I've heard that the bidding is going to *start* at ten million credits."

The Mouse stared at him for a long moment.

"You're a fool," she said at last.

"I thought I was a hero," he said.

"I thought so, too. I was wrong."

"I don't supposed you'd care to tell me why?"

"First, I'm very fond of that little girl, and I'm not about to let you or anyone else sell her as if she were some kind of animal. Second, hasn't anyone told you that there's a reason why she's worth so much?"

"Who cares why?" said Merlin with a shrug. "She's worth a bundle, and we've got her. That's all I need to know."

"No, that's *not* all you need to know," said the Mouse, looking out the grubby window at Penelope, who was standing by herself, watching a trio of girls at play.

"All right," said Merlin, shifting uncomfortably on the straight-backed wooden chair. "Suppose you tell me why she's so valuable."

"She's valuable because she has a gift, an ability, that a lot of people, and even governments, want to control."

"What gift?"

"Precognition."

"Bunk," said Merlin. "If she's got precognition, she must know I plan to hold her for ransom. Why did she agree to come with us?"

The Mouse looked at Merlin and smiled. "Try not to let it hurt your sensitive feelings," she said, "but you are the least menacing alternative that was presented to her. Compared to the Iceman and the Yankee Clipper and some of the others, you're so low on the scale that she hasn't even bothered getting rid of you."

"What do you mean, getting rid of me?" scoffed Merlin. "She's just a kid with a talent. You make her sound like Three-Fisted Ollie."

"Don't you understand what precognition means?"

"Of course I do. It means she can predict the future. It may be a pretty handy talent to have at the racetrack, and I can see why all these high rollers want her around, but I sure as hell don't see why you find it so frightening."

"Then I'll spell it out for you," said the Mouse. "There isn't just *one* future. There are an infinity of them. She has the ability to see huge numbers of them."

"I still don't follow you."

"She can help to bring about the one she most wants to happen."

"Everybody tries to do that," he said, still not comprehending.

"Everybody tries; she succeeds." The Mouse paused. "Let me give you an example. In maybe half the futures she saw, something went wrong with our escape—the cord broke, the guard woke up too early, she lost her grip on you when you were going up to the roof. She has the ability to see each of those futures, and to figure out what she has to do to stop them from coming to pass."

"You're crazy!" he scoffed.

"Remember those two dead bodies we found next to our ship back on Cherokee?"

"Are you trying to tell me *she* killed them?"

"She chose a future in which they died. That's not the same thing," said the Mouse. "She's not a killer. She's just a little girl who protects herself the best way she can."

Merlin considered what the Mouse had said. "If you're right—and that's a big if—it's one hell of an effective way to protect herself."

"Yes, it is," agreed the Mouse. "So you see, if she thought you were anything more than a minor irritant, you'd probably have had a stroke or a heart attack on the way over here. At the very least, you'd have tripped on the way to our room and broken a leg."

"I don't know whether to be insulted or grateful," he said wryly. He paused and stared at her. "And you *like* this kid?"

"Yes."

"Why?"

"She's got the whole galaxy against her," said the Mouse. "I'm the only friend she has."

"That's no reason. Half the people we know have prices on their heads, and you don't like *them*."

"She's very sweet, and very lonely."

Merlin looked out the window, where Penelope was now, playing with the other girls. "I'd hardly call that a lonely little girl," he said sardonically.

"I don't have to justify my reasons to you," said the Mouse, suddenly annoyed. "All you have to know is that she's staying with us."

"All right," said Merlin. "If that's the way it is, that's the way it is. She joins the team and we get the hell out of here first thing in the morning."

"We'd better," said the Mouse, wondering if Merlin had given in too quickly. "You've probably got every bounty hunter on the planet looking for us, to say nothing of the Yankee Clipper and his men."

"Right," he said. "That's a lot of manpower out there. The sooner we get off the planet, the better."

"Do you have your own ship?" asked the Mouse.

"No. I came with Three-Fisted Ollie."

"Then we're going to have to find some way to catch a commercial space flight without being spotted."

"It won't be easy," said Merlin. "They'll be watching the spaceport." He grimaced. "And while they want Penelope alive, I don't think the same applies to you and me."

"No, it doesn't," she agreed.

Merlin got to his feet. "There must be a bar around here, and I do my best thinking in bars. Care to join me for a drink?"

The Mouse shook her head. "I'd better stay here in case Penelope comes back."

Merlin stared at her and finally smiled. "Funny," he commented. "I never thought of you as the maternal type."

"Neither did I," said the Mouse.

The magician walked to the door. "I'll be back in half an hour or so. Maybe sooner, if I can figure a way out of this mess."

"I'll be here."

He left the room, and the Mouse began walking around, checking the holovision and the octaphonic sound system, examining the cabinets in the bathroom and the closets in the bedrooms, more from habit than any particular need.

Penelope entered the room a few minutes later.

"You're back early," noted the Mouse. "Weren't you getting along well with the girls?"

"They were very nice," said Penelope.

"Well, then?"

"We have to leave, Mouse."

"Leave? You mean, leave the hotel?"

Penelope nodded. "Soon."

"Somebody knows we're here?"

"Yes."

"How much time have we got?" asked the Mouse.

"Maybe ten minutes, maybe a little less."

"All right," said the Mouse. "Merlin's in the bar. We'll pick him up and get the hell out of here."

"No!" said Penelope.

"He just risked his life to rescue us," said the Mouse.

"We don't want him, Mouse."

"We don't desert our friends, Penelope," replied the Mouse. "I thought I explained that to you before." She paused. "I wonder how they found us so quickly? I thought we'd be safe here for a few days."

"Merlin is telling them right now."

"They're *here*?"

"No. He's talking to them on a vidphone—but they'll be here very soon."

"You actually saw him calling them?"

Penelope placed a finger to her temple. "In here."

The Mouse stared long and hard at the little girl. "You're sure?"

"Yes."

"That double-crossing bastard!"

"Come on, Mouse," said Penelope, tugging at her arm. "We have to hurry!"

"Where is this friend of yours who we were going to meet on Calliope?" asked the Mouse. "We sure as hell could use a friend right now."

"I don't know."

The Mouse entered the corridor, looked around to make sure Merlin wasn't on his way back to the room, and nodded. "This way," she said, heading off to her left. "The other way takes us by the bar, and I don't want him to see us leaving."

Penelope, her doll clutched against her body, reached out for the Mouse with her free hand.

"Come on," said the Mouse, increasing her pace. "If we're lucky, we can catch a groundcab and be out of here before Merlin knows we're gone."

They walked past a small holo theater, a coffee shop, and a large indoor pool, then carefully approached the lobby.

"Have Merlin's friends arrived yet?" whispered the Mouse.

"Not yet," said the girl.

"All right. Let's go."

They walked rapidly through the lobby, then stood in front of the hotel as the Mouse tried to hail a groundcab.

"Isn't it ever going to end?" said Penelope wearily.

24

If Xanadu showed off Calliope's scrubbed, wholesome face to hundreds of thousands of eager tourists, then New Gomorrah displayed its less affluent side. The city rose up out of the grasslands, a carbuncle on the smooth surface of the western savannah. It possessed seven multi-environmental hotels, and almost all of the aliens who landed on Calliope immediately made their way to New Gomorrah.

There were tourist attractions, to be sure, and the streets were not unsafe, and many a safari started off from the veranda of the Norfolk II—but, perhaps because the aliens had less money to spend, or perhaps simply because they *were* aliens, the attractions New Gomorrah offered seemed less enticing than those of its eastern sister.

Where Xanadu offered circuses with fabulous acrobats and exotic animals, New Gomorrah offered carnivals with sideshows and crooked games. Where Xanadu offered theater, New Gomorrah offered holo shows. Where Xanadu's hotels were palatial, New Gomorrah's were plain, functional structures. Where Xanadu offered fine restaurants with elegantly prepared dishes, New Gomorrah offered a plethora of alien restaurants with foodstuffs most humans had never seen and could not metabolize.

Moreover, there was something about New Gomorrah that seemed to bring out the bloodlust in its clientele. It was here that one came for hunting, rather than holographic, safaris. It was here that animals and occasionally men and aliens fought to the death before crowds both large and very small. It was here that truly huge fortunes were won and lost in the back rooms of gaming parlors. And it was here that almost every perversion known to man or alien could be experienced if enough money changed hands.

The Mouse and Penelope had avoided the spaceport, knowing that it would be under surveillance. With the rest of the planet to choose from, Penelope had looked at a map and immediately selected New Gomorrah. It had taken them three full days to get there via the most obscure and circuitous routes, by which time both their energy and their bankroll were equally depleted. The Mouse, who hadn't seen a bed in three days, had wanted to spend their last hundred credits on a hotel, but Penelope insisted that they go directly to the carnivals that were clustered on the outskirts of the city.

"Why?" asked the Mouse wearily.

"Because we'll meet my friend at one of them."

"You're sure this friend actually exists?" said the Mouse. "I mean, it's not as if he showed up when we needed him before."

"We need him even more now," said Penelope.

"If he's here now, he'll be here in the morning," replied the Mouse. "Let's get a room and catch up on our sleep first."

"I don't want to miss him," insisted Penelope.

"You make him sound like a traveling salesman."

"I don't know what he is. I just know he's here."

"And you think he's at one of these carnivals?" asked the Mouse.

"I don't know. I just have a feeling we should go there."

"Well, your feelings have been pretty accurate so far," said the Mouse with an exhausted sigh. "Let's go."

They caught a courtesy vehicle to the nearest carnival, a relatively small establishment that catered to families with small children. They could hear screams of delight from within the tents, and a number of clowns, both human and alien, mingled with the crowd, passing out free tickets to minor attractions.

"Well?" asked the Mouse.

Penelope shook her head. "This isn't the place."

"Thank God for that," said the Mouse. "All those well-scrubbed, vacant-faced families would drive me crazy."

"Don't you like families, Mouse?" asked Penelope.

The Mouse shrugged. "I don't know. I never had one." She smiled down at the girl. "You're family enough for me."

"You're my family, too," said Penelope earnestly. "You and Maryanne."

"Where to now?" asked the Mouse.

"Let's just keep going," said Penelope. "I'll know when we've arrived."

"Whatever you say," said the Mouse, flagging down another courtesy vehicle.

They passed an open-air zoo that specialized in alien animals, a huge stadium that seemed not to have any events scheduled that day, and a farm that bred gigantic reptiles from Antares, and then they came to a sprawling carnival.

"This is it," whispered Penelope, and the Mouse signaled the driver to let them off.

"This thing must cover thirty acres or more," said the Mouse, standing before the entrance with Penelope. "Do you have any idea what he looks like?"

"I don't even know if it *is* a he," answered Penelope. "But I know we'll find him here, or he'll find us."

"Will you know him when you see him?"

Penelope shrugged. "I suppose so."

The Mouse paid their entrance fee, and they spent the next few hours shouldering their way through the crowds of tourists, walking up and down the rows of games and exhibits, past the hustlers and grifters, the strip shows and the freak shows, the alien exhibits, the pleasurepain palaces, the cheap rides, the display of cattle and hogs from Earth itself.

"I'm about ready to give up for the day," said the Mouse as the midafternoon heat became more intense. She sat down at an empty table near a row of food stands and gestured Penelope to join her. "There must be ten thousand people here," she continued as the little girl sat next to her. "We could have walked right past him and never know it."

"He'll *be* here," Penelope said firmly.

"Soon?"

"I don't know."

"Today? Tomorrow? Next week?" continued the Mouse. "I don't mean to worry you, but we're almost broke. The Forever Kid has most of my money, and I've just about run through the rest of it. Whether we keep looking for your mysterious friend or book passage off the planet, we're going to have to find a way to make some more money. I've got enough to keep us going for maybe three more days, four if we find a cheap enough place to stay." She paused. "Do you know if your friend will show up by then?"

Penelope shrugged. "I don't know."

"You're sure we're at the right place?" asked the Mouse. "There are a lot of other carnivals around New Gomorrah."

"We're in the right place."

The Mouse sighed deeply. "Then we might as well stay right here at the carnival. The less we move around New Gomorrah, the less likely we are to be spotted."

"Will they let us stay here?" asked Penelope.

"Not as tourists. But I saw a few empty booths and tents. All we have to do is come up with some kind of scam and convince the manager to let us go to work for him."

"What can we do?"

"That's a problem," admitted the Mouse. "I suppose I could hire on as a stripper, but I'm so scrawny and ugly that people would pay me to put my clothes back on."

"That's not true," said Penelope heatedly. "You're very pretty, Mouse."

"That's a matter of some debate," replied the Mouse wryly. "Anyway, take my word for it—no one would hire me."

"Then what can we do?"

The Mouse lowered her head in thought for a moment, then looked up and smiled. "You know what I didn't see when we walked up and down the aisles?"

"What?"

"A fortune-teller's booth."

"What's that?" asked Penelope.

"A fortune-teller? It's someone who pretends to do what you really *can* do: foresee the future." She paused briefly. "Do you remember how you saw my cards back at the casino on Last Chance?"

"Yes."

"Do you think you could see who's going to win a particular race or fight?"

"I think so," said Penelope. "I'm much better at it now than I used to be."

"When you can't, will you know that you can't?"

"Yes."

"Then I think we may be in business."

"Good!" said Penelope happily. "Then, after we make some money telling fortunes, I can tell you who is going to win a race or a fight, and you can bet on it, and—"

"No," interrupted the Mouse. "If I win too much money, I'll call attention to myself. Much better to make it in bits and pieces." She stared at Penelope and frowned. "We've got another problem, too. If word gets out that a little girl is picking winners, we're going to have some very unwanted company."

"Maybe we could do what we did on Last Chance," suggested Penelope.

"I just told you—I can't risk being a big winner."

"No," said the girl. "I meant the way we worked the card game. You were the player, and I signaled you. Maybe you could read the fortunes, and I could signal you what to read."

The Mouse considered her suggestion.

"It's a possibility," she admitted at last.

And when no better possibility presented itself, they spent the remainder of the afternoon going over an intricate set of signals by which Penelope could give the Mouse certain basic information about each client who visited her. Then, at dusk, the Mouse hunted up the manager of the sideshow exhibits, gave him a brief demonstration of her skills, offered him a 60-40 split for the carnival in exchange for the use of a booth plus their food and lodging, and they were in business ten minutes later.

They spent the evening decorating their booth and creating a suitable costume for the Mouse, then ate a late dinner in the crew's mess tent and collapsed on the cots that had been provided in the back of their booth.

They awoke early, ate breakfast, and then waited for the carnival to open. Penelope was so excited she could hardly stand still.

"Relax," said the Mouse. "They won't open the gates for another half hour yet."

"I know," said Penelope. "But isn't it wonderful? We're working together again! And look at all the colorful people and all the aliens!"

"A grifter by any other name," said the Mouse.

"What?"

The Mouse smiled. "Nothing. I'm glad you're happy."

"Oh, I am. Can we always work together, Mouse?"

"I'd much rather retire in luxury together," said the Mouse wryly. "But until that happy day, we're still a team."

The other carnival workers began gathering on the midway, setting up their tents and booths. About two-thirds of them were gaudily dressed humans, but there were Canphorites, Lodinites, Mollutei, Domarians, and, just across from them, running a game that seemed to make no sense, was an alien of a race the Mouse had never seen before. It was bipedal, covered with light green scales, and seemed to have a grey, shell-like hump that extended from the back of its neck to just above its buttocks. It stood no taller than five feet, but its thick body and heavy limbs gave an unmistakable impression of great strength. The Mouse nodded a greeting to it, and it opened its horned beak in what she hoped was an answering smile.

Then the gates opened, and a new day's throng of tourists invaded the carnival. It took the Mouse almost three hours to get her first client, and two hours more for her second—but when a 23-to-1 shot came in at the local racetrack, and word went out that a fortune-teller on the carnival grounds had predicted the victory, they were soon lining up to speak to her.

She read the future for unhappy husbands and unfaithful wives, hopeful gamblers and hopeless addicts, the rich and the poor, humans and aliens, good beings and bad. Penelope was never more than ten yards away, acting the part of her shill, collecting her money, urging bypassers to seek her services.

And then, on the third morning, right after she had given a Lodinite the anticipated result of a heavyweight freehand match that would be held later in the day, she looked up and saw a familiar bearded face staring at her.

"You gave us a good run for our money, I'll grant you that," said the Yankee Clipper without any animosity. He held Penelope firmly by the arm, and obviously was pressing a hand weapon against her.

"How did you find us?" said the Mouse.

He chuckled. "Just how many winners did you think you could give away before the press started suggesting there was some kind of racket going on here?"

The Mouse looked around for the pirate's subordinates, but couldn't spot them. "Where are your men?"

"They're hunting for you all over New Gomorrah," replied the Yankee Clipper. "Some are at the track, some are at the arena, some are in the casinos. But I thought I'd try the carnival—and what better place for you to hide than right here, as a fortune-teller?" He smiled in amusement. "It's like a deserter hiding out in the middle of a battlefield."

"And now what?" demanded the Mouse.

"Now you're free to go."

The Mouse frowned. "I don't understand."

"You're a bad influence on the child," said the pirate. "I'm taking her back alone."

"*No!*" cried Penelope.

"Yes, my dear," said the Yankee Clipper. "I know that having the Mouse around was supposed to make you more tractable, but the fact of the matter is that she helped you to escape and thereby caused me considerable embarrassment, to say nothing of the cost of hunting you down. And," he concluded, "since I plan to be rid of you within a day, I really don't care whether your new . . . ah . . . *host* has the means to control you or not."

"You *can't* separate us!" pleaded Penelope.

"I can and I will," replied the pirate. He turned to the Mouse. "If you attempt to follow me, please know that I will not hesitate to kill you."

The Mouse stared at him helplessly, her mind considering and rejecting various alternatives, each more unlikely than the last. Finally her shoulders slumped and she emitted a soft sigh of defeat.

"Then, as we have nothing further to say, I'll be taking my leave of you," announced the Yankee Clipper, tightening his grip on Penelope's arm.

Suddenly the broad, scaled alien from across the aisle approached them.

"I beg your pardon," it said in heavily accented Terran, "but I must speak to the Soothsayer."

"Well, I won't keep you from your work," said the pirate with a grin. He pulled Penelope by the arm. "Come along, young lady."

"No," said the alien, blocking their way. "I must speak to the Soothsayer."

"There she is," said the Yankee Clipper, gesturing toward the Mouse. "Now, step aside."

"I have been observing them for days," continued the alien calmly. "I *know* which is the Soothsayer and which is the imposter."

"What you know doesn't interest me," said the Yankee Clipper irritably.

"It should," said the alien, "for among the things I know is that you have made a serious mistake."

"Oh? What mistake?"

"You may not lay hands on the Soothsayer without her permission."

"Do you know who you're talking to?" demanded the Yankee Clipper.

"Yes," replied the alien tranquilly. "A man who should have known better."

And just as calmly, just as tranquilly, the alien suddenly produced a weapon of a type that was totally unfamiliar to the Mouse. It aimed it at the pirate, there was an almost inaudible humming sound, and the Yankee Clipper collapsed, dead, on the ground.

The alien held out a hand to Penelope.

"Come with me, Soothsayer," it said gently. "I have been waiting for you."

Penelope looked into the alien's hideous face with a happy smile.

"My friend," she said.

PART 4

The Mock Turtle's Book

25

It seemed reptilian, but in truth it was neither a reptile nor in any other way analogous to any life-form with which the Mouse was acquainted. Its powerful limbs and thick torso seemed masculine, but it did not possess a gender, or at least not in a way that any human could comprehend. It had killed the Yankee Clipper in an act of cold-blooded murder, but its behavior was polite and well mannered, and almost deferential where Penelope was concerned.

Its name was unpronounceable, so the Mouse looked at its green scales and grayish hump and soft beak and double-lidded eyes, and decided to call it the Mock Turtle. It neither approved nor disapproved, but it answered to the name, and that was really all that mattered.

Since its weapon had made no noise and attracted no attention, it simply summoned a doctor when the pirate fell to the ground, and during the ensuing confusion the Mock Turtle waited patiently for Penelope to retrieve Maryanne from the booth, then took her by the hand and calmly led her out the carnival's gate. The Mouse quickly took their money from the cash box and followed them to the gate. From there they took a courtesy vehicle to the spaceport and walked directly to the Mock Turtle's ship.

The Mouse was certain they would be spotted by one of the Yankee Clipper's men, but Penelope showed no sign of fear or tension, and a short time later they had left Calliope far behind them and were heading deeper into the Inner Frontier.

"We will have to put down on a human colony soon," announced the Mock Turtle after they cleared Calliope's star system. The three of them were sitting in the ship's cockpit, which had not been designed with humans in mind. The ceiling was much too low, and the chairs were built for beings with the Mock Turtle's hump. The colors, even on the control panels and computer keys, were so washed out that the Mouse decided that the race that designed the ship saw colors very differently from the way that human beings saw them.

"I have no foodstuffs that would be suitable for Men," continued the alien.

"Then you weren't expecting us?" asked the Mouse.

"No."

"Then why did you help us?"

"She is the Soothsayer," said the Mock Turtle.

The Mouse frowned. "What does that have to do with anything? Does your religion anticipate some soothsayer?"

"My religion is a private matter," answered the alien calmly, but in tones that implied the subject was closed.

"Then I must repeat my question," said the Mouse, trying to make herself comfortable on the alien chair. "Why did you help us?"

The Mock Turtle turned to the little girl. "You are Penelope Bailey, are you not?"

"Yes," said Penelope, propping up Maryanne next to her on the broad seat.

"That is why."

"You sound like just another bounty hunter," said the Mouse. "But that can't be. First, you didn't know we were going to show up on Calliope, and second, Penelope trusts you."

"That is true," agreed the Mock Turtle tranquilly. "I did not anticipate your arrival on Calliope, and I am very trustworthy."

"Then perhaps you'd like to tell me what your interest in us is?"

"I am not interested in you at all."

"You are a very difficult person to talk to," said the Mouse in frustrated tones.

"I am not a person at all," replied the alien. "I am a—" It uttered a word the Mouse had never heard and could not pronounce. "But you may call me the Mock Turtle."

"All right, Mock Turtle," said the Mouse, "let's try again: why are you interested in Penelope?"

"She is the Soothsayer."

"You keep saying that!" snapped the Mouse.

"It is the truth."

Penelope giggled as the Mouse tried to control her temper.

"Why do you care whether or not she's the Soothsayer?" continued the Mouse.

"Because if she is not, I have killed a Man for no reason," answered the Mock Turtle.

"Why did you kill the man? And don't say it's because she is the Soothsayer."

The Mock Turtle remained silent.

"Well?" demanded the Mouse.

"You instructed me not to answer you," explained the alien patiently.

"You are driving me crazy!" said the Mouse. She started to stamp her foot in anger, but quickly stopped when she realized that the act would upset her balance and cause her to slide back into the hollow that had been made to accommodate the alien's shell. "Can't you just explain in nice, simple terms why you felt it incumbent upon you to rescue her?"

"Certainly. You had not asked that before."

The Mouse resisted the urge to argue the point, and waited for the alien to continue speaking.

"My world is not a member of the Democracy," said the Mock Turtle, "nor is it a member of the Confederation. We have been nonaligned for many centuries, even before there *was* a Confederation, and even longer, before the Democracy replaced the Republic."

"What has this got to do with Penelope?"

"You have asked," said the Mock Turtle with no show of annoyance. "Allow me to answer."

"Sorry," said the Mouse. "Go ahead."

"My world wishes only to remain neutral. We desire no commerce or treaty with any other world or any other race." The alien paused, as if translating its thoughts into Terran concepts. "We would resist any effort to assimilate us." It paused again. "Men have always hungered for new worlds. The day is not far off that they will hunger for mine. Thus far we have been able to maintain our neutrality by balancing one force against the other . . . but if the men who rule the

Democracy obtain the services of the Soothsayer, they will eventually destroy the Confederation, and then the day will come when they no longer request us to join them, but instead demand it."

"She's just a child!" protested the Mouse. "She can barely keep one jump ahead of the people who are chasing her. How can you possibly believe that she could alter the outcome of galactic power struggles?"

"Children grow up."

The Mouse stared at the Mock Turtle for a long moment, trying without success to discern a facial expression.

"It doesn't sound to me like you have any intention of allowing her to grow up," she said slowly. "The only way you can be sure she doesn't fall into your enemies' hands is to kill her."

"That is because you are a fool," said the alien calmly.

"It's all right, Mouse," said Penelope, laying a hand on the Mouse's arm. "The Mock Turtle is my friend."

"He sure as hell doesn't sound like a friend," answered the Mouse.

"You are mistaken," said the Mock Turtle.

"Then suppose you tell me what you plan to do with us," insisted the Mouse.

"I will take you to my home world, where you will be safe."

"Will we be guests or prisoners? Or do you consider the two terms synonymous?"

"You will be guests," said the Mock Turtle. "She is the Soothsayer. We could not keep her prisoner even if we wanted to."

"And we'll be free to leave whenever we want?" persisted the Mouse.

"You will be free to leave whenever you want."

"Then why not set us down on a human world now?"

"You will not be safe on any nearby world," answered the Mock Turtle.

The Mouse turned to the girl. "Penelope?"

"It's true," she said. "The Yankee Clipper's men are looking for us already."

"All right," said the Mouse, facing the Mock Turtle once again. "So we land on your planet. Then what?"

"Then I hope to convince the Soothsayer that we are a peaceful race that means no harm, so that when she returns to her own people, she will instruct them not to force us to join their Democracy."

"She's eight years old, for God's sake," said the Mouse. "Nobody will listen to her no matter what she says."

The alien stared at her but made no comment.

"Well?" continued the Mouse. "Do you disagree?"

"I have already told you that you are a fool," said the Mock Turtle gently. "Repeating it can only serve to anger you."

The Mouse turned to Penelope again. "Are you absolutely *sure* this creature is our friend?"

"I am *her* friend," said the Mock Turtle. "While I wish you no ill, I care no more for you than you care for me."

"He saved us, didn't he?" said Penelope.

"I am not a *he*, Soothsayer," interjected the alien. "But you may refer to me as a male, if it pleases you."

"I don't care," said Penelope. "You're my friend. That's all that matters."

"What were you doing on Calliope in the first place, if you weren't waiting for Penelope?" asked the Mouse.

"I was waiting for Penelope," answered the Mock Turtle.

"I thought you said you didn't know we were going to be on Calliope," said the Mouse sharply.

"That is true."

"Then how could you be waiting for us?"

"My ship developed engine trouble near the Calliope System, and I was forced to land there to seek repairs. Since my planet's currency is not accepted on Calliope, I was forced to obtain work so that I could pay for the repairs."

"It's working fine now, and no one tried to stop us, so obviously you had paid for the repairs before we met."

"That is true," answered the alien, "but I also had to pay for my food and lodging, and I would not have had enough currency for that until tomorrow."

"So what does that have to do with waiting for Penelope?"

"It is obvious to me that the Soothsayer arranged for me to land on Calliope, and to remain there until I could be of service to her."

"That's ridiculous," said the Mouse. "She didn't even know who you were or where you'd be."

"Ask her," said the Mock Turtle.

"Penelope," said the Mouse, turning to the little girl and staring at her questioningly, "is he telling the truth?"

Penelope shifted uncomfortably on her chair.

"Sort of," she said at last.

26

The Mouse stared intently at Penelope.

"What do you mean: *sort of*?" she asked at last.

"I knew there was a good person on the planet, one who would be our friend," said Penelope. "I wanted him to stay until we could meet him." She paused, trying to order her thoughts. "I didn't know it was the Mock Turtle, or what he looked like, but I thought it wasn't a human. And somehow I thought he'd be in New Gomorrah, and once we got there I knew he'd be at the carnival."

"But he was working right across the Midway from us for two days, and you didn't recognize him."

"We didn't need him until the Yankee Clipper came."

"But you had nothing to do with his landing on Calliope in the first place?"

"I don't think so," said Penelope.

"Don't you know?"

The little girl shook her head. "I have all these strange pictures in my mind. I still don't understand most of them."

"As the Soothsayer grows, so will her powers," said the Mock Turtle. "She will grow in peace and tranquillity on my world"—the alien turned to Penelope—"if she so desires."

"And if she *doesn't* desire it?" asked the Mouse.

"Then she will be free to leave."

"It would be nice not to be hunted anymore," replied Penelope.

"Let's see what his world is like before we start making any long-term plans," said the Mouse skeptically.

"It is an oxygen world with very low levels of pollution, and a gravity minimally greater than your own," said the Mock Turtle. "The seas are green, the grass a rich golden hue, the mountains tall and majestic and snowcapped. Most of our fauna is extinct, but we have set aside vast reserves for those remaining specimens so that we may someday repopulate the planet with their descendants."

"What do you call your world?" asked the Mouse.

The Mock Turtle mouthed an unpronounceable alien word. "In your language," it continued, "it would translate as Summergold." It paused thoughtfully. "It is quite the most beautiful place in the galaxy."

"If it's so beautiful, what were you doing flying a spaceship light-years away from it?"

"Searching for the Soothsayer," answered the Mock Turtle placidly.

"How did you even know there *was* a Soothsayer to search for?" demanded the Mouse.

"Word had reached us that a human child had the power of precognition, and that she and a companion were at large on the Inner Frontier. Further investigation revealed to us that her name was Penelope Bailey, and that she had last been seen in the company of a notorious gambler known as King Tout." The alien paused. "We knew that governments and powerful individuals would be seeking her for their own purposes, and we determined to find her first."

"It's a big galaxy," said the Mouse. "How did you expect to find her with no more information than that to go on?"

"I didn't."

"I don't think I understand."

"I expected *her* to find *me*," said the Mock Turtle.

"Why?" asked the Mouse, surprised.

"Because I, alone of all those who searched for her, meant her no harm."

"And based on your goodwill and nothing else, you expected her to seek you out?" replied the Mouse. "That's the stupidest thing I've ever heard."

"She did in fact seek me out, did she not?" replied the alien gently.

The Mouse had no answer for that, and so fell silent.

"Are there any children I can play with on Summergold?" asked Penelope after a moment had passed.

"It shall be arranged, Soothsayer," said the alien.

"Good," said Penelope enthusiastically. "I finally got to play with some girls on Calliope, and—"

Suddenly she froze, and a look of fear crossed her face.

"What is it, Penelope?" asked the Mouse.

"It's *him*," she said.

"Him?"

"The Iceman. He's after us already."

"Who is the Iceman?" asked the Mock Turtle.

"A bad man," said Penelope. "All the others want to capture me, but he wants to kill me."

"He will not be successful, Soothsayer."

"Then why does he frighten me so?" asked Penelope, tears welling up in her eyes.

"Because you are a child, and do not yet realize what it means to *be* the Soothsayer," answered the Mock Turtle. "We shall protect you on Summergold while you grow tall and strong and confront your destiny, whatever it may be."

"In the meantime, what kind of armaments does this ship carry?" asked the Mouse.

"None," said the alien. "This is not a military ship."

"How far are we from Summergold?"

The Mock Turtle pressed a button, then read the symbols that instantly appeared on the glowing screen of its computer. "Perhaps two Galactic Standard days."

"And if we don't stop for food on a colony planet?"

"The Soothsayer is only a child," noted the alien. "She must have sustenance."

"Don't you have a Deepsleep Chamber?" asked the Mouse. "You can freeze us until we arrive."

"This is but a small, private ship. I have no Deepsleep facilities."

The Mouse turned to Penelope. "How close are they?"

"I don't know," answered the girl.

"Forget the food," said the Mouse. "It's not worth the risk. We're only a few hours out from Calliope. If their ship is even marginally faster, they'll catch us if we stop."

"There is no need for guesswork," said the Mock Turtle calmly. It turned to Penelope. "Is it safe to stop, Soothsayer?"

"No," said Penelope.

"Can you survive without food for two days?" continued the alien.

"Yes."

"Does your race drink water?" asked the Mouse.

"Yes. I will have my ship's galley modify it to human tastes."

The Mock Turtle instructed its navigational computer to lay in a direct course for Summergold, then went to the cramped galley to supervise the filtration of the water's trace minerals.

"He'll never stop," said Penelope plaintively. "Why can't he leave me alone, Mouse?"

"Are you sure he's coming after you to kill you?" asked the Mouse. "Maybe he thinks the Mock Turtle has stolen you, and he and the Forever Kid want to rescue us."

"I don't know," said Penelope. "*He* doesn't know."

"You're not thinking clearly, Penelope. Either he wants to kill you or rescue you. He wouldn't be chasing us if he didn't know which."

"He still doesn't know if he'll kill me," said Penelope. "But he thinks I should die." She turned and faced the Mouse. "*Why?*" she sobbed. "What did I ever do to him?"

"Nothing," said the Mouse. She frowned, once again furious at herself for ever having cared for him. "You know, maybe it's time we considered doing something to him."

"I don't want to hurt anyone. I just want to be left alone."

"Sometimes you can't always have what you want," said the Mouse. "Or at least, sometimes you can't have it right away."

"It's not fair," said Penelope, cuddling Maryanne to her.

"No, it's not," said the Mouse grimly. "Still, maybe our luck's about to change. You've found another friend, and maybe we'll be safe once we get to Summergold."

"I get so tired, Mouse," said Penelope.

The Mouse put an arm around her. "I know."

"Will you always be with me?"

"Always."

Penelope leaned her head against the Mouse's small bosom, and a moment later had fallen into a fitful, disturbed sleep.

"The Soothsayer trusts you," said the Mock Turtle, returning to the cockpit with two containers of water.

"Yes, she does."

"Then perhaps you are not a fool, after all."

"Thanks," said the Mouse sardonically.

"I hope you will urge her to remain on our planet," said
the Mock Turtle.

"I'll have to see what it's like, first."

"She needs time to grow, free from all external pressures,"
continued the alien.

The Mouse looked down at the sleeping child and stroked
her blonde hair.

"She's had a rough time of it, that's for sure."

"Summergold will offer her peace and sanctuary."

"No one ever offers anything for free," said the Mouse.

"I told you what our interest in her is."

"I know you did," replied the Mouse. "Now I'll have to
decide whether I believe you or not."

"*She* will know if I should ever lie to you," said the Mock
Turtle. "You might consider that while you are making your
decision."

"I'll take it under advisement."

They spent the next hour in silence, for neither had anything further to say to the other. Then Penelope awoke,
and the Mock Turtle gave her the container of water, and
then the little girl and the Mouse played a number of very
simple word games to fill the time and take her mind off
the Iceman.

They slept again, and awoke again, and drank again, and
then, when the ship had approached to within nine hours of
Summergold, the Mock Turtle activated its subspace radio
and reported its position and its cargo, concluding with its
estimated time of arrival.

There was a momentary silence as the message was
transmitted, and then a reply came back over the speaker
system. The alien spoke again, waited for another reply,
and deactivated the radio. Finally it turned to Penelope.

"I am sorry, Soothsayer," it said, "but we cannot land on
Summergold."

"Why not?" asked the Mouse.

"We have been denied permission."

"Why?"

"Because even now several ships are approaching my planet, each filled with bounty hunters or members of the Democracy's military. We are not powerful enough to deny them access to Summergold, nor can we risk disobeying the Democracy's official representatives, and hence we cannot protect the Soothsayer's safety."

"What are we supposed to do, then?" demanded the Mouse.

"We must alter our course and go deeper into the Inner Frontier."

"It won't help," said the Mouse. "Every one of those ships left Calliope after we did. If some of them are already approaching Summergold, they're obviously faster than we are. There's no way we can outrun them."

"My ship possesses a Summergold registry, and doubtless someone at the carnival was able to identify my race." The alien paused. "It was much easier for them to anticipate that I would attempt to return to Summergold than it will be for them to predict my next action, for the simple reason that I do not know where we are going."

"Didn't your people give you any instructions except to run away?" demanded the Mouse.

"Most certainly they did," replied the Mock Turtle calmly. "They gave me the best possible instruction, indeed the *only* possible instruction."

"I don't suppose you'd like to share it with us," she said sarcastically.

"It is essential that I share it with you," answered the Mock Turtle. "They told me to ask the Soothsayer where to go, and to follow her orders."

It turned to Penelope and awaited her decision.

27

Penelope stared at the computer simulation of the Inner Frontier.

"This one," she said, pointing to a white-gold star.

"That is Alpha Tremino, also known as McCallister after the human member of the Pioneer Corps who terraformed the second planet circling it," said the Mock Turtle, translating the alien script that appeared on the screen when he entered the coordinates of the star. "That planet is now known as McCallister II. The system possesses six other planets; the inner planet is highly radioactive, and the other five are gas giants. None of them are capable of sustaining life." It squinted at the readout. "McCallister II possesses one Tradertown, which is located in the southern temperate zone. It was mined for uranium until two centuries ago, and is now used primarily as a refueling station for ships bound deeper into the Inner Frontier."

"How long will it take to reach it?" asked the Mouse.

The alien queried its navigational computer. "Approximately six Standard hours."

"And how about our pursuers?" she continued. "How long will it take them?"

"We will gain three or four hours on most of them, as they are closer to Summergold than we are."

"Then lay in a course for McCallister II."

"I did that the moment the Soothsayer selected it," replied the alien.

The Mouse turned to Penelope.

"Do you know anything about McCallister?"

"No."

"Maybe I worded that wrong," said the Mouse. She paused. "Can you see what will happen to us there?"

"No," repeated Penelope.

"Then why did you choose it?"

Penelope shrugged. "I just have a feeling about it."

"Well, your feelings have been good enough so far," said the Mouse with a sigh.

The alien went to the galley and brought them two more containers of water.

"Thank you," said Penelope, accepting the container.

"McCallister II is a human colony," said the Mock Turtle. "You will be able to obtain food there, Soothsayer."

"I hope it's good," said Penelope. "I'm very hungry."

"I am sorry, Soothsayer. I would give you my own if you could metabolize it."

"I know you would." The girl stared thoughtfully at the alien. "Perhaps you'd better pack some of your own food."

"Why, Soothsayer?" asked the Mock Turtle.

"You might need it."

"I shall do so, Soothsayer," said the alien, heading off to the galley once more.

"What was that all about?" asked the Mouse.

"I just think the Mock Turtle will need some food before long," said Penelope.

"He's got a whole galley full of food."

Penelope didn't answer her, and when the Mouse looked to see if she had heard her, she saw a look of intense concentration on the little girl's face.

"She is reading the future," said the Mock Turtle, returning from the galley.

"Sorting it out, anyway," agreed the Mouse.

Penelope remained motionless for almost five minutes, and finally the Mouse reached out a hand and shook her shoulder.

"What is it?" asked the girl.

"You looked like you were in a trance," said the Mouse. "I've never seen you like that, and I got worried."

"I'm fine," Penelope assured her.

"What were you doing?"

"Trying to look ahead."

"You've never gone catatonic before."

"What's 'catatonic'?"

"Rigid and motionless, as if you didn't know where you were or who you were with."

"I was looking further than usual, so I had to concentrate real hard," explained Penelope.

"Did you see anything?"

"Yes."

"Well?" said the Mouse.

"I saw us land on McCallister II," said Penelope. "And the man at the spaceport is going to be very nice to us. He's going to give me a sandwich, and some fruit, and a cup of tea."

"Does anyone else land while we're there?"

"That depends on how long we stay," answered Penelope. "Most of them know we've changed our course."

"How many ships are following us now?"

"Lots."

"Including Carlos and the Kid?"

"Yes," said Penelope. "But they won't catch us before we reach McCallister."

"How long will we stay on McCallister II?" asked the Mouse.

Penelope frowned. "I don't know."

"An hour? A day? A week?"

"It depends on what I tell the Mock Turtle," said Penelope. "And I have to decide if it's right or wrong to tell him."

"To tell him what?"

"I have to decide," repeated Penelope, falling silent. A moment later she was cuddling Maryanne, as if for comfort.

Five hours later the Mock Turtle began braking its ship to sublight speed, and twenty minutes after that it set the ship down at the small spaceport just beyond the Tradertown.

"I shall add fuel to the ship's reservoirs while you seek nourishment," announced the Mock Turtle as the three of them climbed through the hatch.

"Don't," said Penelope, who had taken Maryanne out of the ship with her.

The Mouse was startled, but the alien merely inclined its head.

"It shall be as you wish, Soothsayer," it said. "I will wait for you here."

"Please come with us," said Penelope. "We shouldn't be separated now."

The Mock Turtle fell into step behind them without another word.

They entered the spaceport's small restaurant, and the waiter was as pleasant as Penelope had predicted. While they were waiting for their food, the Mouse turned to the girl.

"All right," she said. "Are you ready to tell me what's going on?"

"Yes," said Penelope unhappily. She paused. "We have to do a bad thing."

"What thing?"

"We have to steal a spaceship."

"I thought that was what you had in mind," said the Mouse.

"I don't want to," said Penelope. "It's wrong to steal. But if we don't change ships, they'll catch us very soon."

The waiter returned with their order, and the Mouse remained silent until he had once more moved out of earshot.

"Will changing ships fool all of them?" she asked.

"Most of them," replied Penelope. "They'll all find out what we did, but then we'll be so far away that they won't be able to follow us."

"They have subspace radios," said the Mouse. "Why won't they stay in contact with each other?"

"Because each of them wants the reward for me," answered Penelope. "None of them will help any of the others to catch me."

"Which ship must we appropriate, Soothsayer?" asked the Mock Turtle.

"That one," said Penelope, pointing to a sleek blue ship that was standing, poised for takeoff, on the field beyond the hangars.

"The blue one?" asked the Mouse.

"Yes."

"It's right out in the open," she said dubiously. "Maybe we'd be better off taking a different one."

"You must not dispute the Soothsayer," said the Mock Turtle calmly. "She has foreseen that we need this particular ship. That is all we have to know."

"I'm not disputing her," answered the Mouse defensively. "I'd just like to know why she chose that one."

"Most of the others have people aboard them," said Penelope. "Or else they aren't fast enough, or they need fuel."

Penelope finished her sandwich and started picking pieces of fruit out of her fruit cup.

"This is very good," she said. "But I don't like my tea very much. Can I have some milk instead?"

"Yes, Soothsayer," said the Mock Turtle, getting to its feet and walking off to find the waiter.

"I wish he'd call me Penelope," the little girl confided to the Mouse. "I feel funny when he calls me Soothsayer."

"Well, that's what you are, you know," said the Mouse. "A soothsayer is someone who can see the future."

"It doesn't work that way," said Penelope. "You see lots of futures, and then you try to make the one you want happen." She looked at the Mouse's plate. "You only ate half your sandwich. Aren't you hungry?"

"I'll take the other half along with me," answered the Mouse. "What I mostly am is anxious to get moving again. We've still got thirty ships closing in on us."

"They won't catch us, Mouse," said Penelope as the Mock Turtle returned carrying a glass of milk. "Not on McCallister, anyway."

"Just the same, I'll feel a lot more secure once we're back in space," said the Mouse.

"We're not ready to leave yet," said Penelope. She smiled at the Mock Turtle. "Thank you for the milk."

"When *will* we be ready to leave?" asked the Mouse.

"In a few minutes." She drained the glass of milk. "That was very good. I *like* milk."

"You're not being very communicative," said the Mouse, trying to keep the irritation from her voice.

"I don't know what that means."

"I mean you're not telling me what you're thinking."

"I'm sorry, Mouse," apologized Penelope. "I was just thinking that I'd like to get Maryanne a lace dress. The ones that we had sent up to our suite on Calliope were nice, but she needs something really pretty."

The Mouse sighed deeply. "All right. Have it your way."

"You look mad, Mouse," said Penelope with a worried expression on her face. "Did I do something wrong?"

"The Soothsayer cannot, by definition, do anything wrong," said the Mock Turtle, its voice as placid as ever.

"I'm not mad, just frustrated," said the Mouse.

"What did I say?" asked Penelope.

"It's what you didn't say," explained the Mouse. "I know you have a reason for not going to the ship right now, just as you had a reason for landing on McCallister II and for wanting to steal that particular ship. But I can't see the future, and since the only thing I know for sure is that all those bounty hunters are getting closer to us with each passing minute, I'd like to know why we're sitting here and exactly what we're waiting for."

"Oh, is that all?" said Penelope, relieved that she had not done something more serious to offend the Mouse. "Do you see the fat man in the leather tunic who's sitting at the far end of the restaurant?"

The Mouse glanced quickly across the restaurant.

"Yes."

"It's his ship that we're stealing," said Penelope. "In about five or six minutes, he's going to get up from his table and walk into the bathroom. He'll be there a long time, and we can just walk out across the field and get into the ship and leave."

"Won't he report us to spaceport security?"

Penelope shook her head. "He's got something on the ship he doesn't want anyone to know about. He'll buy another ship and try to find us himself, but he won't report us."

"What's he smuggling?" asked the Mouse. "Drugs? Money?"

"I don't know."

"And security won't stop us?"

"He's already given them money not to pay any attention to the ship. They'll think we're working for him." She looked at the Mouse with a worried expression on her face. "Do you like me again now?"

"Of course I like you," the Mouse assured her. "I just get a little upset when I can't see what you can see."

"I wish *I* couldn't see it," said Penelope earnestly. "Then maybe everyone would leave me alone."

"You have been blessed with a great gift, Soothsayer," said the Mock Turtle. "In time you will learn to appreciate it."

Penelope seemed about to argue with the alien, then shrugged and went back to picking pieces of fruit out of the cup. A few minutes later the heavyset man got to his feet and walked to the rest room. As soon as he was out of sight the Mouse, Penelope, and the Mock Turtle rose from their seats and casually walked out to the ship.

"It's not locked," said Penelope as they approached the hatch.

The hatch door slid back as they came within range of the ship's sensor, and one by one they climbed into the interior of the ship. It was considerably larger than the Mock Turtle's vessel and was designed for human occupants. There was a cockpit, of course, and a well-equipped galley, two sleeping cabins, and a locked storage compartment.

"The controls are unfamiliar to me," said the Mock Turtle after examining the instrumentation. "And while I can speak Terran, I have great difficulty reading it."

"No problem," said the Mouse, moving past him into the cockpit and seating herself on the pilot's chair. "Its computer has a Gorshen/Blomberg module. We just tell it what we want, and it takes care of the rest." She turned to her companions. "Strap yourselves in."

They took off less than a minute later, and ten minutes after that the computer announced that it was ready to break out of orbit and attain light speeds.

"Time for a decision," said the Mouse. "I've got to give the navigational computer a destination."

"Soothsayer?" said the Mock Turtle, turning to Penelope and awaiting her decision.

"I don't know the name of the world," said Penelope.

The Mouse ordered the computer to create a holographic map of the Inner Frontier.

"All right," she announced. "This is Summergold, this is McCallister, and that's Last Chance 'way over there."

The little girl studied the simulation for a long moment. Finally she extended an index finger and pointed to a distant star that had no near neighbors.

"This one," she said.

The Mouse instructed the navigational computer to lay in a course for the indicated star, then asked for a readout.

"Where are we bound?" asked the Mock Turtle.

"The star is called Bowman 26," replied the Mouse.

"A curious name."

The Mouse squinted at the readout. "It was the twenty-sixth star system mapped by Pioneer Milton Bowman almost

3,200 years ago. The third of its five planets was colonized in 288 G.E., and was initially named Van der Gelt III, after the man who financed the colonization."

"Initially?" asked the Mock Turtle. "Then its name has been changed?"

She nodded. "The entire colony was slaughtered by a madman named Conrad Bland in 341 G.E., which was when it received the name it's now known by: Killhaven."

"Does anyone reside there now?"

"Let's see," said the Mouse, looking at the readout again. "Yes. It was deserted for almost three millennia, but now it's got a couple of hundred farmers, and a small religious group trying to create their own Utopia, based on an agricultural community from the days when we were still Earthbound. I gather than the planet itself is very scenic, and most of the dwellings were designed to look like Victorian farmhouses from old Earth. There's nothing in the readout about a Tradertown, but I suppose there must be one; Killhaven's so far off the beaten track that I imagine the cartographers are a few years behind the times."

The Mock Turtle had no more questions, and the Mouse ordered the holographic map to dissolve. Then she left the cockpit and made her way back to the storage compartment.

"Now let's see exactly what kind of contraband we're carrying," she said.

The alien showed no interest in helping her, but Penelope, with a child's curiosity, joined her at the door to the compartment.

The Mouse ordered the computer to unlock the door. It replied that it could not do so without the proper code.

"Damn!" she muttered. "I guess we'll have to do it the hard way."

She looked around for a tool kit, found one, and spent the next two hours tinkering with the lock mechanism, all the while wishing that Merlin, to whom no lock was a mystery, had not joined the opposition.

Finally, when she was all but ready to admit defeat, she heard a faint beeping sound, and the door slid back into a bulkhead. She crouched over and entered the low-ceilinged compartment.

"Well, how about this!" she exclaimed a moment later. "Four bags of alphanella seeds."

"What are alphanella seeds?" asked Penelope.

"A hallucinogenic drug. They're outlawed everywhere in the Democracy, and on most of the Frontier worlds as well."

"A *what* kind of drug?"

"Hallucinogenic," repeated the Mouse. "When you chew on the seed you go into a trance and see all kinds of strange things. As often as not the experience kills you . . . but if you survive the first time, you're an addict the rest of your life. You forget to eat, you don't sleep, all you do is chase after the seeds."

"Why would anyone want to chew the seeds, then?"

The Mouse shrugged. "The ultimate thrill," she said without much conviction. "Don't ask me. I never did understand seed chewers." She patted the bags fondly, then walked back out of the storage compartment. "Alphanella seeds! Who'd have thought it?"

"What difference does it make?" said the Mock Turtle. "None of us will partake of them."

"In case it's escaped your attention," she pointed out, "we're not exactly swimming in money. I've got about twenty-five hundred credits left from Calliope, and I suspect you have even less."

"That is true," admitted the alien.

"Well, then? These bags must be worth a few hundred thousand credits apiece. What do you say?"

"I say leave them aboard the ship," replied the Mock Turtle. "They will destroy anyone who uses them."

"The way I look at it, anyone stupid enough to become a seed chewer deserves whatever happens to him," said the Mouse with a shrug.

"Let us ask the Soothsayer."

"That's not fair," said the Mouse heatedly. "If she says no, we'll be stuck on a strange world with no money and half a dozen bounty hunters chasing us, and if she says yes, you'll have made her an active participant in drug dealing. No child should have to make such a decision."

"She is the Soothsayer," replied the Mock Turtle. "She will choose correctly."

He turned expectantly toward the little girl.

"We should leave the alphanella seeds where we found them," said Penelope without hesitation.

"But we've barely got enough money to get by for a few days on Killhaven," said the Mouse.

"We won't need it."

"What about when we leave?" insisted the Mouse. "We'll *have* to have money then."

"We're not leaving Killhaven," said Penelope.

"But we're still being followed."

"I know."

"Then why—?" began the Mouse.

"Because it's time to stop running away," said Penelope.

28

It wasn't a Tradertown, not as the Mouse understood Tradertowns. It was just a little cluster of buildings: a restaurant, a general store, a farm implement shop, a seed warehouse, a church, and a two-story frame rooming house.

There wasn't even a street, just a dirt track that passed in front of the buildings, and it was so filled with ruts that the few vehicles they saw drove about ten feet to the right of it.

"This is a hell of a place to make a stand against a couple of dozen bounty hunters," muttered the Mouse as they walked the mile from their spaceship to the town.

"You must have faith in the Soothsayer's judgment," said the Mock Turtle placidly.

"Let the first five ships crash and I'll have a lot more faith," remarked the Mouse caustically.

As they passed a pasture of mutated beef cattle, each weighing close to 2,500 pounds, grazing contentedly on the native grasses, Penelope walked up to the wire fence to stare at them.

"They're lovely," said the little girl.

"They're just cows," said the Mouse. "A little bigger than most, but no smarter, I'll wager."

"Can I pet one, Mouse?" asked Penelope.

"I don't know why not," replied the Mouse. "You'll know better than me if it's safe or not."

"Thank you."

Penelope leaned up against the fence and called to the cattle. Most of them ignored her, but a calf, almost as large as a full-grown Earth cow, stared at her with large, curious eyes and finally came over to the fence.

"He's very nice," said Penelope, rubbing the calf's broad forehead between its eyes. "I think he likes me."

"I'm sure he does," said the Mouse.

Penelope petted the calf for another minute, then rejoined the Mouse and the Mock Turtle. As they began walking toward the buildings again, the calf followed them on its side of the fence until it could go no farther, then began bleating plaintively, and finally returned to its gargantuan mother.

"I wonder if all the animals are that big," said Penelope.

"I doubt it," answered the Mouse. "Probably just the meat animals."

Penelope frowned. "I hope nobody wants to eat him when he grows up."

"Perhaps they won't," said the Mouse reassuringly. "I'm sure they keep some for breeding."

"Wouldn't it be nice it we could come back here someday and see him all grown up, and pet one of his children?" said the little girl.

"I'll settle for just getting off the planet in one piece," said the Mouse.

They walked past fields of corn and sugar berries and finally came to what passed for the town.

"What shall we do now, Soothsayer?" asked the Mock Turtle, oblivious to the curious stares it elicited from within the various shops.

"Now we wait," answered Penelope.

"Right here?" asked the Mouse, surprised.

"No," said Penelope. "They won't be here for a while."

"Good," said the Mouse. "Then let's rent some rooms. I could do with a shower."

"Me, too," said Penelope. She examined her doll thoughtfully. "And Maryanne's all covered with dust."

The Mouse headed for the rooming house and entered it a moment later. It seemed much like the farmhouses of ancient Earth: it was made of wood, and the floor was covered with an inexpensive rug rather than carpeted. The furniture was sturdy and functional, but far from elegant, and despite the displays of fresh flowers there was a scent and feeling of mustiness about the place.

A floorboard creaked as she walked up to the registration desk, which in this case was simply a wooden table with a thin, weatherworn, elderly man sitting behind it.

"How much are your rooms?" asked the Mouse.

"Eighty credits a night. One hundred if you want the one with its own bathroom."

"We'd like three rooms, please," she said as Penelope and the Mock Turtle entered the house. "Including the one with its own bath."

"Only got two," said the man. "Your green friend will have to make other arrangements."

"We'll take two, then," said the Mouse with a shrug. "The little girl and I can double up."

"Only got one in that case."

"If you don't accept aliens, why don't you post a sign to that effect?" demanded the Mouse.

"That's the first alien I've seen in almost thirty years," answered the man. "Only been renting out rooms for the last seventeen."

"Since there's no sign to the contrary, we'll take two rooms," said the Mouse firmly.

"I only got one to rent," said the man.

"Look," said the Mouse. "We've come a long way, and we're tired and hungry. We want two rooms."

"I know what you want," said the man. "You keep it up, and you might find yourself sleeping out in a cornfield."

"*You* keep it up, and you might start wondering what your ugly little world looked like when your head was still attached to your shoulders."

The Mouse felt a hand tug at the sleeve of her tunic.

"Offer him more money," said Penelope.

"Why should I?" said the Mouse. "He hasn't posted any restrictions."

"Mouse, just *do* it," said Penelope wearily.

The Mouse shrugged and turned back to the old man. "Five hundred credits a night for two rooms."

"A thousand," replied the man.

The Mouse was about to protest, but Penelope squeezed her hand, and nodded her approval.

"All right. A thousand."

"In advance."

The Mouse dug into the pouch where she kept her valuables, pulled out a thousand credits, and slapped them down on the table.

"Up the stairs," said the old man, indicating a wooden staircase. "First two rooms on the left."

"Where are our keys?" demanded the Mouse.

"Where's your luggage?"

"That's none of your business."

The old man seemed to consider her answer, then opened a drawer and pulled out two keys.

"Thanks," said the Mouse sardonically.

"If you don't like our service, you can always go to our competitors," said the old man.

"You could *use* a little competition," snapped the Mouse.

"We got some," he replied with a broad grin. "Another boardinghouse, halfway around the planet. Just a good stretch of the legs."

The Mouse picked up the keys and led the way upstairs. When she reached the landing, she handed one of the keys to the Mock Turtle.

"Why didn't you say anything?" she demanded, still furious.

"What was there to say?" responded the alien placidly.

"I've seen you shoot the Yankee Clipper down in cold blood, so don't tell me that you've been taught to turn the other cheek. Why didn't you stand up for your rights?"

"The Soothsayer did not instruct me to argue."

"And if the Soothsayer tells you to jump off the edge of a cliff, will you do so?"

"Most certainly," replied the Mock Turtle.

The Mouse muttered an obscenity and entered her room, followed by Penelope. The Mock Turtle watched her for a moment, then entered its own room.

The Mouse's room contained two narrow beds, a dresser with a large mirror, a rocking chair, a pair of small throw rugs—one between the beds, the other just outside the door to the bathroom—and each wall was covered with two-dimensional photographs of the old man at the desk, an equally aged woman, a number of middle-aged men and women, and children of various ages from infancy to young adulthood, which the Mouse assumed were their children and grandchildren.

"There's no holo set," noted Penelope.

"I'm surprised there's a window," said the Mouse. She sighed deeply. "Well, let's see what the facilities are like."

She walked to the bathroom door and waited impatiently.

"Open," she commanded.

The door remained shut.

"Try the handle," said Penelope.

The Mouse reached for the door's handle and twisted it.

"I'll be damned!" she said. "Do you know how long it's been since I've seen one of these?"

She entered the bathroom, grimaced when she discovered that there was no dryshower, walked to the tub, said "Hot," waited for a moment, then shook her head in disbelief and turned the faucet.

"How do people live like this?" she muttered.

She bathed, dried herself, and got back into her clothes, then rejoined Penelope in the bedroom.

"I don't think I'd better wash Maryanne in real water," said Penelope, sitting cross-legged on her bed and looking thoughtfully at the doll. "I was hoping the bathroom would have a dryshower."

The Mouse sat down on her own bed.

"We have more important things to worry about," she said.

"I know," answered Penelope seriously.

"When will they start arriving?"

"Soon."

"Today?"

"I think so."

"How many of them?"

"Today? Just one ship."

"Can you tell who's aboard it yet?"

"Not yet."

"Carlos and the Kid, perhaps?"

Penelope frowned. "I hope not."

"If you're still afraid of him, why are we sitting here waiting for him?" asked the Mouse, puzzled.

"I told you: we're all through running away."

"Why here? Why weren't we all through running away on Calliope or McCallister?"

Penelope shrugged. "It just *feels* right here."

"Well," said the Mouse with a sigh, "I suppose it makes sense, after all. Most of the ships that were chasing us got left behind at McCallister." She paused. "I wonder what would happen if we went back to the ship right now and took off again? How many more of them would we lose?"

"They'd catch us before we reached the next world and kill us," said Penelope.

"No, they wouldn't—you're much too valuable to kill."

"They wouldn't mean to," said the little girl. "They'd try to disable the ship—but it's not very sturdy. The first time it was hit, all three of us would die."

"So that's why we're through running?"

Penelope nodded her head.

"Shit!" said the Mouse. "I was hoping it was because you saw some way to make them finally stop chasing us. I didn't realize it was because we'd die if we kept running away."

Penelope sighed deeply.

"Whatever happens here, at least it will finally be over," she said. "I'm *so* tired."

"I know," said the Mouse sympathetically.

There was a momentary silence as Penelope continued brushing dust from the doll. Finally she turned to the Mouse.

"Can we eat now?"

"Sure," said the Mouse. "I don't know if the restaurant has any food the Mock Turtle can eat, though."

"It will hurt his feelings if we don't ask him to come," said Penelope.

"If he *has* any feelings," said the Mouse, remembering the little scene at the desk.

"Everyone has feelings, Mouse," said Penelope.

The Mouse sighed and tousled the girl's blonde hair. "I know," she said. "I guess I'm just tired, too."

They left their room and knocked on the Mock Turtle's door. The alien emerged a moment later.

"Have they arrived?" it asked.

"We're hungry," said Penelope. "We're going across the street to eat at the restaurant. Would you like to come with us?"

"If you so wish it, Soothsayer," said the Mock Turtle.

"I think we should stay together," said Penelope.

They walked down the stairs and past the desk, which was now deserted. The Mouse opened the door, almost stepped on a small, catlike marsupial that had been sunning itself, and headed off toward the restaurant, followed closely by Penelope and the alien.

"Mouse?" said Penelope when they had covered half the distance.

"What is it?"

"Whatever they charge us for the food, pay it."

"But the Turtle can't even eat human food," said the Mouse. She turned to the alien. "Can you?"

"No," answered the Mock Turtle.

"So why should I let them overcharge us?" continued the Mouse. "If they object to his presence, he can wait outside."

"Pay it," said Penelope. "It's not polite to make him wait outside."

"At this rate we'll be out of money by tomorrow night," said the Mouse. "I'm sure the Turtle will understand."

"We won't need the money by tomorrow night," said Penelope.

"Why not?"

"Because whatever's going to happen will be over by then."

"Let's be optimistic and assume we're all going to live through it," said the Mouse. "If we do, we'll need money."

"If we do, then you'll take it off the bodies of the people who *don't* live," answered Penelope, dismissing the subject.

She climbed the steps of the restaurant's broad veranda, then paused to look at a wooden porch swing. "That's very nice," she said. "Can I sit on it when we're through eating?"

"I don't know why not," said the Mouse, still preoccupied with what the girl had just said about the impending events.

They entered the restaurant, which consisted of eight tables, all empty, each covered with an inexpensive, faded tablecloth. A pudgy, middle-aged woman walked out from another room and approached them.

"Can I help you?" she said coldly, regarding the Mock Turtle with open contempt.

"We'd like to have lunch," said Penelope.

"Too late for lunch," said the woman.

"Dinner, then," said the Mouse.

"Too early for dinner."

The Mouse walked to a table and seated herself. "We'll wait," she announced, signaling Penelope and the Mock Turtle to join her.

The woman disappeared into the room from which she had emerged, then came out again a moment later.

"All we've got is stew," she said.

"What kind of salad do you have?" asked the Mouse.

"I said all we've got is. stew."

"What's it made of?"

"Beef and vegetables," said the woman.

"Can you make more if you have to?"

"I suppose so. Do you plan to eat twelve pounds of it?"

"No. But I want you to take some of those vegetables you would use to make more stew, and make me a salad," said the Mouse.

"You ever have a salad made of potatoes before?" asked the woman with a harsh laugh.

"No, and I don't plan to have one now. However long it takes to make a simple salad, I'll wait." She paused. "We'll *all* wait."

"I'd like some stew, please," added Penelope.

The woman jerked a thumb in the Mock Turtle's direction. "What does *it* eat?"

"Nothing, thank you," said the alien.

The woman turned on her heel and left the room.

"I've never seen a place like this," said the Mouse. "You'd think they'd never met an alien before."

"Probably most of them haven't," said the Mock Turtle. "Killhaven is an insular, isolated world."

"Then they ought to be curious."

"It is my experience that your race manifests its curiosity in unusual ways," said the alien with no show of emotion. "This experience is not unfamiliar to me."

"Then why are you risking your life to save one of us?" asked the Mouse, suddenly feeling defensive.

"Because she is the Soothsayer," said the Mock Turtle, as if explaining the obvious to a small child.

The pudgy woman suddenly reappeared, placed a garden salad before the Mouse and a plate of stew in front of Penelope without uttering a word, then turned to leave.

"We'd like some water, too," said the Mouse.

She glared at the Mouse, then left and returned with two glasses of water a moment later.

"Thank you," said Penelope as she left again.

The Mouse began eating her salad, made a face, and searched through it for a sign of dressing. She couldn't find any, and finally she shrugged and continued eating. "You know," she remarked, "I get the distinct feeling that they're not very happy to see *any* of us."

"They lead very rigid, insular lives," said the Mock Turtle. "We have disrupted them."

"But we can't be the only visitors they've ever seen," said the Mouse. "After all, they *do* have a hotel and a restaurant."

"They are probably patronized by farmers who come to town to shop for seeds and supplies, and by off-planet agents who come here to buy the crops."

"Perhaps," said the Mouse.

"We make an unlikely party," continued the Mock Turtle. "Furthermore, you and I are both heavily armed, nor did we announce our arrival in advance."

"Well, I hope they're no more hospitable to the others when they show up," said the Mouse. Suddenly she grinned. "Maybe they'll all starve to death trying to get service here."

As if on cue, the pudgy woman returned to the dining room.

"That'll be five hundred credits, cash," she announced.

"Five hundred credits for one bowl of salad and one plate of stew?" demanded the Mouse.

"If you don't like the price, you shouldn't have eaten the food," said the woman.

"Mouse . . ." said Penelope softly.

The Mouse looked at the little girl, then pulled some bills out of her money pouch.

"How much of a tip do you think we should leave?" she asked caustically.

"I don't want any tip from you," said the woman. "Just pay up and leave."

The Mouse handed over the money.

"We'll leave when we're ready to," she said.

The woman glared at her. "When the shooting starts, just see to it that you're not in my restaurant."

"What shooting?" asked the Mouse.

"Don't play dumb with *me*," said the woman. "We heard on the subspace radio that there's a bunch of bounty hunters bound for Killhaven. Since no one here has broken any laws, it stands to reason that you're the ones they're after." She paused. "I want you out of my restaurant. If we had any police here, I'd turn you in myself."

"I told you," said the Mouse coldly. "We'll leave when we're ready."

Penelope reached across the table and laid a hand on the Mouse's wrist. "It's all right, Mouse. I'm through eating."

"All right," said the Mouse, getting to her feet. "Let's go try out that swing."

"I don't want to anymore," said Penelope.

"Don't let her frighten you," said the Mouse, still angry.

"I'm not afraid of her, Mouse."

"You're sure you don't want to sit on the swing?"

"I'm sure," answered the girl.

The Mouse shrugged. "All right," she said. "Let's go back to our room."

They left the dining room, walked out the door, and started climbing down the steps of the veranda.

"Well, maybe it wasn't xenophobia, after all," said the Mouse.

"Maybe it wasn't *only* xenophobia," the Mock Turtle corrected her.

They began walking back to the rooming house. When they were in the middle of the dirt street separating the two buildings, Penelope suddenly froze in her tracks.

"What is it?" asked the Mouse solicitously.

"He's here already."

"He?"

Penelope stared fixedly at a point just beyond the Mouse's left shoulder.

"*Him!*" she whispered.

The Mouse turned and saw two men standing at the door of the hotel. One was the Forever Kid.

"Hello, Mouse," said the other. "You led us one hell of a chase."

"Hello, Carlos," said the Mouse.

29

"Come no closer," said the Mock Turtle.

"And who are *you?*" demanded the Iceman.

"I am a friend of the Soothsayer," replied the alien. "That is enough for you to know."

"So she's the Soothsayer now?"

"And I am in her service."

"If she was anyone else in the galaxy, I would say that she needed all the friends she could get," said the Iceman. "I suppose you know that half a dozen ships are due to land before nightfall."

"Yes—but you are the only one she fears," said the Mock Turtle. "Keep your distance."

"He's not going to touch the little girl," said the Forever Kid. He turned to the Mouse. "I'm still on your payroll; I figure that includes protecting the girl." He paused. "Unless you want the rest of your money back, that is."

"Keep the money," said the Mouse as an enormous surge of relief swept over her. "You're still working for me."

"Well, Iceman?" said the Kid. "We haven't settled what we were going to do when we caught up with them. It seems to me that it's about time we found out where you stand."

"We have time, yet," said the Iceman. "Anything we decide right now is going to be disputed by a dozen or more bounty hunters. If we start shooting each other, there will be that many less of us to stand against them."

"Why should we believe you, Carlos?" demanded the Mouse.

The Iceman stared into the little girl's eyes. "Tell them," he said.

"He's not going to do anything to me at least until we're safe from the others," said Penelope.

"What about later?" asked the Mouse.

"I don't know."

The Mouse turned to face the Iceman once again. "Carlos?"

"She doesn't know because *I* don't know," he replied.

"I'm still wondering if I can trust you," said the Mouse.

"It is impossible for the Soothsayer to err," said the Mock Turtle tranquilly. It began walking toward the rooming house. "Come. Let us go inside and make our plans. We are very visible targets here on the street."

The Iceman nodded his agreement, and the five of them entered the rooming house. The old man was back at the desk.

"No rooms left," he said sullenly. "We're all sold out."

"We don't want a room," replied the Iceman.

"We don't allow visitors."

The Iceman stared at the old man for a long moment.

"Leave," he said at last.

"This is *my* rooming house!"

"Don't make me say it again," said the Iceman. He didn't raise his voice; if anything, he spoke even more softly. But there was something in his tone that convinced the old man to get up and walk out the door without saying another word. At the same time the Mouse became aware of Penelope pressing very hard against her hip and leg, as if she were trying to keep the Mouse between herself and the Iceman.

"We've got a little time," said the Iceman. "About an hour or so. Where can we talk?"

"There's a lounge over there," said the Mouse, pointing to an adjacent room that was dominated by a large brick fireplace.

They entered it, with the Forever Kid leaning against the doorjamb, where he had a view of the empty street. Penelope waited until the Iceman had seated himself on a chair, then sat as far away from him as possible. The Mouse joined her a moment later, and the Mock Turtle, finding no furniture that would accommodate the huge, horny hump on its back, stood in a corner, from which it could observe all of them.

"Well?" said the Mouse. "What do we do now?"

"Now we wait," said the Iceman.

"Then we kill 'em all," added the Forever Kid happily.

"Don't ask *him* what to do," said the Iceman wryly. "He can't wait to take them all on single-handed."

"Why aren't we trying to get away before they arrive?" asked the Mouse. "I know why we can't use *our* ship, but why can't we all leave in yours?"

"Because the Democracy's got a couple of battle cruisers on the way here," answered the Iceman. "They won't arrive for a couple of days, but we can't outgun them, and while our ships are a little faster, they can carry a lot more fuel—they'd catch us the first time we put into a port with a fuel depot." He paused. "The only way to get away cleanly is to do to them what you tried to do to us: change ships and hope they don't figure it out as quickly as we did."

"And the only ships worth taking belong to the bounty hunters," added the Forever Kid.

"So there's no alternative," said the Mouse. "We stay and fight."

"There's an alternative," said the Iceman.

"What is it?" asked the Mouse.

"Leave the girl here and get out now. They're not interested in any of the rest of us."

"*No!*" shouted Penelope.

"Never!" said the Mock Turtle.

"That was a foolish suggestion, Carlos," said the Mouse, trying to control her anger.

"Probably," he replied. "But you *did* ask for alternatives." He stared at Penelope again. "You'd never let us get away with it, would you?"

"Why do you hate me so?" asked Penelope, edging closer to the Mouse and holding her hand as if for comfort.

"I don't hate you at all," replied the Iceman.

"But you want me dead."

"Probably."

"Then you *do* hate me."

"No more than I hate a cancer that has to be removed, or a scavenger that has to be shot. You can't help what you are, but you're too dangerous to be allowed to live."

"If you lay a finger on her, it'll be over my dead body!" said the Mouse.

"And mine," chimed in the Mock Turtle.

"Your money doesn't run out for four more days, Mouse," said the Forever Kid easily. "I'm sure we'll have this all sorted out by then."

"And what happens when the money runs out?" asked the Iceman.

The Kid smiled at him. "Then I might go up against you just for the hell of it."

"Maybe you'd better worry about who you have to face today," said the Iceman emotionlessly. "They're due to arrive within the hour."

"I'm looking forward to it," the Forever Kid assured him.

"I'll just bet you are," replied the Iceman.

"Soothsayer," interjected the Mock Turtle, "how may we help in your defense?"

"You don't listen very well, do you?" said the Iceman. "She doesn't *need* any help."

"You don't listen too well yourself," shot back the Mouse. "They're not coming to kill her, but to capture her."

"How long will she stay captured?" replied the Iceman. He turned to the girl again. "How many people have captured you so far, and where are they all now?"

Penelope's grip on the Mouse's hand tightened. "Make him leave me alone, Mouse."

"You heard her," said the Mouse.

The Iceman shrugged. "That being the case, I think I'll go across the street and get a drink while there's time."

"That's a restaurant, not a bar," said the Mouse.

"They'll find some liquor," said the Iceman confidently. He got to his feet, walked across the room, and a moment later he had left the rooming house and crossed the empty street.

The Mouse turned to Penelope. "Will you be all right if I leave you for a few minutes?"

"Where are you going?"

"To have a talk with Carlos," she answered. "I've got to know whether we can count on him—or even turn our backs on him—once the shooting starts."

"He's a very bad man," said Penelope.

"I'm starting to agree with you."

"Then don't go," pleaded Penelope, clutching at the Mouse's arm with both of her hands.

The Mouse hugged her reassuringly, then gently disengaged herself and got to her feet. "I'll just be a few minutes," she said, "and you'll be safe here with the Kid and the Mock Turtle."

"He'll just say terrible things about me," said Penelope. "Promise me you won't listen to them."

"Of course I won't." The Mouse smiled. "We're still a team, remember?"

She hugged the girl again, then left the rooming house and walked across the street to the restaurant.

"You again?" said the pudgy woman as the Mouse walked up the stairs of the veranda and into the building.

"Let her in," said the Iceman, who was sitting alone in the dining room.

As with the old man, the woman detected something in his voice that made her decide not to argue with him.

"A beer for her, and another Cygnian cognac for me," said the Iceman.

The woman left the room, and the Mouse sat down opposite the Iceman.

"I had a feeling you'd come over here," he said. "I suppose it's just as well. We've got to talk."

"Yes, we do," agreed the Mouse.

The woman returned with the drinks.

"Thanks," said the Iceman, placing a couple of bills on the table. "Now leave us alone."

"How will I know if you want more?" she demanded.

"We won't."

The pudgy woman turned and left the room without another word.

The Mouse leaned forward and stared at the Iceman.

"Why did you come here, Carlos?"

"Because I was thirsty."

"You know what I mean," she said irritably. "You're not here for the reward, and you're certainly not here to save me—so why *are* you here?"

"You still don't believe it, do you?" said the Iceman. "You're sitting on a time bomb, and you still haven't realized it."

"You make her sound like Evil incarnate," said the Mouse. "There's not a malicious bone in her body. She's just a little girl, and I love her."

"I never said she was malicious."

"Well, then?"

The Iceman sipped his drink, put it back down on the table, and met the Mouse's gaze.

"Wherever she goes, people die."

"Only people who mean her harm."

"She's just a child, Mouse," said the Iceman. "As she grows older and stronger, her definition of harm is going to change. Right now it's people who want to take her away from you, but one day soon it'll be anyone who opposes anything she wants."

"Nonsense."

"You think only bounty hunters can trip on ladders and break their necks?" continued the Iceman. "You think a planetary governor can't choke on his food, or that the Secretary of the Democracy can't slip in the rain?"

"She would never do that!"

"Why not?"

"She's a decent, sensitive child. You don't know her like I do."

"Nobody knows her like you do," agreed the Iceman. "But she'll even kill you if you stand in her way."

"Stand in her way?" repeated the Mouse. "In her way to *what*?"

He shrugged. "I don't know. But the first duty of power is to protect itself, and the first instinct of the strong is to eat the weak."

"You're a fool, Carlos!"

"Perhaps."

"She's never harmed anyone who didn't try to harm her first."

"She's never had the opportunity to."

"She has the opportunity right now," said the Mouse. "If she's what you think she is, why haven't you choked to death on your drink, or keeled over with a heart attack?"

"Obviously she needs me—probably to face the bounty hunters," said the Iceman, still with no display of emotion. "That's why we have to talk." He stared at her intently. "If one of the bounty hunters manages to get his hands on her, then she's the Democracy's problem, and good luck to them." He paused. "But if you're the only one who survives this mess, you'd better start giving some thought to how you're going to kill her."

"You're describing a monster, not a little girl!"

"A potential monster, anyway," agreed the Iceman. "The longer you wait, the harder she'll be to take on."

"Did it ever occur to you that she could be a force for good?" demanded the Mouse.

"What's good for her won't be what's good for us."

"She's a human being!"

"She's more than a human being," replied the Iceman. "And the more she grows, the less like a human being she's going to become."

"Then why didn't you try to kill her the minute you saw her out on the street?"

He stared at his drink for a moment, then looked across the table at her.

"There's a possibility that I'm wrong."

"That's the first rational thing you've said."

"Everything I've said is rational," he replied. "I could be mistaken about how much harm she could do. It wouldn't be the first time I was wrong." He paused. "But I doubt it."

"Then I repeat: why are you here at all? Why don't you just stand back and let the bounty hunters take her away?"

"I plan to stand back."

"I don't understand."

"If she can arrange for the Forever Kid to kill them all, then she's as dangerous as I thought. If she can't, then I'll take a hand."

"That won't prove a thing," said the Mouse. "I've seen him kill eight miners all by himself."

"Those were miners," said the Iceman. "These are bounty hunters. There's Three-Fisted Ollie and Jimmy the Spike and Cemetery Smith and half a dozen others just as formidable. The Forever Kid's good, but he's not *that* good."

"Then you're telling me that you plan to sit back and watch him die defending Penelope?"

"First, nothing would make him happier than dying, and second, I don't expect him to die."

"What *do* you expect?"

"I expect him to kill them all, and then I expect I'll try to kill her, whether he tries to stop me or not." The Iceman paused. "And if I fail, I expect you to remember this conversation, and put your emotions aside, and do what has to be done."

"Not a chance," said the Mouse in level tones.

"Then I feel very sorry for you." He paused. "You always seem to love the wrong people. Once it cost you a year in an alien prison. This time it may cost you your life."

"*You* never cared for me!" said the Mouse. "Penelope loves me!"

"She loves you because she needs a mother and that's what you've been to her," said the Iceman. "What happens when she stops needing a mother?"

"Sooner or later all little girls grow up and stop needing their mothers," said the Mouse. "That doesn't mean they stop loving them."

"But you're *not* her mother," he pointed out. "By the time she's mature she'll have no more in common with you than you have with an insect."

"You don't know her, or you wouldn't say that."

"I freely admit I don't know her," said the Iceman. "My point is that you don't, either. She looks and acts like a normal little girl, but she isn't one." He paused. "I asked you a question back on Last Chance. Let me ask it again: how many men and women and aliens has this normal little girl killed?"

"I told you," said the Mouse. "Anytime she's hurt or killed somebody it's been in self-defense."

"You still haven't answered me. How many?"

"I don't know."

"More than the Forever Kid?"

"I doubt it. But that's not the point. She's not a paid killer. She's just trying to stay alive."

"I know. But let me ask another question now: has she ever expressed any remorse or regret over having taken so many lives?"

"No," said the Mouse, Then she added defensively: "Would *you* feel remorse over killing someone who was trying to kill you?"

"No, I wouldn't," replied the Iceman.

"Then why is she any different from you?"

"Because when I was eight years old, I couldn't kill ten or twenty or however many bounty hunters she's killed," said the Iceman. "She's still a little girl, and her needs are simple: she wants to stay alive and she wants to stay free. But what will her needs be when she grows up?"

"I don't know, and neither do you."

"Nobody knows," he admitted. "Probably not even Penelope. But I do know this: if her power keeps growing, and there's no reason to assume it won't, she can have anything she wants when she grows up. A planet? A star system? A trillion credits? Hers for the asking—or for the wanting and the manipulating."

"That's no different than a politician or a businessman."

"There's a difference," said the Iceman. "*They* can be stopped. *She* can't. Hell, she's already killed more men than most of the bounty hunters who are after her. Can't you see what lies up the road?"

"You're guessing!" she half shouted. "You want me to kill her because you think she *might* grow up to be some kind of monster! Well, she isn't, and she never will be! You don't know her like I do!"

"No," he said. "But I know something else. I know that we've had monsters before—Caligula, Hitler, Conrad Bland—and that they all had mothers who loved them."

"What is that supposed to mean?"

"Think of how many lives could have been saved if just one of those mothers had seen her child for the potential monster it really was." He paused and stared at her. "You might consider that while there's still time."

Then he rose and walked out of the dining room, leaving her with her beer and her thoughts.

PART 5

The Soothsayer's Book

30

An hour had passed.

The Mock Turtle, the Mouse, and Penelope were sitting quietly in the lounge of the boardinghouse. The Iceman was leaning against a wall, looking out at the street through a window, and the Forever Kid stood in the open front door, totally relaxed while idly fingering the handle of his sonic pistol.

The Iceman lit a cigar, took a deep puff of it, and turned to stare expressionlessly at the little girl.

"Don't do that," said Penelope.

"Don't do what?" he asked.

"Don't look at me like that," she said. "It frightens me."

He took another puff of his cigar, then walked out into the foyer and sat down on the corner of the desk.

"Where the hell are they?" said the Mouse, getting to her feet and crossing the room to stand by the doorway.

"They'll be here, never fear," said the Iceman.

"I just wish we had some plan," she said nervously.

"The Soothsayer will tell us what to do when the time comes," said the Mock Turtle placidly.

"Why are you so goddamned calm?" said the Mouse, turning to glare at the alien. "Don't you ever get excited about anything?"

"Why are you so excited?" responded the Mock Turtle, its voice calm and steady. "Have you no faith in the Soothsayer?"

The Mouse was about to reply to the alien, then thought better of it, and continued her pacing.

Penelope held Maryanne to her chest, rocking back and forth on the ancient sofa and half singing, half whispering a lullaby to the doll. She stopped every now and then to see if the Iceman was still in the next room, then lovingly smoothed the doll's dress and began crooning to it again.

The Forever Kid pulled his sonic pistol out of its holster and checked its charge.

"You keep fiddling with that thing and you're going to inadvertently deactivate it," commented the Iceman. "If you're nervous, go across the street and have a drink."

"Bored, not nervous," corrected the Kid. He paused. "I've never seen the Spike or Cemetery Smith before. I want to see what they can do."

"They can kill you, that's what they can do," said the Iceman.

"You really think they've got a chance?" asked the Kid with an almost hopeful note in his voice.

"Everyone's always got a chance," said the Iceman noncommittally. "Out here, if you carry a weapon, you're undefeated so far."

The Kid smiled one of his rare smiles. "I never thought of it like that."

"You're young yet," said the Iceman sardonically. "You'll learn."

The Kid actually chuckled at the remark, then replaced his pistol in its holster.

"He's crazy," said the Mouse, finally sitting down next to Penelope.

"Who is?" asked the girl.

"The Kid. He's about to take on some of the best bounty hunters on the Inner Frontier, and he's actually laughing. I haven't seen him laugh since I met him."

She got up and paced across the room once more, then seated herself uneasily on a wooden chair, tried to hold still, and immediately began fidgeting.

Suddenly Penelope looked up from her doll.

"They're here," she announced.

"Where?" demanded the Mouse.

"On Killhaven," said Penelope. "Two ships, and a third is about to land."

"I know," said the Kid from his position in the doorway. "I just saw them come down. They're at least three miles away, maybe five." He paused. "Here comes another one."

"Well, we've probably got half an hour or more until they get here," said the Iceman, remaining seated on the desk. "If they get here at all, that is."

"What do you mean?" asked the Mock Turtle.

"There's a huge reward for the girl, and these guys probably aren't planning to divide it ten or twelve ways. They might kill each other off before they even come to town."

"I hope not," said the Forever Kid devoutly.

"How many more ships will be arriving?" asked the Mouse.

"Two that I know of," said the Iceman. "There were five of them on our tail."

"Three more," corrected Penelope.

The Iceman shrugged. "We must have missed one—or else somebody radioed for reinforcements."

"They better get here soon," noted the Kid. "It'll be dark in less than an hour."

"Maybe they'll wait until morning," said the Mouse hopefully.

"Not very likely," said the Iceman. "By morning the other three ships will be here. They'll want to grab the girl and get out of here as quick as they can."

"Well, let's not make it too easy for them," said the Mouse. She turned to Penelope. "I want you to go upstairs and keep out of sight."

"I want to stay with you, Mouse," protested the girl.

The Mouse turned to the Mock Turtle. "Go with her, and protect the door if they get that far."

The alien stared at her politely, but made no reply and didn't move from where it was standing.

"Didn't you hear me?" snapped the Mouse. "Take her upstairs."

"I obey only the Soothsayer," replied the Mock Turtle. "When *she* tells me to go upstairs, then I will go."

"Listen, you," began the Mouse. "When I say to—"

"*Don't!*" shouted Penelope, and suddenly all eyes turned to her. "You're my friends," continued the girl. "I don't want you to fight."

"You're what they've come for," said the Mouse. "You've got to let us try to protect you."

The Mock Turtle held up its hand for silence, then stared intently at Penelope. "What do you see, Soothsayer?" it asked. "Who will live and who will die?"

"I can't tell," answered the girl. "There are still too many futures."

"And I'll wager a castle to a credit that you live in all of them, don't you?" said the Iceman.

"No," said the girl. "I don't."

"If you live in even one, that's enough," said the Mouse. "Just tell us how to make that future come to pass."

"I don't know yet," said Penelope, obviously agitated. "But I know I want to be with you, Mouse. Please don't make me go upstairs."

The Mouse looked at the girl for a long moment, then sighed and shrugged.

"How can I give an order to a soothsayer?" she said with a wry smile.

Penelope ran over to the Mouse and hugged her. "Thank you, Mouse," she said. "I love you."

"I know," said the Mouse, returning her embrace. "And I love you, too. That's why I worry so much about you."

"I think I see another one," said the Forever Kid, drifting out to the porch. "Could be a bird, though." He paused. "No, it's a ship, all right." There was another pause, longer this time. "Looks like it's landing to the north. That means they'll be approaching from both ends of town."

"Maybe we'll just lock the doors and let them fight it out for the privilege of facing you," suggested the Iceman. He got up and walked to the door, where he shaded his eyes and scanned the sky.

"From what I hear, that means I'd wind up facing Jimmy the Spike," replied the Kid, considering the possibility. He spat on the dirt. "Damn! I want to face more than one of them." He paused thoughtfully. "Maybe they'll come in teams."

"If I'd known it meant so much to you, I'd have radioed our position to one of the Democracy's battle cruisers," said the Iceman with dry irony.

"I wonder how many of them I could take out before they killed me?" mused the Kid.

"Not enough," said the Iceman.

Suddenly the Mock Turtle walked through the foyer and joined the Forever Kid on the porch.

"What are you doing here?" asked the Kid.

"In the absence of instructions from the Soothsayer," replied the alien, displaying its odd, silent weapon, "I have elected to make my stand here with you."

"I don't know about that," said the Forever Kid. "I planned to face whoever shows up alone."

"What about the Iceman?"

The Kid snorted contemptuously. "He doesn't like to get his hands dirty. He'll probably watch the whole thing from inside the house and then take credit for all the men I kill."

"Sounds good to me," said the Iceman dryly.

"Besides," continued the Forever Kid, "you ought to stay with the little girl, in case anyone gets past me."

"She will summon me if she needs me," said the Mock Turtle.

"And if she doesn't summon you?"

"Then she never needed me," answered the alien.

"I'm glad someone besides me understands what we're dealing with here," said the Iceman.

"I have always understood what we are dealing with," said the Mock Turtle serenely. "That is why I am here."

"Then you're the biggest fool of all," said the Iceman.

"Why should you think so?" asked the alien curiously.

"The Mouse still doesn't understand what she is, and the Forever Kid couldn't care less. But you—you know and you're *still* trying to help her."

"And why are *you* here?"

The Iceman shrugged. "I wish I knew."

"Then who is the bigger fool?" continued the Mock Turtle. "I, who understand my motivations, or you, who do not begin to understand your own?"

The Iceman considered its statement. "Maybe you have a point at that," he admitted wryly.

The Forever Kid stepped off the porch and into the street. "Are you two through arguing about who's a bigger fool?" he asked.

"Yes," said the Iceman. "I think we'll call it a draw."

"Good," said the Kid. "Then get inside."

"No," said the alien calmly.

The Forever Kid turned to the alien. "I'm working for the Mouse, and I'm being paid to protect the girl," he said, "but I never saw you before today, and the way I see it, I don't owe you a damned thing. I've been waiting a long time for a chance like this, and if I have to kill you first to make sure I get it, then I will."

The Mouse walked to the doorway. "Leave him alone, Kid. I'll tell you who to kill."

"Right," agreed the Kid. "But nobody tells me who not to kill. Not even you."

"Well, somebody better remind you who the bad guys are," said the Mouse. She pointed to the cornfields beyond the small cluster of buildings. "The enemy's out *there*."

"Right now the enemy is anyone who tries to stop me from what I want to do," answered the Kid.

Penelope appeared beside the Mouse in the doorway, still holding Maryanne.

"Come inside, Turtle," she said. "If you don't, he'll kill you."

"If it is your desire, Soothsayer," replied the alien, immediately turning and walking back into the interior of the rooming house.

"I've had pets before," remarked the Iceman, "but I never had one that well trained."

"That's enough sniping, Carlos," said the Mouse. "We can sort out our differences later. I'll tell you what I told the Kid: the enemy's out there."

"Not any longer he isn't," said the Forever Kid, as six men came into view half a mile down the dirt road. "Iceman, get off my street."

"Your wish is my command," said the Iceman ironically, stepping back into the doorway. He glanced quickly toward the north. "By the way, I don't want to intrude on your idyll, but it looks like you've got two more friends coming from the other end of town."

The Kid's fingers dropped to the handles of his pistols. "The more the merrier," he said.

The Iceman suddenly noticed that the Mouse was still standing next to him.

"You'd better get inside," he told her. "You're not even carrying a weapon."

"You're really going to let him face all eight of them alone?" she demanded.

"I told you before that I was. Besides, it's what he wants." The Iceman looked at the progress the approaching men were making. "They'll be here in about two minutes," he said to the Kid. "I hope you're ready."

"I've been ready for two hundred years," replied the Forever Kid, a smile of anticipation on his handsome, unlined face.

31

The eight bounty hunters—five men and three women—reached the cluster of frame buildings that formed the tiny town within a minute of each other. One hung back, some hundred yards or so behind the others. The remaining seven stopped opposite the boardinghouse and stared at the Forever Kid, who stood before them, hands on hips, completely relaxed.

"I know who you are," said one of the men.

"Then you must know why I'm here," answered the Kid.

"You're no bounty hunter," said a woman. "You've got no interest in the girl."

"My interest in her is the same as yours: financial," said the Kid.

"We've got no fight with you," continued the woman. "Why don't you walk away now while you can?"

"Got no place to go," said the Kid.

"Surely you don't think you can take all eight of us?" demanded the woman.

"I only count seven," replied the Kid calmly. "One of your friends is showing rare good judgment."

"He's no friend of mine," said the man who had spoken first. "And he'll be along, never fear."

"Are you planning to split the reward seven ways?" asked the Kid. "If not, I have no serious objection to your going over to one of the cornfields and sorting things out." He paused. "I'll still be waiting here to face the winner."

258

"As a matter of fact, we spoke by subspace radio, and that's exactly what we plan to do," said the man. "There's more than enough money to split seven ways."

"Or eight ways, if you'd like to throw in with us," added another man.

"What about your friend down the street?" asked the Kid curiously. "Or the two ships that haven't landed yet?"

"We made them the offer. They turned it down. It's their loss. Yours, too, if you plan to stand against us."

"All I'm losing is money," said the Forever Kid. "If you don't walk back to your ships right now, you're going to lose your lives."

"You're crazy!" said the woman, as three of them started fanning out in a semicircle. "Do you really think you can take seven armed bounty hunters?"

The Kid smiled confidently. "Do you really think I can't?"

As he spoke he drew both of his hand weapons, panning the area with his laser pistol and firing short bursts of almost-solid sound with the sonic gun. Two women and two men dropped to the ground almost instantly, while the third woman clutched her belly and doubled over in agony.

The two remaining men had their weapons out—one a sonic gun, one an old-fashioned projectile pistol—and began firing while running for cover. The Forever Kid neither ducked nor crouched nor sought out shelter. He stood his ground, oblivious to the bullets and sonic blasts flying about him, aimed his laser pistol carefully, and brought both men down. Then, almost casually, he turned back to the wounded woman, aimed his laser pistol between her eyes as she desperately sought to reach her own weapon, and fired. She collapsed without a sound.

And now the eighth bounty hunter, the man who had lagged behind, began approaching the Forever Kid.

"Not bad," he said. "Not bad at all."

"Damned good, if you ask me," responded the Kid.

"Oh, I don't know about that," continued the man easily. "Four of them were dead and one was as good as dead before they even knew the fight had begun."

"When you're outnumbered seven to one, you don't wait for a referee to drop a flag," said the Kid. "If they weren't ready, that was their problem."

"I fully agree," said the man. "In fact, I suppose I should be grateful to you. After all, you saved me the trouble of killing them myself."

"I take it you're not much for sharing," said the Kid with a smile.

"I work alone."

"Maybe you'd better consider whether you want to die alone, too," suggested the Kid.

"I might say the same thing to you."

"You might," agreed the Kid. "But I probably wouldn't listen."

"No, I suppose not," said the man. "We're a lot alike, you and I."

"You think so?"

The man nodded. "I don't give a damn about the money or the girl, and neither do you. Men like us, we live only for the competition."

"Or die for it," answered the Kid.

"Or die for it," agreed the man. "You're the Forever Kid, aren't you?"

The Kid nodded.

"I've heard of you."

"I don't know if I've heard of you or not," replied the Kid.

The man grinned. "I'm fresh out of business cards, but my name is Jimmy the Spike."

"You know, I was wondering if you were in that batch," said the Kid, indicating the dead bounty hunters as the sun glinted off their weapons. "But from what I knew of you, I didn't figure you could be."

"My reputation precedes me. How very gratifying."

"I've been looking forward to meeting you," said the Kid.

"I'd kind of hoped we might get together over a drink someday, and maybe swap stories," answered the Spike. He sighed. "But I suppose this way is better."

"Much," agreed the Kid as a number of avians began circling lazily overhead.

"I notice you haven't told me to go back to my ship," said the bounty hunter with an amused smile.

"That's because I don't want you to."

"You *are* a man after my own heart!" chuckled the Spike. "In another life, we could have been great friends."

"Well, you're going to get to that other life first," said the Kid. "Maybe when I finally join you, we'll be friends, after all."

"I hope so," said the Spike. "Where *we're* bound, I have a feeling a man needs all the friends he can get." He glanced at the boardinghouse. "The little girl's in there?"

The Kid nodded his head.

"Is she alone?"

"It doesn't make any difference," said the Kid. "You've got to get past me first, and you're not going to."

"That remains to be seen," said the Spike, taking a step forward.

The Forever Kid reached for his sonic pistol. As he did so, Jimmy the Spike made a quick backhanded motion with his forearm, and a trio of long, ugly darts buried themselves in the Kid's chest. He stood motionless for a moment, then stared in disbelief at the blood running down the front of his tunic.

"Well, I'll be damned," he whispered, the trace of a smile on his face. "It finally happened."

Then he fell to the ground.

Jimmy the Spike walked over to the Forever Kid's body, rolled him over on his back, and looked down at him. He stared at the boyish face for a long moment, then sighed and turned to the boardinghouse. He had taken only two steps toward it when the Mock Turtle stepped up to a window and aimed his weapon. There was a faint humming noise, and then the Spike collapsed, almost falling on top of the Kid's lifeless body.

The Iceman stepped through the doorway and surveyed the carnage, followed a moment later by the Mouse, Penelope, and the Mock Turtle.

"What a waste," muttered the Iceman.

"He sacrificed himself for us," intoned the Mock Turtle. "He was a noble man."

"You're wrong on both counts," said the Iceman.

"I don't understand," said the alien.

"First, there was nothing noble about it. He's been trying to get himself killed for the better part of a century; he finally succeeded." He paused. "And second, he didn't sacrifice himself for us."

"Certainly he did."

The Iceman shook his head. "Someone else sacrificed him for us." He turned and stared at Penelope. "Or am I wrong?"

"Leave her alone, Carlos!" snapped the Mouse.

He looked from the girl to the Mouse, back to the girl once more, shrugged, and walked off to see if he could identify the various corpses.

"I think I know two of them," he announced. "This one's Buzzard Stone, and that woman"—he indicated the woman who had done most of the talking—"is Nina Pallone. He wasn't much, but she was supposed to be one of the best." He paused. "I never saw the other five before."

"What shall we do with the bodies?" asked the Mock Turtle.

"After I've had a drink, I'll bury the Kid out behind the rooming house," answered the Iceman. "You can help."

"And the others?"

"Let's leave 'em right where they are," said the Iceman. "There are two more ships due to land. Maybe this will give them something to think about."

He turned and walked off to the restaurant.

The Mouse turned to the Mock Turtle. "Thank you for avenging the Kid's death."

"He meant no more to me than I meant to him," replied the alien. "I was protecting the Soothsayer."

"Well, whatever your reason, thanks," said the Mouse. "Maybe you'd better start digging his grave out back. I'm sure Carlos will be by to join you in a few minutes."

"Have I your permission to leave you, Soothsayer?" asked the Mock Turtle.

"Yes," said Penelope.

The alien stepped down off the porch. "I have no digging instruments," it announced.

"There's a shed behind the building," said the Mouse. "I'm sure you'll find a spade or a pick inside it."

The Mock Turtle walked around the rooming house without another word.

"Come inside, Penelope," said the Mouse.

"Why?" asked the girl.

"We have to talk, and I'd just as soon not do it where we can be overheard, even by the Turtle."

The Mouse went into the house and walked across the foyer to the lounge, followed by Penelope.

"Sit down," said the Mouse.

Penelope sat on a couch, and the Mouse sat down next to her.

"What's the matter?" asked the girl. "You act like you're mad at me."

"I'm not mad, but there's something I have to know."

"What?"

The Mouse looked into Penelope's eyes. "Was Carlos telling the truth?"

"I don't know what you mean," said the girl.

"Did the Forever Kid have to die?"

"He wanted to die," answered Penelope. "You don't have to feel sad about it."

"You didn't answer my question," said the Mouse. "Did he have to die?"

"Jimmy the Spike was faster."

"But Jimmy the Spike was our enemy and the Forever Kid was our friend."

"But he died the way he wanted to."

"Look at me," said the Mouse. "Did you interfere with the fight?"

Penelope met her gaze. "No."

"You're sure?"

"Don't you believe me, Mouse?"

The Mouse stared at her for a moment, then put her arms around the little girl. "Yes, I believe you."

"She's telling the truth," said a voice from the doorway.

The Mouse jumped up, startled. "I thought you were having a drink."

"They locked up the building when the shooting started," said the Iceman.

Suddenly the Mouse frowned. "If you agree that she's telling the truth, what were you talking about before?" she demanded.

"You asked her the wrong question."

"What do you think I should have asked?"

The Iceman stared at Penelope. "Ask her if the Kid would have lived if she *had* interfered."

"Go away and leave me alone!" shouted Penelope, half hysterical.

"Please, Carlos," said the Mouse.

He nodded. "I've got a body to bury." He turned to leave. "Besides, I already know the answer."

Then the Mouse was alone with Penelope again.

"Well?" she said.

Penelope, her body still tense, continued to stare at the spot where the Iceman had been standing.

"Penelope," said the Mouse, "is it true? Could you have saved him?"

"He *wanted* to die."

"He was *prepared* to die," said the Mouse. "That's not the same thing."

"It is."

"No," said the Mouse. "If he had wanted to die, he wouldn't have drawn his guns against the first seven bounty hunters. He'd have just stood there and let them shoot him down."

Penelope gradually relaxed, but made no answer.

"Could you have saved him?" asked the Mouse again.

"Maybe," said Penelope grudgingly.

"That's not an answer," said the Mouse. "Could you have saved him—yes or no?"

"Yes."

"How?"

"By breaking the window just when the Kid tried to draw his gun. Jimmy the Spike would have been startled, not for long, but long enough for the Kid to kill him."

"Then why didn't you do it?"

"He didn't care whether he lived or died."

"But *we* care," said the Mouse. "First, because he was our friend, and second, because we needed him to face the last two men—the two who haven't landed yet."

"They would probably have killed him," said Penelope.

"Probably?" repeated the Mouse.

"It depends where they stood."

"You could have told him where to stand."

"What difference does it make?" asked Penelope. "He wasn't important, anyway. *You're* the one I love." She threw her arms around the Mouse and buried her head against her small bosom. "You and Maryanne and maybe the Mock Turtle. He didn't matter." She started crying. "Say you're not mad at me, Mouse."

The Mouse stroked her blonde hair absently and stared out the window at the bodies on the street.

"No, I'm not mad at you, Penelope," she said, her voice troubled.

"And do you still love me?"

"I'll always love you."

"And we're still partners, and we'll always be together?"

The Mouse sighed deeply and continued stroking Penelope's hair.

"You didn't answer me," said the little girl.

The Mouse hugged her tightly, but remained silent, a troubled frown on her face.

32

Night had fallen.

The Iceman had pulled a rocking chair out to the porch so he could watch for the final two ships against the darkened sky. Penelope was sleeping in the lounge, where the Mock Turtle sat watch over her.

The Mouse, who had been walking restlessly through and around the rooming house, finally approached the Iceman.

"I've been thinking about what you said," she began softly.

"And?"

"She's been on the run all her life. She's never stopped long enough for anyone to teach her right from wrong."

"I know."

"She's not malicious," added the Mouse quickly. "She doesn't mean to hurt anyone. She just doesn't know any better." She paused. "She thought she was doing the Kid a favor by letting him die."

"I'm sure she did," said the Iceman. "But the end result is that he's dead."

"She needs guidance, that's all," said the Mouse.

"And you're going to give it to her?"

"I'm going to try."

"And what happens when she doesn't agree with what you say?"

"I'll just have to be patient, and explain it until she understands," answered the Mouse.

"Children aren't notorious for being patient," he pointed out.

"Most of them just cry, and a few break things. This one could destroy whole worlds."

"I *can't* kill her, Carlos. She loves me."

The Iceman stared into the darkness for a long time before answering.

"Then you'd better never leave her side for an instant," he said. "You'd better never give her a reason to doubt that you love her, or that she's the most important thing in your life." He paused. "The *only* important thing in your life."

"She'd never harm me, Carlos."

"She's just a child, and an untrained one at that," replied the Iceman. "She'll have doubts and fears and jealousies, just like any other child—only *she* won't recognize them for what they are." He turned to her. "Other children wish terrible fates on their parents and siblings every day; it's a normal part of growing up. The difference is that what she wishes will come true."

The Mouse made no reply.

"And you'd better watch out for the Mock Turtle, too," continued the Iceman.

"Why? He worships her."

"You call it a 'he' and you give it a name like 'the Mock Turtle,' and that makes you forget it's an alien, with alien perceptions and alien motivations. It's got a polite, almost servile manner, but it killed the Yankee Clipper in cold blood, and it showed no hesitation in shooting down Jimmy the Spike."

"He was protecting her."

"I know . . . but it's going to be giving Penelope as much input as you are, and for all you know it kills someone every day before breakfast."

"He seems very gentle and very caring to me," replied the Mouse.

"You've only seen it in the presence of a little girl that it worships. You know nothing about its beliefs and its ethics, except that it's willing to kill humans for what it considers valid reasons."

"What do you want me to do?" demanded the Mouse. "Kill both of them?"

"Kill the little girl, and the alien doesn't matter," said the Iceman. "But if you let her live, then you'd better get rid of the alien, and the sooner the better."

She stared at him. "You're a hard man, Carlos."

He was about to answer her when the sky was lit up by the retro burn of an incoming spaceship.

"How far away would you say it is?" asked the Iceman when the ship had finally vanished from their sight and presumably landed on the planet's surface.

"Four or five miles, just like the others."

"Whoever's flying it must have picked up the others with his sensor and decided that was the spaceport." He paused. "Well, we've probably got until sunrise."

"Why won't he come after us right now?" asked the Mouse.

"Because for all he knows, we've got the whole route mined and booby-trapped," answered the Iceman. "No, he'll wait until he can see where he's going." He looked up at the sky. "Besides, his partner isn't here yet."

"How do you know who it is, or that he has a partner?" asked the Mouse.

"Because I saw who the Kid killed, and Three-Fisted Ollie wasn't among them," explained the Iceman. "Ollie is too good at his work to have lost our trail, and he'll have kept in contact with Cemetery Smith." The Iceman smiled grimly. "*That's* who we're waiting for."

"Maybe we ought to mine the road," suggested the Mouse. "We have enough time. It won't be daylight for another four or five hours."

"I don't have the equipment," said the Iceman. "Besides, it doesn't make any difference."

"Why not?"

"Because these are two of the best in the business. They're not going to make a second foolish mistake."

"A *second* one?" said the Mouse. "What was their first?"

"The same as yours," he replied, leaning back on the rocking chair to wait for Cemetery Smith's ship to streak through the atmosphere. "They thought Penelope Bailey was a helpless little girl."

33

Dawn broke with surprising suddenness on Killhaven. One moment it was dark, the next moment it wasn't, and a moment after that a score of avian raptors swooped down and recommenced feeding on the dead bodies that littered the street.

"They're coming," announced Penelope from inside the house.

"I'll tell Carlos," said the Mouse's voice.

"Not necessary," said the Iceman, still sitting on his rocking chair. "I'm awake."

The Mouse appeared in the doorway and looked up the long dirt road.

"I can't see them yet."

"They're probably still a couple of miles away," said the Iceman.

"What do you plan to do?" asked the Mouse.

"I'll play it by ear," answered the Iceman.

"You mean you're just going to sit here?"

"That's what I mean."

"That's stupid, Carlos," said the Mouse. "We still have time to take defensive positions. You could get on the roof, the Turtle can hide behind the restaurant, I can—"

"I'm too old to climb on top of buildings," interrupted the Iceman.

"But you can't just do nothing!"

"Why not?" replied the Iceman calmly. "It's usually best."

"What's going on, Carlos?" she demanded. Suddenly she stared intently at him. "You're going to join them, aren't you?"

269

"I doubt that they'd have me."

"Then what are you going to do?" she insisted.

"I don't know."

"Well, you've got about ten minutes to come up with an idea."

"I don't want one."

She frowned. "What the hell are you talking about, Carlos?"

He turned to her. "If *I* don't know what I'm going to do, then *she* doesn't know what I'm going to do."

"It doesn't work that way, Carlos," said the Mouse. "She sees lots of futures, and then tries to manipulate things so that the one she wants will come to pass."

"Not knowing what I'm going to do will make it harder for her to manipulate anything," answered the Iceman. "Maybe she'll want me to sneeze when I'm going for my gun, and maybe she won't—but if even *I* don't know if or when I'm going for it, it's got to hamper her."

"If I were you, I'd be more worried about Three-Fisted Ollie and Cemetery Smith," said the Mouse.

The Iceman shrugged. "They're just killers."

The Mouse stared at him again, then disappeared back inside the house.

The Iceman pulled a thin Castorian cigar from his pocket, lit it, and continued rocking on his chair. The sun peeked up over the restaurant, and he squinted up the road, wishing that he had remembered to bring a hat to shade his eyes.

And then two figures, one human, one definitely inhuman, came into view. As they came closer he saw that the alien wore a silver outfit, and had either one arm too many or one too few, and he knew that it was Three-Fisted Ollie. The other wore the dull browns and greens of a man used to blending in with his surroundings, but there was no doubt in the Iceman's mind that it was Cemetery Smith.

"I am standing in the window of the lounge," said the Mock Turtle's voice. "I will keep my weapon trained on the human."

"Don't shoot until I tell you to," said the Iceman. "We tried this the Kid's way yesterday, and all we have to show for it is a batch of dead bodies and fat birds."

"Two more dead bodies and we can leave in safety," responded the Mock Turtle.

"These guys aren't that stupid," said the Iceman. "And they've worked as a team before. One of them will approach me, but the other will stay out of range, and if anything happens to his partner, he'll blow the whole rooming house straight to hell."

And, almost as if they had heard them, Cemetery Smith came to a halt some eight hundred yards away while Three-Fisted Ollie continued approaching with his powerful, lumbering walk.

"That's close enough," said the Iceman, getting off the rocking chair and stepping down from the porch when the alien was about fifty yards away.

"I know you," said Three-Fisted Ollie, stopping and peering at the Iceman through his many-faceted eyes. "You're Mendoza."

"I know you, too."

"I haven't seen you in many years," continued the alien.

"I've been around."

"Are you working for the girl now?"

The Iceman shook his head. "Just working."

"We have come for her."

"I know."

"Do you plan to stand against us?" asked Three-Fisted Ollie.

"Not if I can help it."

"Then step aside."

"I thought we might talk first," said the Iceman.

"Briefly."

"You know that the Clipper's dead?"

"Of course. We were on Calliope when he was killed."

"Then who are you working for?"

Three-Fisted Ollie smiled a very alien smile. "I cannot tell you that, Mendoza. You might think of delivering her there yourself and claiming the reward."

"The thought never crossed my mind," said the Iceman, returning his smile.

"You have not changed, Mendoza."

"Sure I have," said the Iceman. "I don't work for the Democracy anymore."

"Who do you work for now?" asked the alien.

"Me."

"What has this to do with the girl?"

"I'll buy her from you."

Three-Fisted Ollie frowned. "That makes no sense, Mendoza. You already possess her."

"You were never the brightest bounty hunter on the Frontier," said the Iceman. "Think it through, Ollie."

The alien was silent for a moment. "You are offering to pay us to leave?"

"That's right."

"Why?"

"Because I don't want to kill you, and because she'll help me recoup whatever I pay you."

"You won't kill me, Mendoza," the alien assured him. "You are not a young man anymore."

"But I have friends."

Three-Fisted Ollie suddenly tensed. "Oh?"

The Iceman nodded. "Nine of them. They're in every building in town, and each of them has a weapon trained on you."

"I don't believe you, Mendoza."

The Iceman gestured to the eight bodies that lay on the street. "Do you think I could have done that all by myself?"

"You were accompanied here by the Forever Kid," said Three-Fisted Ollie. "*He* could have done that."

The Iceman walked over to Jimmy the Spike's body and turned it over with his foot.

"Could he have taken all eight of them at once, including the Spike?" he asked.

"No," answered Three-Fisted Ollie. "Not including the Spike."

"Then maybe you'd better accept my offer."

"Where is the Forever Kid now?"

The Iceman pointed to the seed store. "In there, with a gun pointed at your head."

The alien grinned again. "I almost believed you, Mendoza. But I know the Forever Kid, and if he was alive, nothing could keep him from facing me. Therefore, he is dead and you are alone."

"You're half right," admitted the Iceman. "He's dead. But I'm not alone."

"We have spoken enough," said Three-Fisted Ollie. "Now it is time for me to get the girl."

"Two million credits," said the Iceman.

The alien stared at him. "That was a fair price a year ago. Now she is worth much more."

"But if you accept two million, you'll walk away with it in your pocket. If you don't, you'll be buried along with the rest of them," he said, indicating the dead bounty hunters.

"I do not fear you, Mendoza."

"No one ever said you did. The question is whether you believe me."

"I do not think so."

"I'm offering you two million credits to say you do," said the Iceman. "That's a hell of a profit for avoiding a fight."

Three-Fisted Ollie stared at him for a long moment.

"And two million more for my partner," he said.

"Just take the money and tell him the girl isn't here."

"He knows that she *is* here," said the alien.

"That's pretty dangerous knowledge," said the Iceman.

"What do you mean?"

"I mean that every bounty hunter who knew she was here died for his trouble," said the Iceman. "All the ones who believe she's somewhere else are still alive."

"You're suggesting I kill him?" said Three-Fisted Ollie with another inscrutable grin.

"You don't need a partner if she's not here," answered the Iceman. "And you won't have anyone to split the money with."

"I have always said that you were the most interesting human I ever met, Mendoza," said Three-Fisted Ollie.

"I'll accept that as a compliment."

"Tell me," continued the alien, "when you were a young man, would you have made me this offer?"

"Probably," said the Iceman. "That's how I lived to be a middle-aged man."

"It's a very interesting proposition, Mendoza," said Three-Fisted Ollie after some consideration. "I think I shall have to discuss it with my partner."

"I'll wait here," said the Iceman. "I wouldn't want to intrude on your deliberations."

"One thing first," said the alien. "I must see the money."

"How do I know you won't kill me and take it, and still go after the girl?"

"How do I know you have the money at all?"

"We'll have to trust each other," said the Iceman.

"Maybe I'll just kill you now."

"You can try," said the Iceman. "But there really *is* a weapon pointed right at you."

"Now it's only one?"

"Now it's only one," agreed the Iceman. "But one is enough. If I were you, I'd think very carefully before I did anything I might not live long enough to regret."

The alien stood silent and motionless for a moment.

"Three million for the pair of us," it said at last.

"Deal," said the Iceman. "Signal him to join us."

"I'll take the money to him."

The Iceman shook his head. "I've got to know he agrees to leave without the girl before I pay either of you."

Three-Fisted Ollie seemed to consider it for a moment, then waved to Cemetery Smith, who began approaching the cluster of buildings.

The Iceman watched the human walk down the dirt road, trying to keep his mind absolutely blank, to avoid even the hint of a decision about what he might do next.

"What's going on here?" demanded Cemetery Smith when he was still about two hundred yards away.

"This is Mendoza," said Three-Fisted Ollie. "Do you remember him?"

"Thought he was dead," said Smith, continuing to approach them. He squinted in the bright sunlight. "You've changed, Mendoza."

"He's made us an interesting proposition," said the alien.

"Yeah?"

"Yes. He has offered us three million credits to—"

As Smith turned his attention to the alien, the Iceman pulled out his hand weapon and shot the bounty hunter through the chest, then hurled himself to the ground, rolled over once, and fired at Three-Fisted Ollie. The alien clutched his belly and fell onto his side.

"All right," said the Iceman, getting painfully to his feet and facing the rooming house. "You can come out now."

The Mouse was the first one out the door.

"I didn't think you could pull it off!" she exclaimed.

"Neither did somebody else, I'll wager," said the Iceman meaningfully, brushing the dust from himself and panting heavily.

Penelope and the Mock Turtle came out of the house and climbed down off the porch to join the Mouse.

"Well, we can finally leave," said the Mouse.

"It can't be that simple," said the Iceman. He looked at the little girl. "Can it?"

Penelope glared at him, and suddenly the fear was gone from her face.

"No," she said.

Suddenly the Iceman felt a searing pain on the back of his left leg as a laser beam burned through cloth and flesh, right down to the bone. He fell to the ground and clutched his leg with his hands, turning his head to see what had happened.

Three-Fisted Ollie had propped himself up on his side and held a laser pistol in his free hand.

"You lied to me, Mendoza!" he whispered hoarsely. He aimed the pistol at Penelope and tried to steady his hand. "We had a deal. If I can't have her, nobody can!"

"Shoot him!" screamed Penelope, running toward the Mouse.

The Mouse instinctively threw her arms around the little girl as Three-Fisted Ollie's laser pistol and the Mock Turtle's silent weapon both came to life and meted out death.

Three-Fisted Ollie grunted once, rolled over, and died. The Mouse fell to her knees, a smoking burn mark on her torso.

"Penelope?" she said, trying to focus her eyes.

"I love you, Mouse," said Penelope sadly, but with neither tears nor hysteria.

The girl stepped back, and the Mouse fell to the ground.

"I am sorry," said the Mock Turtle. "She died to save you." It paused. "I should have fired sooner. It was my fault."

The Iceman, still clutching his leg, turned back to the girl and the Mock Turtle.

"You're as big a fool as she was!" he grated. "Tell him whose fault it was, Penelope!"

"I loved her," said Penelope.

"Then why didn't you tell the Turtle to shoot sooner? You knew what he was going to do."

"It's your fault!" shouted Penelope, her face filled with childish fury. "You made her stop loving me!"

"You killed her, as surely as if you had fired the gun yourself," said the Iceman, trying to ignore the burning pain in his leg.

"She wasn't going to be my friend anymore," said Penelope petulantly. "She was going to leave me."

The Iceman looked at the alien.

"Well?" he demanded. "Aren't you going to finish the job?"

The Mock Turtle turned to Penelope. "What is your desire, Soothsayer?"

Penelope looked at the Iceman, sprawled in the dirt, his leg blood-soaked and useless.

"He's just an old man," she said contemptuously. "He can't harm us anymore."

"You'd better kill me now," said the Iceman. "If you don't, I'll come back and hunt you down."

"You can't hurt me," said Penelope confidently. "No one can hurt me."

"You were lucky," he answered, his face contorted with pain. "Next time you won't be."

She approached the wounded man and stared down at him. "Do you really think it's just luck that my friend and I are the only two who lived? Do you really think that?"

"Come, Soothsayer," said the Mock Turtle placidly. "It is time to leave."

The Iceman tried to reach his pistol, but it had fallen too far away, and he couldn't drag his body over to it.

"I'll find you," he promised.

"No, you won't," said Penelope. "The Mock Turtle and I are going to go away now, not to Summergold, but to some place where no one can find me. And I'm going to grow up, and I'm going to learn more about being the Soothsayer, and someday, when I'm ready, I'll come back." She turned to look at the Mouse's body. "And I'll never love anyone ever again."

"I'll be waiting," said the Iceman, his vision becoming blurred.

"You?" said Penelope. "You'll be an old man with one leg." She smiled. "If they don't come out to help you, you won't even live through the day." She turned to the Mock Turtle and reached for its hand. "It's time to go."

"Yes, Soothsayer," it replied, taking her hand and walking down the long dirt road to its ship.

The Iceman watched them until he lost consciousness.

34

When he awoke, he was in a hospital on McCallister II, and he spent the next few weeks getting used to his prosthetic leg.

After he had completely recovered, he went back to Killhaven. The twelve bodies had been buried out behind the boardinghouse. Since nobody had known who they were, there were no identifying markers on the tombstones. He arbitrarily decided that the one on the left belonged to the Mouse and laid a handful of wildflowers on it.

Then he went to the restaurant before returning to his ship.

The pudgy woman wasn't there, and nobody recognized him, and he had a quiet meal. Finally the waiter, a young man with dark brown hair and the start of a sparse mustache, approached him with his bill.

"I couldn't help noticing you looking at the graves over there," he said. "Were you related to any of them?"

"No," said the Iceman.

"It was a hell of a battle," said the young man, his face flushed with dreams of heroism. "I wish I'd been there." He paused, then added confidentially: "They say the Forever Kid was one of them."

"You don't say?"

The young man nodded. "As near as anyone can tell, the whole thing was about some little girl. There were ten bounty hunters after her, and the girl was hiding right in the rooming house across the street! Isn't that exciting?"

278

"Sounds exciting to me," agreed the Iceman, waiting patiently for his check.

"We ought to hang a plaque or something," continued the waiter. "After all, ten people died because of her."

"Twelve," the Iceman corrected him.

"That's right," said the waiter enthusiastically. "I'd almost forgotten. There was a man and a woman who gave their lives to protect her." He smiled. "At least they died heroes' deaths."

"If you say so," replied the Iceman.

He paid his bill and walked out into the dry, dusty street.